K. L. MIELKE

OCEAN DWELLERS' LEGEND

1

OCEAN DWELLERS' TRILOGY

First paperback edition October 2021

Book design by Jamie Dalton of Magnetra's Design
Editor: Whitney Morsillo of Whitney's Book Works
Author photo: Alesha Becker Photography

ISBN: 979-8-9850260-0-9

Published through Amazon KDP & Ingram Sparks

*Book One is dedicated
to my oldest son*

*We had such dreams of what you might become,
Sweet Boy.
Such dreams…*

You have already surpassed them all.

Table of Contents

Holly

One

I wrung my hands together nervously while Cecille scanned the contents of the letter I received the day before. I had read and reread it since its arrival and nearly had it memorized.

Finalist in the New Writers and Photographers of America contest.

The trip of a lifetime.

A massive grand prize for the winner.

And a huge step toward my dream of becoming a full-time photographer.

I would be gone for two weeks, though, and I was not sure the café where I worked could spare me. While I waited, I pulled my long curly hair back into a bun, before pouring myself a cup of coffee.

"Of course, you must go!" Cecille crowed, clutching my hands in her gnarled ones and squeezing them. "You *must* go, Holly!"

Cecille Vanden Hooven.

Five-two, one hundred pounds soaking wet, Einstein's hair, Mr. Magoo's glasses, and prone to wearing neon colors with bulky gold accessories. My eccentric, wild, and utterly loveable boss and owner of Cecille's café. I had been working at her small, lost-in-time restaurant for the last two years since my sister Abby and I had moved to Hartford. From the black and white checked floors to the pink booths to the immaculate ancient jukebox that only charged a nickel per song, it was a little piece of Hartford history, having been in operation for nearly fifty years. Cecille greeted every customer with the love of a long-lost aunt, a little rough around the edges and quirky but well-meaning. The walls were filled with photographs—major events with her previous husbands, Hartford fifty years ago, and framed photos of famous people she'd met throughout her life. If you asked, she'd tell you how she met them too. Some stories were normal, just passing through town, and others were wild and almost unbelievable. People came for the food and stayed for the quick wit of the tiny woman who ran the place.

"I'll be gone a while—almost two weeks. Are you sure?"

Cecille waved her hand as she reached for the coffee pot. "When life hands you a cruise to Hawaii, you find a different cabin boy for each night."

I choked on my coffee, barely preventing it from spraying across the counter in front of me. "Cecille!"

She pointed a finger at me. "Make each one bring you a cocktail too, for after all the sex. Or during. God rest Bob, Number Two. He knew what to do with ice cubes."

"Cecille!" I cried.

She waved a hand again at my horrified expression. "I was much younger then—not much older than you. Don't waste your youth, Holly. Flaunt your body before it starts to sag."

"Holy crap on a cracker," I muttered, willing my cheeks to quit burning as she walked away. "That woman has no modesty."

"She's like a hybrid of all the Golden Girls," Jonah, Cecille's cook, remarked when I passed the window that separated the kitchen from the dining room.

I laughed. "I suppose she's learned a few things in her life."

"How to find men?"

"Yes, all the men."

Jonah and I had several theories on how Cecille had found Joe, husband number six. He was a man easily twenty years younger than her, who still followed her around with puppy eyes. He brought her flowers almost every day and was thanked with a very public, visually awkward make-out session. Cecille walked away with a bubbly smile and a sassy comment. Joe did a blushing walk to the counter for a cup of coffee, grinning like a fool. "Did I miss Joe this morning?" I asked, noting the new bouquet beside the cash register.

"About ten minutes ago," Jonah replied, making a face.

I found much more entertainment in their displays of affection than Jonah. As her nephew, Jonah had had a lifetime of Cecille.

"Free cruise, huh?"

"Yeah." I tucked the letter back into my purse and tied my apron around my waist. "Remember that competition I entered a few months ago? I got a letter yesterday saying I'm a finalist."

"Congratulations. That's a hell of an opportunity."

"The grand prize is one hundred thousand dollars and publication."

His eyes widened. "Wow."

"I know." I glanced back at Cecille, who was happily chatting with one of the regulars. "She blows it off like it's no big deal. She only has two other waitresses," I said with a sigh.

Jonah laughed. "She'll be fine. Maybe Number Six will bus tables."

I guffawed as I grabbed the plates warming on the counter between us. "If he does, I'll need photographic evidence."

"Deal."

I delivered plates piled high with eggs and bacon to the older couple at the far end of the restaurant to save Cecille a trip before heading to my first table. "Hello, everyone. My name is Holly. What can I get you to drink?" I asked the sweaty, burly construction workers who filled the pink booth.

"How 'bout lemonade on the house, boys?" Cecille chirped, appearing with a pitcher and a stack of glasses. "Eye candies like you need to stay sweet."

"What else is on the house? Her number?" one of the younger guys asked, a wink in my direction. The others rolled their eyes.

"Not on the menu today, I'm afraid," I said, clearing my throat to buy myself a moment to collect my wits.

"But I'm sweet eye candy, just like she said," the man persisted.

"Oh my god, shut up, James," one of them mumbled.

"It's the sun," another said apologetically. "His damn pea brain melted. What are the specials today?"

"BLT, clam chowder soup, and bacon double cheeseburger."

"I'll have the burger with fries."

"Same."

"Same."

I scribbled on the pad before looking back to James. "And you, sir?"

"House waitress, with a side of whipped cream."

Two of the men groaned and one dropped his head into his hands. My cheeks flushed as I tried to compute a response.

"Young man," Cecille said calmly. "'I think thou art an ass.'" She turned to the man beside him. "Vegetarian?" she asked, crooking a finger at James. When he shook his head, she turned to me. "Four of the same. Off you go, dear."

I hurried back to the counter to post the ticket. Cecille followed.

"*Macbeth*?" Jonah asked her.

"*A Comedy of Errors*," Cecille said as she breezed past me. "Give 'em hell, Holly."

Cecille, a Shakespearian mastermind, relied on lines from the famous playwright for many things. It was not the first time she had used them to put a man in his place, nor would it be the last.

"Yeah, give 'em hell, Holly," Jonah taunted.

I made a face at him as I passed, smiling at his laughter when my back was turned. When I first started working for Cecille, her well-placed Shakespearian quotes to ward off guys and Jonah's quiet humor put me on edge. However, with each experience, I came to realize Cecille was simply protecting me with a dollop of love and a gallon of wit. And to her credit, I had yet to hear the same quote twice. This was, I learned from Jonah, thanks to Number Four, who was a Shakespeare scholar and had taken her to see all the plays. While I fully appreciated her epic ability to effectively silence rude customers, demons from my past still tortured the corners of my mind.

The door chimed as I was grabbing change for one of my tables, and I looked up to see my sister, her perfect dark curls bouncing behind her. I dropped the change off with table four and returned to the counter.

"Hey, Holly!" Abby flopped down on a stool at the counter, dropping her bag at her feet. "Could I have a cup of coffee, please?"

"Sure."

"Hi, Jonah," she sang sweetly, waving at him with her fingers and giving him a wink.

He grinned, resting his forearms on the ledge of the warming station. "Hey there, Abby. How's my favorite girl?"

"Only a few months from legal."

"I'll be sure to ask Cecille for a raise so I can buy a ring."

My sister nodded. "I'll take *all* the diamonds."

"Of course, my love."

I shook my head with a chuckle as I poured a cup of coffee for my sister. "You two are something else."

Abby just laughed. "Thanks." Whether it was for the coffee or my comment, I decided I did not want to know.

"What brings you in?" I asked her.

"She's here for a job interview," Cecille said brightly, giving Abby a bear hug.

"A job interview?" I repeated.

Abby's smile was soft. "I asked Cecille not to tell you. I want you to go on the cruise. One, because you're an amazing photographer. And two, because you deserve this trip more than anyone else I know. I thought that maybe if I started working here, you'd worry less." She held up her hand before I could protest, ticking off more reasons on her fingers. "You will know where I am. You will know Jonah and Cecille would have their eye on me. And you will not need to worry about Cecille being short-handed."

"That's an awesome sister right there," Jonah muttered.

"No, *that's* an awesome sister right there," Abby said, pointing to me.

I reached across the counter to squeeze her hand. I had been the older sibling, responsible for my sister since she was eight years old. Yet her continued selflessness and loyal kindness made me wonder how I had gotten so lucky with the sister card that had been given to me.

Our mom died when I was twelve, so we moved in with our grandmother. When she died, I became Abby's legal guardian. I worked my tail off and went to school on a full scholarship, completing a degree in photography and media in three years. By then, Abby was plowing through middle school, head held high, despite all the crappy taunts and jabs about her family.

We desperately needed a change. Hartford, the mid-sized Wisconsin town, had a great school for Abby and anonymity for both of us, two states away from those who had made my life a living hell. Abby and I had pooled our savings to make the trip—one moving truck, one car, and a lifetime of emotional baggage.

Just last night, she had been over the moon thrilled, flapping the envelope at me from our second-story apartment while I gathered the grocery bags from the car. I chuckled remembering her reaction—jumping around wildly in our kitchen before snatching the letter to read the rest.

"Seriously?" she squealed. "An all-expenses-paid cruise from San Francisco to Hawaii?"

"Abby, you're going to shatter a window."

"This is a big deal!"

I grabbed the letter from her flailing hand. "I know it's a big deal. I just don't think the screeching is necessary."

I had submitted a series of photographs to the competition just before the April first deadline. As May became June, I figured I had not been a finalist. I skimmed the rest of the letter. "I have until the end of June to decide if I'm going. The cruise leaves July fourteenth."

"Of course, you're going," Abby said, tucking away the bread and her favorite chips.

I sighed. "Two weeks. That's a long time to be gone."

"From me? Holly, I'm seventeen years old. I'm perfectly capable of looking after myself for two weeks.

It's summer. I'm working on finding a job, and when I do, it's going to be: get up, workout, go to work, and go to sleep. On repeat. All summer long."

"I know, but it's my responsibility to—"

"To take this opportunity to step toward your dream career. You're going. I'll pack your bags myself if I need to," she said, putting her hands on her hips. "And I'll be sure to pack the skimpiest outfits I can find to show off your rockin' bod. You're going, Holly. I won't let you back out of this."

Shaking my head at the previous night's discussion, I gathered the construction crew's plates from the warmer and headed to their table. Cecille adored Abby. I had no doubt she'd hire her on the spot. With my two major worries out of the way, I had no reason not to say yes to the cruise. And yet, years of being constantly responsible for everything still caused me anxiety.

Two

"You know she'll be fine, right?" Jonah asked later that evening when I went to the fridge for more coffee creamers. "Abby, I mean."

I smiled at him. "Yeah, I know. It just doesn't make leaving her any easier."

Jonah turned and leaned against the stove, crossing thick arms over his chest. "Overprotective sister."

"We have been through a lot together. I'll gladly accept that title," I said with a shrug. I returned to the dining room, empty after hours. Cecille had gone home with Joe at seven, leaving the two of us to clean up and close.

"You haven't talked much about your life before you guys came to Hartford. Except that you used to live in Ohio."

I moved to each booth, filling creamer and jelly bowls. If I stayed quiet, perhaps he would change the subject. Upon my return to the kitchen, however, Jonah looked up expectantly. I sighed. "To say we've been through a lot of crap together would be an understatement. I just try not to focus on the past." I picked up the large pot he washed and began drying.

"Sounds like you need a well-deserved break. A fully-paid cruise seems perfect."

"Oh, I'm not disagreeing there," I grinned. "Some of it seems too good to be true, though. If I got into the finals, surely there are others better than me. That reward money is a pipe dream."

"One hundred thousand dollars," he remembered. "What would you do with it?"

"Put Abby through college."

Jonah glanced up at me, raising an eyebrow. "Isn't that money supposed to help your photography business?"

"Abby's education comes first," I replied firmly. "After that, if there's anything left, new equipment or a studio."

"What does Abby want to go to school for?"

"She's still undecided."

"Has she picked a school yet?"

I shook my head. "It's her project for the summer, to narrow down her choices."

"And if she chooses somewhere further away?"

Jonah knew me all too well, but I only shrugged. "We'll cross that bridge when we get there."

He laughed. "I can already see it. In a year, she will be coming to Cecille and I, asking us to keep an eye on you while she's gone."

"We only have each other."

"It's been that way a long time, hasn't it?"

I flinched under the weight of his gaze. No one liked to talk about trauma. "Yeah."

"How long?"

I cleared my throat. "Um… eight years, since our grandma died."

"You were young."

"Eighteen." I cleared my throat again before meeting his eyes. "Can we talk about something else, please?"

"Yeah, sorry," he replied, immediately backing off. "I just—I was only trying to say that if you've been Abby's guardian for so long, that it might be easy to forget who you are. If you've been her guardian that long, you *need* this trip. You have more than earned it."

"Thanks."

When I first met Jonah, my initial reaction was intimidation. He towered over everyone, made even more noticeable when you added in the heavily-tattooed, well-toned arms and broad shoulders. He had long chestnut hair tied back in a man bun, a style that only seemed to work for him. Add to that perfectly tanned skin, a well-groomed short beard, and emerald green eyes, and you had a recipe for disastrously handsome. Luckily, his charming, kind nature set me at ease. We had become friends, and he rarely asked personal questions. I gladly returned the favor.

When the dishes were washed, dried, and put away, I moved to count the cash drawers and tip jars while Jonah mopped the floors. We worked quietly to the sounds of Elvis, Billy Joel, Neil Diamond, and a few other classics. It was an eclectic collection, pieced together over decades by Cecille and her husbands.

We finished the nighttime duties just before nine. I waited while Jonah locked the doors and then we walked together to the parking lot. My car, a geriatric sedan, looked small and pathetic beside Jonah's immaculate, brand new black pickup.

"Maybe a new car," I sighed. "If I won first place."

"It is a miracle that that thing even starts when you turn the key."

"Hey, she's sturdy! Don't hurt her feelings."

Jonah barked a laugh. "Sturdy? She's a rust bucket."

I patted the hood when I reached it. "Don't you listen to him, Felicia. He's just jealous."

"Jealous," Jonah chuckled, shaking his head.

"Your truck must drive like a bus. There is no way you could ever win a race—you'd run out of gas just accelerating to race speed."

Jonah's eyes narrowed. "Care to make a bet?"

"Care to give up all your tip money?" I countered. "Because I'd waste you."

"Pick a day and time."

I laughed, shaking my head.

"Wuss," he taunted.

"Not a wuss, I just need to get home."

"Big plans?"

"Abby and I have a pool date and then it's time for Netflix and ice cream."

"Sounds girly."

"What are you doing tonight?"

"Baseball. Beer. Pizza." Each word was grunted like a caveman.

"Huh, sounds manly."

"Very," he responded proudly.

I laughed. "Goodnight, Jonah."

"'Night, Holly."

I drove home humming to whatever was on the radio and went up to the apartment. "Abby? Are you here?" I called, dropping my keys in the bowl by the door.

"Yeah. Time for a swim?" Abby asked.

"Yes, please."

"Cecille called this afternoon. I got the job. She told me at the café, but she said she had to call and make it official," Abby chuckled while I changed. "I start on Thursday."

"Do you have all your paperwork ready?"

"I just need to get my birth certificate from the safety deposit box tomorrow."

I changed, grabbed my things, and joined her as we started the trek downstairs. "You didn't have to do that, you know. Apply for a job at Cecille's."

She laughed. "Yes, I did, because you're a worrywart. And besides, I was already planning on applying there anyway. Beats scooping ice cream all summer. You don't mind, though, do you? I won't be cramping your style?"

I thought of the construction workers from the lunch crowd. "You'll be in good hands. But there are creeps at every job. Just be careful, please."

"When I have Jonah and Cecille to keep an eye on me? Please."

"I'm serious, Abby."

Her sigh echoed in the stairwell. "I know, but I'm not worried. You shouldn't be either. Besides, I have to keep an eye on my future fiancé."

"You two are ridiculous."

Abby tossed her hair dramatically. "Yes, we are. Fabulously so."

Abby had come to the café a few times shortly after I started working there and occasionally brought her friends from school. They all stared at Jonah, giggling, and whispering to each other when he wasn't looking. When prom approached, her friends heckled her about finding a date despite her assurances that she *wanted* to go alone. She finally announced, during lunch with said friends at Cecille's, that she was taking Jonah. He went along with it for the remainder of the meal. Since then, Jonah and Abby's faux relationship had blossomed most exaggeratedly.

"I got asked about you today," Abby told me, holding the door to the pool room.

"Oh?"

"Yep. The blond guy at the grocery store—the cute one that works in the deli. He asked where you were today. Then, he asked if you were seeing anyone."

I groaned, dropping my towel on the bench. "What did you say?"

Abby skipped past me, leaping into the pool. "That I wasn't at liberty to say. My comment may or may not have been accompanied by a wink."

"Abby!"

"Holly!" she said, matching my lamenting tone. "He is cute, and seems nice, and obviously noticed you. Take a chance."

"I don't date."

"Don't or won't?"

"Can't," I corrected.

"Holly, it has been a long time since high school. Isn't it time to move on from the past?"

"I'm not dating, Abby," I said firmly.

She recognized the edge in my tone and backed off with a shrug. "I just want my sister to be happy. And I know you, Holly. You are a romantic at heart. You don't need a man to run your life, but you do need to find someone to love and to love you."

I chose not to respond, donning my cap and goggles and diving into the pool. She did know me well, but one too many heartbreaks had led to the major construction of walls around my emotions. Abby was right, sort of. It had been nearly a decade since high school, and we had moved far away from the guys who had destroyed my high school career and social life. A series of boyfriends, all meeting unusual accidents in their lives while dating me. Eventually, they had bonded together, nicknaming me Holly Heartbreaker, or Holly Arm-breaker, or whatever fit their purpose. A floozy for a mom and a drunk or high (or both) grandma had not helped the situation either.

I tapped Abby's foot as I came up behind her, telling her to let me pass at the next wall. While I had the speed, she had the endurance. She was planning on joining the swim team again in the fall for her senior year and told me she wanted to attend a college where she could continue to swim competitively. I had quit swimming in my junior year of high school when the teasing had reached the worst. I had accidentally knocked my ex-boyfriend, Brayden Jones, into the pool. We had just broken up the week before when I discovered he was cheating on me with one of the other swimmers. Though he denied it at the time, he had shown up at the swim meet to support her. When he fell, he twisted his leg and ended up tearing several muscles in his knee, causing an early end to his football season. He had rolled away on the stretcher swearing he would get me back. True to his word, he ostracized me from the swim team, pitting me against each of the other members with well-placed insults, tricks, or rumors.

I screamed into the water on my next breath, pushing myself faster. Years had passed, but the pain was still fresh. I had tried so hard to pretend everything was all right, but he told all his enemies in the school that I was easy and his friends that I was bad luck. It was not obvious at first but as more guys took any opportunity to get me alone, copping feels, or trying to steal kisses, I realized what was happening. He told girls I had slept with their boyfriends. He even went so far as to hide my clothes for the girls to find and to convince guys to display extra hickies and scratches claimed to be left by me. By the end of my junior year, my grades plummeted, as I fought depression and anger. I begged Gram to let me finish my senior year online, but she refused, believing traditional schooling was the only way.

"Holly!" Abby shouted, grabbing my leg when I did a flip turn past her. "I thought we were doing one hundred S.K.I.P.S. You just did two hundred."

"Sorry." I took a drink from the water bottle she handed me. S.K.I.P.S—swim, kick, individual medley, pull, swim. One hundred yards each, with a one-minute break in between.

"I'm sorry too."

"It's fine."

"No, it isn't."

"It is," I told her. "I promise."

"It doesn't have to be Cute Deli Guy, but you should try dating again. Make a goal. Maybe… one date every month. You could try online dating if you don't feel comfortable asking a guy."

"I'm *not* doing online dating."

"Why not?"

I made a face. "It's so… awkward."

"Okay, but maybe there's someone who you see often that you could hang out with, or flirt with, or you know, mention you're looking for Mr. Right."

"No."

She caught me in a trap. "Wait. Who did you just think about?"

"No one."

"Come on, Holly."

"Go." It was sooner than a minute, but I knew she would press harder. Unfortunately, the next lap was kicking, so we were both above the water.

"Come on, tell me."

"I didn't think of anyone."

"Fine, I'll guess."

"Please don't," I moaned.

"Is it the hot guy who orders pie and Mountain Dew every Tuesday?"

"No."

"What about… Jack, the guy who stops at the café every Friday?"

"Nice guy," I said. "Married."

"The guy who calls you Hotty Holly?"

The fifty-something, overweight trucker who came through each week. He didn't shower on his week-long trips and insisted on having leftovers for Pickles, his obese feline companion. "Eww. No."

"Come on, Holly. Just tell me."

"I wasn't thinking of anyone in particular. When you said that, I simply went through the Rolodex of Cecille's regular customers. There isn't anyone I'd be interested in seeing romantically, and I don't want to date anyone."

"What about the people you work with?"

"There's only Kevin and Jonah. And Kevin is married."

"What about Jonah? What's wrong with him?"

I paused at the wall to face her. "You're not serious."

Abby shrugged. "What if I was?"

"I could *not* date Jonah."

"Why not?"

I raised my eyebrows. "Besides the fact that you've claimed him? Jonah is my friend."

"You friend-zoned him before he had a chance to ask you out."

"He would never have asked," I snickered.

"How do you know?"

"He wouldn't have asked." I tried to picture dating Jonah and giggles bubbled out of me. A big, tattooed, perfect specimen Jonah, holding the hand of a curvy, broken, sarcastic, only-works-out-so-she-can-eat-ice-cream Holly.

Abby's eyes narrowed. "What?"

The giggles wouldn't stop. "I just pictured it. And… I just can't."

"Is he seeing anyone?"

"I always pictured him with a short, petite blond with tattoos and piercings."

"Okay, but is he dating anyone?"

I shrugged. "I never asked."

"Who else? Come on, Holly, live a little! Oh, maybe you'll meet Mr. Right on the cruise," she decided. "Someone who likes photography as much as you, who sweeps you off your feet, and—oh, you better not have a destination wedding while you're in Hawaii. I need to be there. Maybe he'll be loaded and fly me out there. Maybe he'll have a hot friend."

"You're ridiculous."

Abby belted out a few lines of "Don't Rain on My Parade" in response.

Three

On Thursday, Abby came with me to work as planned. The summer before, she had worked at an ice cream shop. She came home every night exhausted but never complained, as she was spending all day with her friends. This year, she had mentioned finding a job that paid better rather than adding a second job to the ice cream shop, so that she could have a little more free time.

She practically skipped into the building, hugging Cecille when she saw her.

"She reminds me of a puppy," Jonah muttered, as I passed him to drop off my things. "All energy and innocence."

"That's Abby," I agreed. As I tied my apron, Abby's suggestion of dating Jonah came back to me. I let out a snort of laughter.

"Care to share with the class, Miss Douglas?" Jonah asked.

"No, sorry. What's the latest gossip today?"

Jonah shrugged. "Nothing out of the ordinary. Cecille is bubbling with excitement over the fact that Abby is working here now."

Before I could leave the bar, Cecille appeared with Abby at her side. For such a tiny woman, she could deal bone-crushing hugs. "Hi, Holly. Take your sister with you. I want you to teach her your shorthand for meal tickets, please."

"Sure. I usually bring water with me," I told Abby.

"I'll grab some glasses and meet you in a minute."

"Thanks." I moved to the table. "Hello, gentlemen. Welcome to Cecille's. What can I get you to drink?"

I started taking orders as Abby appeared, distributing the drinks with a bright smile. She then turned her attention to my notepad. It irked me to see all three men sit up a bit straighter, eyeing Abby. This was nothing new. Everywhere we went, it happened, but it never ceased to amaze me that her being a minor did not seem to matter. She had black lazy curls pulled back into a messy bun with big green eyes. She had spent many of her younger years experimenting with makeup and had perfected the task, always choosing natural makeup tones that accentuated her eyes and lips. She was as tall as me with curves in the form of boobs and hips rather than my thighs and ass. Everything else was lean and perfect, just like her sunny personality. I couldn't blame the guys, I decided, but honestly.

ooooo

Abby shadowed me for the rest of the day, finding ways to make herself useful when I did not have any tables. Seventeen years old perhaps, but a good head on her shoulders and a go-getter attitude.

"Abby is doing well," Jonah said, resting his hip on the prep counter behind him as I made another pot of coffee.

"She is. I think a lot of the things we do here are similar to what she did at the ice cream shop last year." I grinned as she sent an elderly couple at a booth into gales of laughter, gesturing wildly. Her laughter floated through the noise of the café. I sighed. "I envy her spirit sometimes."

"You have spirit."

"It isn't the same."

"It shouldn't be." When I looked up in surprise, Jonah shrugged. "Sure, you might be sisters but wishing to be more like her is like… the waves asking to be more like the wind."

I put my hands on my hips. "What is that supposed to mean? That I can't be as fun as my sister?"

"Nope," he said coolly, ignoring my ruffled feathers. "Abby is young, innocent, protected. Thanks to you, she can stay that way a bit longer. You… You have just as much spirit but exert it differently. Puppy," he said, pointing to Abby. Then, he pointed to me, "Kitten."

"Kitten? Ah, pet names. Number One used to call me that," Cecille grinned. "Suits you much better than me, though, Holly."

"See?" Jonah crowed.

My cheeks flushed as I tried to block out Jonah's laughter. "On your way out?" I asked her.

"Yes, Joe just pulled up. Going to the movies tonight for some Jujubes and neckin'."

"Cecille!"

"'To thine own self be true,' Kitten."

"*Macbeth*?" Jonah asked.

She put her fists on her hips, dealing him a dark scowl. "Really, Jonah, have I taught you nothing? *Hamlet*. See you all tomorrow."

"Cheese and rice," I muttered, covering my cheeks with my hands, willing them to cool.

"What's up?" Abby asked, as she approached.

"Nothing," I answered quickly. It only made Jonah laugh harder. "How's it going?"

"I was just talking with Mrs. Williamson and her husband. She was my English teacher last year and just retired. Jonah, my love," she said, addressing him as she had all day. "I need one BLT with fries and one bacon cheeseburger, well done, with fries, please. Holly, did I get the abbreviations right?" she asked, showing me the notepad. I nodded. "Yes! Okay, I'm going to take a quick snack break. I'll be back in five minutes. What time do you usually start your closing routine?"

"Seven." Jonah stopped cooking around seven-fifteen and cleaned up the kitchen while the last customers finished their meals.

She glanced up at the clock, nodding. "Got it. Be right back."

She bumped past a man on his way in, apologizing before jogging out to the car. He paused to watch her before turning to enter. My heart dropped as I spun back to the kitchen, breathing deeply.

"Holly? You all right?" Jonah asked, catching my quick movement.

"Oh," I said, swallowing several times. "Yeah, I'm good."

Aaron Jones, Brayden's older brother, sat at the counter, hardly looking up from his phone when I turned to him. "Welcome to Cecille's," I stammered, as he picked up a menu. "What can I get for you?"

"Coffee. Any specials today?"

He didn't recognize me, I realized, though my heart was still racing. The years had added a few pounds to his waistline, and he sported a new hairstyle to hide the receding blond hairline. I could see the start of crow's feet around his eyes. Be cool, Holly, relax. "Ham and cheese melt, fish sandwiches, and potato soup."

"I'll take the ham and cheese," he said, setting the menu aside to look up at me. His eyes widened and then narrowed. "I know you. How do I know you?"

Thank goodness Cecille didn't require name tags. "I-I'm not sure," I said with a quick shrug.

"You look so familiar to me," he said, tapping a finger on the counter. "Are you from the area?" I nodded. "Not me. Do you work anywhere else?" I shook my head. "Dang it. Well, this is going to bother me. What's your name?"

"Jane."

"Jane… huh."

I handed the meal ticket to Jonah, who had watched the exchange with curiosity. I gave a slight shake of my head before grabbing the coffee pot. After pouring Aaron a cup, I moved around the restaurant, timing Abby's return to hurriedly whisper the situation to her.

"I'll do recon," she whispered.

"Abby, no, please." She was already gone. I took my time refilling glasses, checking that everyone had what they needed before steeling myself against the inevitable.

"One ham and cheese," Abby said, setting the plate in front of him.

"Thanks. This looks great." He spotted me and was about to speak again when his phone rang. "Excuse me."

Abby took my elbow and led me away from the counter through the swinging doors. "I think it's about time for your break, isn't it?"

"You need—"

"I've got it. If I have questions, Jonah can help me." She gave me a quick hug. "He's here on business. Small world maybe, but this is a one-time thing. You're good." She poked her head into the kitchen. "Jonah my love, my sister is on her break. Is there any soup left? She will take a cup, please. Thanks."

I sat down in the small room that was Cecille's office and put my head down on the desk. I had spent years convincing myself I was better, stronger. I had even gone to a couple of therapy sessions to work on it. And yet, at the first challenge since high school, I had dissolved into a terrified, stupid mess. "What is wrong with me?" I groaned.

"Nothing. You just got dealt shitty cards in life," Abby replied, setting a bowl and spoon down before me. "He just took his sandwich to go. Said he had a business emergency. I can hold down the fort until you get back."

Breathing a sigh of relief, I pulled myself together. The potato soup was amazing, as always. Cecille spent every Monday making large batches of soup, freezing them for the week in gallon tubs. I had never been much of a soup lover, but Cecille's magic recipes had changed that. How she could make vegetables taste so damn good was beyond me.

"You good?" Jonah asked when I returned to the dining room.

"Yeah," I sighed. "How's Abby?"

"She's fine."

"Good." As it approached six-thirty, I moved to collect and refill condiments, sugar, salt, pepper, and jelly bowls. Abby ran the tables, finishing up the last four.

I laughed when she locked the door after the last couple left, dramatically leaning against it with her best rendition of Etta James's "At Last". Laughing, she perched on a stool at the counter. "My feet," she moaned.

I handed her a glass of soda. "You've been busy. Take a few minutes while I count the money drawer. Cecille said she would teach you that job tomorrow. When I'm done, I will take you through the closing list."

"Sounds good." She took a sip before moving to the jukebox. Producing a coin, she perused the track lists. "Jackpot!" she squealed. In moments, the deep, soothing voice of Howard Keel filled the empty room as she danced back to the counter.

"I thought you said you were tired," I chuckled.

"How can I be with Mr. Keel singing straight to my soul? Right, Jonah?" she asked, sticking a hand out as he passed with the mop bucket. He grabbed her hand and spun her on the stool like a dance. Her surprised look quickly turned to curiosity. "Wait, wait, wait!" she squealed, bouncing off her chair. "Jonah! You've got some moves. Smooth moves!"

Jonah shrugged. "A few."

"Come on! Holly, did you know about this?"

"Am I not supposed to have moves?" Jonah countered. "Too old?"

Abby laughed. "No! Well, how old are you, anyway?"

"Twenty-eight."

She waved her hand. "That's not old. No, I'm just… You don't strike me as the type."

"She's nicely telling you you're too old to be cool," I remarked.

Jonah barked a laugh as Abby argued. "Holly! Not helping!" She pestered him for a bit, giving up when she realized he would not give her any details. "Alright, sir, you leave me no choice," she decided, fisting through her apron for another coin. Punching a number into the jukebox, she slipped her shoes off and crooked a finger at him. When the music started, she began the *Footloose* line dance, taunting him to join in.

Jonah paused his mopping to watch before turning to me. I smiled, clucking like a chicken much to Abby's delight. Jonah narrowed his eyes at me, setting the mop aside. Glaring at me, he moved across the room to the open space beside Abby, smoothly joining in with her. He was extremely light on his feet and could ad-lib his moves with the music, easily catching Abby's hand to dance with her too. I stared in shock.

He only danced a few minutes before gliding back to his mop. "If you'll kindly pick your jaw up off the floor, *Kitten*, I have to mop there."

My cheeks reddened as I guffawed. "As you wish, Twinkle Toes."

Abby was laughing too as she put her shoes back on. "All right, Jonah, you win this round. Holly, what can I do?" I had her wipe down the counters and tables while I started the dishes. Images of Jonah dancing kept me grinning to myself.

When he joined me later, I burst out laughing all over again. "I'm sorry. I just… I did not expect that from you."

"That I have rhythm?"

"That you line dance. To *Footloose*!"

Jonah shook his head. "I had something to prove, not that you helped."

"My sister's persistence knows no bounds."

"Noted." He picked up the pan I washed and began drying. "She's also incredibly talented."

"Theater and choir."

"Yes, that too." When I looked up at him, he added, "She's also very good at drawing attention away from you when you're upset."

"Oh," I said, blushing fiercely. I had never thought of it that way before, but he had a point.

"Who was that guy?"

"I shook my head. "He's from Ohio. I knew his brother. He caught me by surprise, that's all."

"What happened, Holly? I've never seen you panic like that before."

I turned my eyes back to the pan I was washing. "There are a lot of reasons we moved to Wisconsin. That guy and his brother were two of them."

"That doesn't answer my question." I looked back at him, trying to gauge his feelings. His face remained passive, simply studying me in return.

Abby bounced through the swinging doors. "Holly? What else can I do?"

Four

Abby only needed to shadow me for the remainder of the weekend before being scheduled for hours on her own. Two other waitresses worked at Cecille's since Therese had retired in April. Diane and Judy, two of Cecille's closest friends, were also approaching retirement age. Both ladies had mentioned wanting fewer hours, which was why Cecille had hired Abby. With her filling in and covering my cruise, Cecille would not need to look for part-time help until Abby went back to school in the fall.

My sister hovered over me as I accepted my spot on the cruise and scoured the website on her phone that had a Q and A menu about the competition. There were one hundred people total, and she gave me their stats as I did the grocery shopping.

"Okay, they picked twenty men and twenty women, half for photography, half for writers." She was quiet for a moment, waiting for her phone to load. "Here we go. Seven people have filled out their 'about me' page. Five women, two men. One guy is… Fred Cunningham, photographer, age seventy-four. Oh, look! He's adorable!" She showed me a picture of a small, burly man who resembled something between Richard Gere and Santa Clause. "Guy number two. Oh my. Name is Nick Grable, age thirty-five, and sexy as hell."

"Abby!"

"He is, look." The second man was built like a brick house with curly hair, dark eyes, and skin that suggested a Latino background. "Dreamy," she decided. "And he's a photographer too."

"Abby… I see where you're trying to take this."

"Where?" she asked innocently. "Oh, it is my week to pick cereal. Yes! Trix, come to Mama." She dropped a family size box in the cart. "What are you going to write on your bio?"

"Is it required?"

Abby scrolled again. "No, I don't think so."

"I probably won't if I don't have to."

"What? Why not? I'll do it."

"Abby…" I sighed.

"What? How about if I write a blurb in a note on my phone, and you can decide later if you want to use it? Please?"

I threw a hand up in frustration. "Fine."

"Okay." She followed me around like a puppy, barely looking up as she typed furiously. Until we got to the deli, of course.

"Hey!" the deli guy said, resting his elbows on the counter with a grin. "How's it going?"

At that moment, I felt bad that I had not noticed his name before. He was there most times I shopped and had always been very friendly. I glanced at his nametag. Chad. "Hi. Could we have a pound of ham and a pound of turkey, please?" I asked, feeling my cheeks heat.

"Sure thing. Both of you off today?"

"Yep. Girls' Day," Abby chirped.

"Any big plans?"

"Swimming, chick flicks, and ice cream."

Abby rested a hip against the glass. "What's your preferred sport, Chad?"

"To play? I was always a soccer guy."

She raised an approving eyebrow at me. "Holly played soccer in high school too."

Holy cheese and rice, Abby. Subtle. "Thanks," I said when he handed me the first bag.

"You play soccer?" Chad asked with a friendly smile, grabbing another handful of sandwich meat.

"Ah… played. I haven't been to a soccer field for a long time."

"Well, if you ever want to practice, you know where to find me."

"Thanks." When he handed me the second bag, I turned the cart away. "Have a good day."

"Thanks, you too," he called after me.

Thankfully, Abby waited until we were out of eyesight to pounce. "Oh my God, Holly! You know he basically asked you on a date just now, right?"

"I'm not an idiot, Abby. I heard him."

"So…?"

"So what?" When she just put her hands on her hips, waiting, I shook my head. "I am not looking to date anyone, Abby."

"Holly, come on!"

I stopped and turned to her. "Why?" I demanded. "You've never been bothered by my single status before. Why are you pushing this now?"

"Holly, I've *always* been bothered by your single status. I've taken many opportunities to try and get you back into the dating world. Because you are awesome, and the world needs to know. *You* need to know." She threw her hands up in frustration. "I have one year left of high school. After that, college. I don't know where that will be yet. If it's farther away, I want to know you aren't lonely. That you aren't all work, sleep, repeat, holed up in the apartment. I want to know you are happy, in love, and taken care of by someone who loves you as much as I do." I watched in surprise as her eyes filled with tears. "And apparently, the grocery store is where we have our deep conversations now."

I chuckled, pulling her into a hug. "Apparently," I said, my eyes not entirely dry. "Look, I appreciate it, now that I know where you are coming from. Please, stop worrying. That's my job, remember? And no," I said, speaking before she could argue, "it won't just be work, sleep, repeat. I have my photography to continue perfecting. If I win this competition, I'm going to get a studio. If I don't win, I will just convert your room."

"Hey," came her muffled response.

I laughed. "Come on. Pull yourself together, and let's go out for lunch."

She took my list and grabbed a few more items as my mind wandered. She was not completely wrong, I decided. If Abby went to a college farther away, unable to commute home on weekends, I would be lost.

Abby, my mom, and I had been involved in a car accident when I was twelve years old. Abby had been just three at the time. She and I had walked away from it with minimal injuries. Mom had not. She ran a stop sign and was hit by a pickup truck, the impact all in her door. Thankfully, Abby and I had been on the other side of the vehicle. Since neither of us knew our fathers—only that they weren't the same—we had gone to live with her mom, Gram. The mother and daughter shared a love of social ostracism, choosing things that made them happy rather than things that would help make them friends or be good, contributing members of society. Gram's interests included men, gambling, whiskey sours, and dabbling in prescription medicine. She was kind enough to us, but at twelve, I assumed most of the household chores and caring for Abby. I was angry, so angry with both Mom and Gram, but I kept it locked away, needing that feeling of normalcy. Or at least the "normal" I saw when visiting friends.

A month after I turned eighteen, Gram's whiskey and medicine recipe proved fatal. Despite being a few months into college, I did not bat an eye, adopting legal guardianship of nine-year-old Abby. There were a few fights and disagreements but we had managed well enough. We had taken life one day at a time for so many years. It was hard to picture life without her. So, I simply hadn't thought about the future. I did not know what I was going to do, but I sure as hell wasn't going to tell her that.

Taking care of Abby... That had been my life since I was twelve. Maybe it was time for something new. I just wasn't sure if dating was it.

ooooo

A week before I was to leave on my trip, Louis, our landlord, dropped a bill at our door, giving us a warning that our rent would be rising three hundred dollars a month in January. His reasons were: he was promoting the handyman to full-time and moving into partial retirement.

"Three hundred!" Abby fumed, as we drove to work. "Three hundred, times twenty apartments, times twelve months." She pounded the keys on her phone and barked out a laugh. "Seventy-two *thousand* dollars. Either that's a *very* well-paid handyman, or Louis has another gold-digger in his life. Cheese and rice! The rent is high enough already. Nine hundred dollars a month is too high!"

"Let me worry about that."

"We should find a new place before school starts. I can pack while you're on your trip."

"Abby, it's fine. Don't pack. We will figure out a plan when I get back."

She was still seething when we got to Cecille's, storming past the window to the kitchen.

Jonah cocked an eyebrow at me. "No greeting for her future husband?"

I shook my head. "She's never been shy about her emotions. Worn her heart on her sleeve since I can remember."

"What's going on?"

"They are raising our rent. She's very upset about it."

I had spoken loud enough for her to hear, knowing she needed one last vent session to move on. "No. They aren't just *raising our rent*," she said, whipping out a pair of angry air quotes. "They are shoving our rent up our ass. Six hundred to nine hundred dollars a month, effective January first. Six hundred square feet, no in-unit laundry, and fixes take weeks! It's ridiculous!"

"Sounds like you need a new apartment," Jonah remarked.

"Exactly!" Abby cried. With a growl of exasperation, then a sigh, she plastered a smile on her face.

Jonah chuckled as she walked away. "You weren't kidding. That girl's a wild child."

"She'll be fine now," I grinned. "Just a little emotional regurgitation and she's good."

"It does sound like you're getting screwed, though. I don't know of any apartments here that would be worth nine hundred bucks."

"It's new news. We will figure something out."

"I'm happy to help if you need me."

I laughed. "Do you have about six friends with your scary and imposing stature? Because our landlord reminds me of Mr. Roper from *Three's Company*, cocky and arrogant but easily intimidated."

"I'll let you know when I decide if your description of me was an insult or a compliment, Kitten."

ooooo

The free time I had that day was spent creating to-do lists: one with things to do before I left, one for packing. There were only six more days until my plane ride, seven until the cruise left the continental states. I had managed to snag a cheap ticket to California as well as a discounted hotel room. Granola bars and snacks would tide me over until I could find breakfast on the cruise in the morning.

I also spent my time laughing at Cecille's verbal berating of Jonah's new purchase.

"He bought a damn motorcycle," she snapped when I asked. "A motorcycle. Damn death contraption!"

"Cool it, Cecille. It's just a motorcycle. Saves gas. And it's not like I'm driving it cross-country. I only live a few blocks away."

She flapped her hands furiously at him. "I don't care if you lived one block away! I don't like it. Take it back."

"Nope."

"Don't make me come back there."

"You probably should go back there, Cecille," Abby commented as she passed, fueling the fire. "He is not listening."

"Not helping," Jonah sang.

"I know," she sang back.

Jonah's eyes narrowed at his aunt. "Didn't Number Two have a bike?"

Cecille's eyes narrowed through the thick lenses. "And Number Three and Four. But it's not the same."

Jonah guffawed. "How is it any different?"

"Because you are my nephew, and I love you."

"So, you didn't love Two, Three, or Four?"

"Of course, I did, you rampallion! It's different because I love you and want to keep you safe."

"I'll be fine."

Cecille threw up her arms and let out a growl of exasperation. "Maybe you can talk some sense into him!" she told me, grabbing the coffee pot to make a round of refills.

"A motorcycle, huh?" I asked when she was gone.

"Yeah. The black one in the parking lot."

I looked in the direction he nodded. I knew nothing about motorcycles, but it was shiny, sleek, and looked expensive. "Traded the gas guzzler?"

Jonah looked at me as though I'd suggested putting fish on a grilled cheese. "Of course not!"

"So, you own two vehicles. When you can only drive one at a time?"

"Ever ridden on a motorcycle?"

"Ha! Nope."

He winked as he grinned. "Never too late to try new things."

Abby overheard and giggled. "Holly ride a motorcycle? When pigs fly."

"Hey, now!" I chided, though I laughed anyway, refilling the coffeemaker.

Five

The whole day. I made it the whole day.

Almost.

After a slow day, I had begun the nighttime chores early. My back was to the door when it rang.

"Oh good, she is here. Maybe you can help me figure out how I know her."

I spun around to meet the gaze of a too-familiar face. "Well, holy shit. It's Holly Douglas. Fancy meeting you here in this backwater town."

Brayden Jones, the man who had ruined my teenage life. Blond and fair-skinned like his brother, but less round, apparently keeping up his fitness routine. He used the same cologne from high school, some overwhelming fresh scent. The memory of it sent my stomach spiraling.

"What are you doing here?"

"I was invited. You remember my brother, Aaron?"

Aaron's eyes lit with recollection. "Heartbreak Holly! But you told me your name was Jane."

"What are you doing in Hartford?" I asked again.

"I'm here on business. My brother and I started a software company," he said, sitting on a stool at the counter. His smile was slow and lethal. "Tell me about you, though. I cannot wait to hear about you."

"You aren't welcome here."

Brayden turned at my sister's snarl, and his brows rose. "Abby Douglas? Well, holy shit."

"I said you aren't welcome here."

"You two own this joint?"

"Abby, it's fine," I said before she could continue. "It's fine. Could you check table four, please?" I watched her hesitate before doing as I asked. Then, I turned my attention back to Brayden, summoning my courage. "I have no authority to kick you out, so I will serve your food. However, I am under absolutely no obligation to talk about my life with you. Is that understood?"

"Aww, come on, Heartbreak Holly," they coaxed together.

"You need to stop, now," I snapped. "Do you want food or not?"

"We are starving," Aaron said, grabbing a menu. "The sandwiches are good. I'll have the bacon cheeseburger with fries."

"Me too."

I put the order up for Jonah without making eye contact with him and moved to the soda fountain. "Drinks?"

"Mountain Dew."

"I bet Holly still remembers what I like best," Brayden taunted.

I did remember, but I waited for him to tell me before pouring another Mountain Dew. Slamming them down on the counter, I moved back to the sugar canisters I was filling.

"Come on, Holly Heartbreaker. It's been so long! What's new? Besides working here. You haven't changed much, at least not on the outside. Still swimming?"

I kept my back to him, trying desperately to keep my emotions in check. I tried to imagine what Cecille would say if she was still there.

"Aw, come on, Holly. Don't be so uptight. High school was ages ago. Get off your high horse. I just wanted to see if you—"

"Is there a problem here?" Jonah asked, emerging from the kitchen to stand beside me. With his arms crossed, leaning casually against the counter beside me, he looked formidable.

"No," I said quietly. I replaced the sugar canisters and reached for the saltshakers.

"No," Brayden drawled, leaning back to cross his arms. A lazy smile spread across his features. "Holly and I went to high school together. Old friends."

"You aren't friends now," Jonah observed.

"All right, you've got me," Brayden laughed, raising his hands. "We may not be friends now, but we dated a while. We were just catching up."

"No, they weren't," Abby hissed, as she passed. "This guy is a douche canoe."

I turned to look up at Jonah, who bore a look of fury. "It's fine," I said quietly, giving his arm a gentle squeeze.

Brayden crowed. "Oho, don't tell me! The waitress and the cook! Holly, have you told him about your unlucky streak?"

I turned to him, wondering how I had ever been attracted to the man before me. "Brayden, you need to stop. Now."

"You haven't told him! Well, sir, she brings bad luck to anyone she dates." He clapped his hands, rubbing them together as he leaned forward. "Ruined my high school sports career when she pushed me in the pool. She caused a car accident for her next boyfriend, stole boyfriends, made enemies with every girl in school. She's easy, though, but awful luck. I was told she even gave an STD to one of her boyfriends. Bad, bad luck, our Holly Heartbreaker."

Aaron, to his credit, had the decency to look slightly abashed. "Lay off her, Brayden. It wasn't that bad."

My face burned with embarrassment. "Get out. Now."

Brayden, however, wasn't done. "Holly's Kiss of Death. That was what the football team called it. One kiss, and your fate was sealed."

"I believe she asked you to leave," Jonah growled.

"We ordered food already," Brayden retorted, as though that excuse was good enough. "Aren't you the cook?"

Jonah pushed off the inside counter to rest his hands on the outer, putting his face inches from Brayden's. "You bet your ass I'm the cook. Trust me, you would not want the food I'd make for you. The kitchen is closed. Get out."

Brayden leaned back, but only a little. "Hey, just trying to give you a head's up."

"Get the hell out of this establishment. And get the hell over yourself."

"Holly, honestly. Call off your dog." Before he could continue, he let out a howl, jumping up from his chair and wiping at his pants.

"Suppose you should probably go clean that up," Abby said matter-of-factly, setting an empty water pitcher on the counter.

Aaron pulled Brayden out the door, though he was still spewing insults as he left. When he was gone, I held up my hands before anyone could say anything.

"Close the doors when your last table leaves," Jonah told Abby.

After the scene, the last couple seemed anxious to leave, and so Abby was able to lock the doors nearly half an hour early. I went through the motions of the nighttime cleanup, fighting to keep tears of humiliation at bay. Brayden had found me. A one in a million chance, and he had come to Hartford. High school may have been a long time ago, but the wounds were still fresh.

Abby and I waited outside while Jonah locked the doors behind us. We walked out to our vehicles in silence, and I fished my keys out of my bag, looking up in surprise when Jonah tossed them to Abby. "Drive safe. I'm taking your sister for a ride."

"Okay!" Abby grinned. "Stay out as late as you want. I'll be up waiting."

My shoulders slumped. "Jonah, as much as I appreciate it, I just want to go home, curl up under a blanket, and forget the last two hours ever happened."

"No."

I stared up at him. "What do you mean, 'no'?"

"Your sister is already leaving, first of all," he said, raising a hand as my car backed out past us. "And you need a mental break. I can help. Come on."

"Jonah…"

"Holly…"

I did not want to go anywhere on a motorcycle. I wanted to go home and wallow in ice cream and sappy chick flicks. It only took a moment to realize how pathetic it sounded. "Fine!" I cried, hoisting my bag over my shoulder and stomping toward the bike.

Jonah was chuckling behind me. "Sorry if I'm your last choice, Kitten."

I watched as he maneuvered gracefully onto the bike, kicking it off the kickstand with an ease I envied. He extended a helmet to me, and we stared at each other for a moment. Nerves sizzled as I hesitated.

"I promise not to drive like a bat out of hell. Come on, Holly. Channel that sense of adventure," he coaxed with a grin.

"Where are we going?"

"You'll see."

"Fine," I grumbled. "You and Abby seem to think I am some boring mother hen," I said, snatching the helmet. "You're going to kill me on this contraption, and I won't even get to say I told you so. If you make it and I don't, I am going to haunt you relentlessly." I swung my leg over the back, wrapped my arms around Jonah's waist, and prayed.

Jonah was still laughing as he revved the engine and we took off. It was what we called a crotch rocket—one of those bikes you had to lean forward to ride. Thus, passengers looked like piggy backers. My chest pressed to Jonah's back, my arms wrapped around his waist, gripping his shirt for dear life. I yelped as we began to accelerate, burying my face in Jonah's back.

And damn it, I enjoyed it.

Jonah maneuvered the bike easily down the roads, quiet for a weekday evening. Cecille's was on the main drag of Hartford, part of a series of townhouse-style shops all crammed together in just a few blocks. We drove out of Hartford north to the neighboring city of Acreage. It matched much of Hartford but was a smidge larger, boasting a main street twice as long, an extra eight hundred people, and a Walmart. Nothing but farms and fields between the two towns.

We pulled into Hog's Head Bar beside three other motorcycles. I had driven past the place many times but had never been inside.

"Biker bar?" I asked skeptically when I removed my helmet.

Jonah shook his head. "Coincidence. Let's get a drink," he said, guiding me inside the building. Country music was blaring, but the bar was fairly empty. An older man behind the bar waved to us, and Jonah returned the gesture. Putting a hand at the small of my back, he guided me to an open table. "What would you like to drink?"

I had not had a drink in so long, I realized. Only a glass of wine here and there with Abby stealing sips. "Beam and Coke."

His brows rose in surprise. "I didn't have you pegged for a bourbon girl. I was thinking you'd be an Irish coffee drinker."

"Tonight's a special occasion. And I'm only having one."

Jonah moved to the bar to order as I took in my surroundings. Bars had never been my preferred hangout space, but Hog's Head was not the worst. As the name suggested, someone was a big fan of hunting, or taxidermy, or both. Various animal heads and plaques lined the walls, as well as photographs of beautiful landscapes and wildlife.

"Thanks," I said when Jonah returned. "Is this a bar you frequent?"

"I play darts here every other week with a few friends."

I took a sip carefully. *Only one—the bartender had a heavy hand.* "I didn't know you played darts."

Jonah grinned. "We've worked together awhile, but we don't really talk about what happens after we punch out."

"Like playing darts and riding motorcycles."

"Or asshole ex-boyfriends?" When I did not respond, he continued. "What happened with that guy?"

"It… doesn't matter."

"Then, why did you turn white as a sheet when he walked in? You scared the daylights out of me. I thought I was going to have to scrape you up off the floor. And it happened with the brother last time, too."

"I-I don't like to talk about it. I should say, I don't talk about it."

"Why not?"

I took a long drink, hoping he would drop the subject. When he waited, I sighed. "It hurts. I don't like talking about it because it hurts. He hurt me, and I've spent years licking my wounds privately, trying to grow a thicker skin."

He remained determined. "What happened?"

"Jonah…"

"Tell me."

Whether it was the crazy day, or the relaxed atmosphere, or the first drops of alcohol warming my body, the story suddenly began to spill out. How we had dated and broken up, how I had to avoid social situations from then on. He knew I was my sister's guardian, but stories of my mom and Gram were worked into the story and how we moved to escape it all. One drink turned to three, and that dizzy, buzzy feeling took away some of the sting.

"I don't have the emotional capacity for love anymore," I told him, voicing things I had not even told Abby. "I have enough on my plate. Even if I could date, he made me realize I shouldn't. Every decision I've made in the area of relationships has been a complete disaster. I'm not trying to play the pity card. I don't want pity. But Abby keeps trying to set me up with someone. I'm Holly Heartbreaker. I'm bad luck for every guy I date."

"No, you're not."

"I am! I dated Brayden, and he tore up his knee and lost out on scholarships. One guy got in a car accident on his way home after our first kiss. Another—"

"Holly, stop." I tried to argue with him, but he reached across the table to cover my lips with his hand. "Accidents happen. Freak accidents we cannot control. You believe you caused these things because he put the idea in your head. Let them go."

I pushed his hand away. "How do you know the universe isn't just trying to tell me—"

I didn't finish my thought because Jonah's lips were on mine, his hand on the back of my neck. I could taste the beer he'd had on his lips. While I didn't like beer, I found I enjoyed it immensely. The kiss too. His beard was soft, tickling my chin now and again as his mouth moved on mine. Heaven. That's where I was. Hog's Head Bar was heaven, animal heads and all.

When he finally broke the kiss, he pulled away slowly. "I've been waiting to do that a long time," he murmured.

"Oh," I whispered.

"And to prove that if—*if*—you had a bad luck streak, it's over."

"Oh," I repeated. In the awkwardness that followed, I sipped my drink. "So… now what?"

"Nothing." I looked up at him in surprise. With a grin, he elaborated. "Look, it's clear this Brayden guy messed with your head. Why? I don't know. Probably just because he could. Teenage boys are assholes. You need to understand something, Holly. You are a strong, beautiful, spunky woman who can love and be loved, just like anyone else. You've got scars—we all do. And yes, you've overcome obstacles some of us couldn't even imagine, but you're all the stronger for it. Abby is not a child anymore and can look after herself well enough. It's your turn to relax and live life to its fullest. Let go of the responsibilities and the fears. Be free."

I smiled as I closed my eyes. "Free," I whispered, relishing the idea. "I hardly know what that word means."

"It means you're going to play darts with me and have as many drinks as you want, simply because you can."

My eyes shot open. "Darts? I've never played before."

"No time like the present, Kitten," he said, rising and holding a hand out to me.

His pet name made me laugh. I put my hand in his and grabbed my drink. "You've given me bourbon, and you're going to put sharp objects in my hands to throw. Are you sure this is a good idea?"

"I've got good reflexes. Ninja skills."

ooooo

He spent the next hour teaching me the rules of the game, encouraging me, demonstrating, gently critiquing. Whether it was the booze or the company, I felt stress begin to seep away. As always, Jonah was sarcastic and sweet, keeping a smile on my face. I let go of the kiss we had shared, focusing instead on the unexpected fun the evening had presented.

"So, what's your story?" I asked boldly between games.

Jonah lifted an eyebrow at me. "My story?"

I crossed my arms over my chest. "Yeah. No girlfriend you've mentioned, but you're cute and kind and sexy and funny and—"

"You think I'm sexy?" Jonah asked, leaning casually against the bar.

My cheeks reddened, but I stood my ground. "Jonah, *everyone* thinks you're sexy. You know how many phone numbers I have given you from female customers, and that's just at work! Come on, let's hear your story."

"I'm shy," Jonah said, as he took a sip from his beer.

"Oh, bullshit."

He nearly choked. "Get a few drinks in her, and she develops a potty mouth," he crowed.

I poked him in the chest. "You're avoiding my question."

He only laughed more. "I don't have a story. I work a lot. Not much time for relationships."

I remembered his catering business in California. He went back and forth on his days off and when the café was closed. Cecille had invested in it when he graduated from culinary school and had happily announced that she was paid back in full shortly after I started working there. "Seriously? No girlfriends? Not even a prospect?"

"Can I tell you a secret?" he asked, leaning in conspiratorially. "There is one prospect. She's beautiful, talented, funny, and hard to convince she's worth it."

"Smooth," I said, pulling away with a giggle. "Get me drunk and whisper sweet nothings to me."

"All true nothings."

I shook my head. "It's like you said, we don't have time for relationships."

"I would make time for you, Holly. The question is, would you make time for me?"

Some of the lightness melted away with his pointed tone. "Why?" I asked. "Why now? Why wait so long to tell me you liked me? And why wait until I'm inebriated to try to have such a serious conversation?"

"The drinking wasn't planned," he admitted with a sheepish smile. "Though it has gotten you to open up and relax more. I guess I can't give an honest apology for that. When you started working for Cecille, I knew you had come from something rough, but we never talked about it. I was afraid… Well, until I knew what happened, I didn't want to act on my feelings. Tonight, you told me what happened. Moving forward, I understand a little better what will trigger your emotions and how to help."

"A boyfriend is not meant to be a therapist, Jonah."

"Sure, he is. He's supposed to be around for the highest highs *and* the lowest lows. To offer support, or advice, if needed."

I shook my head. "That's too much for anyone to handle."

"Are you speaking from experience?" His green eyes pierced my soul. He did understand me better than most guys, but still, I hesitated. He seemed to understand that too. "No decisions tonight," he said with a gentle smile. "I will be here tomorrow, and the next day, and beyond."

My stomach fluttered as I nodded, hoping that his words were sincere.

"Good, now I believe I have another match to win."

I sneered. "Whatever. I will beat you just like the last four times."

"What!" Jonah cried, laughing. "You haven't won a game yet."

I gave him my sweetest smile. "No one knows that except you and I. Who will they believe?"

Jonah's eyebrows rose further. "Really? Well then, let's do this. I have been going easy on you too!"

Six

"Holly?"

I groaned as I rolled over. Abby chuckled as she came in, pulling the shades open and moving about the room. "You're a monster," I grumbled, squinting into the offensive sunlight.

"Why? Because you're tired or hungover?"

"Yes."

She chuckled, flopping onto the bed with a bottle of water and ibuprofen. "Did you have a good time last night?"

I could not help the grin that spread across my face. "Yes."

"Judging by the fact that Jonah gave you a piggyback ride up to our apartment, it would seem so. Details, please!"

My cheeks heated, vaguely remembering giggling up the steps and burying my face in Jonah's neck to keep from waking our neighbors. "Too many drinks made stairs challenging."

"Jim Beam kicked your ass, huh?" On the rare occasion I drank, Abby knew my preferred beverage.

I shrugged. "As usual." Some of the ride home was hazy, but I did remember Jonah helping me into an Uber when the bar closed, and him carrying me up to the apartment into Abby's waiting arms before catching his ride home.

"Well, good. I am glad you went and that you and Jonah had fun. I wasn't sure I'd be able to distract you enough from Brayden and Aaron."

Funny how that part of yesterday had become insignificant. I climbed out of bed, headed for the bathroom. "Well, it's easy to be distracted when you are with a tattooed, hunky guy who kisses like heaven."

"WHAT!" Abby squealed, hurtling off the bed. I beat her to the bathroom, closing and locking the door. "Holly Jane Douglas, you open this door right now and tell me everything!"

I turned the shower on, drowning out her shouting. "Sorry, I can't hear you, Dear Sister," I called sweetly.

Despite the headache, the more I moved around, the better I felt. I had gone out, had a great time after a particularly crappy day, and nothing bad had happened. Time had not stopped, everyone was fine, and I had *fun*. I had spent most of my life believing that the world needed me to spin, that I had to work my butt off to make it so. Jonah forced me to take a step away from that mindset, only to realize that it was completely ridiculous. Especially now that Abby was grown. It was time for me to loosen the reins on her life and mine, and have some fun. It wouldn't be easy to change my mentality, but perhaps with a push from the right person...

I let the cool water penetrate my thoughts and skin. Jonah's kiss had caught me by surprise, true enough, and his admission of a crush even more so. He had been my closest friend beyond Abby since moving to Hartford. I looked forward to seeing him every day. But he was

Jonah—impossibly gorgeous and sexy—and me… I had a wanna-be swimmer's body that had succumbed to too many bowls of ice cream. He was calm, cool, laid back. I was uptight and prone to stress and anxiety.

I grinned. And yet he had a crush on *me*.

ooooo

"What does this mean?" Abby squealed, as we drove to work. "Are you two dating?"

"No!"

"No? He took you out, kissed you, brought you back home safely when you were drunk, and didn't try to take advantage of you. That's what *boyfriends* do."

"That's what friends do," I corrected. "Minus the kissing." When she grinned in victory, I sighed. "We agreed to wait a little while to talk about it. Maybe after the cruise."

"That's a long time to wait. Poor Jonah. Two years in the friendzone, and you're making him wait even longer."

"It was his idea!"

"Even still!" Abby persisted. "What is there to think about? He likes you; you like him. You know you can work well together, and I have yet to hear about any arguments. You both know at least some of each other's family and get along with them. He knows your past now and is willing to help you in the future. The way I see it, you've got so much going already that it's hard to imagine it *not* happening."

"What if it doesn't work out?"

Abby shrugged. "You find good terms to end it, so you guys can still work together peacefully. I have a good feeling about this, Holly. I'm cautiously optimistic, and you should be too."

My stomach did flip flops as we pulled into the parking lot. I didn't see Jonah's truck or motorcycle. Panic filled me. It was happening again.

Ping. I parked the car and rummaged through my bag to read the incoming text message.

J: Don't worry. I'm fine. I had an emergency meeting with my catering company. Took a red-eye flight back to California.

I exhaled a sigh of relief before responding.

H: Who said I was worrying? And how did you time that text so perfectly?

J: You're a creature of habit. Hungover today?

H: Not too bad. Thank you for last night. I had a great time.

J: Me too. But if you tell people I lost at darts, I may have to exact my revenge.

H: Ha! Abby thinks I'm a darts champion. Like, Olympic quality. Way better than you. And she can't frequent bars for another three years, so...

J: Watch your back, Kitten.

"Aww," Abby cooed when I snorted a laugh. "Not even twenty-four hours and you guys are already sending love texts. Look at you, giggling at your phone. You're so cute."

I rolled my eyes. "You are ridiculous. Come on, we're going to be late."

Kevin, our backup cook, was a nice enough guy, but work wasn't the same without Jonah. Another of

Cecille's nephews and fellow chef, Kevin was a family guy, married with four kids. He kept mostly to himself, usually with earbuds in while he cooked.

Abby stuck in any jabs and teases she could, noting I spent less time behind the counter when Jonah was not around. She wasn't wrong—I had to think of more tasks to pass the time. As closing time finally approached, I glanced up to find Brayden outside the door. When our eyes met, he beckoned for me to join him.

"What the hell?" Abby fumed. "I'll tell him to go f—"

"I'll take care of it." I untied my apron and stepped outside, less emotional than I had been the day before. Instead, a small, unexpected wave of confidence washed over me as the summer's heat warmed my skin. "What are you doing here?" I asked when I got outside.

Brayden raised his eyebrows. "Not even a hello?"

"No. What are you doing here?"

"I was made aware that an apology was in order."

I crossed my arms over my chest. "You were 'made aware'? What does that mean?"

"My brother and your boyfriend."

"My boyfriend?"

"Yeah. You know, big tattoo chef guy."

"Jonah. And he isn't my boyfriend." *Yet.*

"He wants to be. And the asshole can have you as far as I'm concerned."

"You're not concerned," I snapped.

"Not anymore. Turns out, he works for Seeley Catering, one of our biggest clients, and told his boss.

Now the CEO is threatening to switch, taking many of our other clients with him. All over you."

I shook my head, not understanding any of what he was saying. "Say what you need to say and go."

Brayden put his hands in the pockets of his tailored gray suit. "That's it, I guess."

I crossed my arms over my chest again. "You didn't apologize."

"Huh?"

"You said you owed me an apology, but you didn't *actually* give me one."

"Sorry," he replied, the word dripping in sarcasm.

"Try again."

"Jesus, Holly. I'm sorry. There, is that better?"

It wasn't. "For what? What are you sorry for?" I said slowly when he stared at me.

"Seriously?"

"Seriously."

Brayden threw up his hands. "I don't know, Holly! For trying to irritate you? For teasing you? For picking a fight with your sister and your boyfriend?"

"So, you're sorry for what happened last night." At his noncommittal shrug, I continued. "What about everything else?"

"Everything else?"

"That happened in high school, you stupid, stupid man!" I shouted.

"Oh my God, Holly, that was high school. People did dumb shit all the time in—"

"No. No! Toilet papering the school was dumb. Food fights were dumb. What you did was harassment."

He scoffed. "Oh, come on."

"No! You messed me up, Brayden. With your gossiping and setups and tormenting, you made me think I wasn't good enough! You made me think I could not be loved by anyone. You made me afraid of dating and relationships. I deserve an apology for that."

"It wasn't that bad."

I slapped him then, hard. My hand burned as red began to bloom across his cheek. We both stared at each other, momentarily stunned. I recovered first. "Your actions caused depression, Brayden, so deep that I attempted suicide. If Abby hadn't found me at just the right moment, I would not be standing here today. So, don't you dare brush off what you did as 'silly high school stuff.' For me, it was that bad." When he just stared at me, I added, "I don't want to see you, ever again. Do you understand me? If you have to come to Hartford for work, fine, but skip Cecille's as a dining option. Agreed?"

"Holly—"

"Goodbye, Brayden." I stepped back inside the restaurant, holding back tears of anger and pain, and beneath them, relief. I had finally shared a part of my story with Brayden. It was both humiliating and healing. Abby rushed to my side as soon as the door was closed. "I'm okay," I said before she could ask. "Between Jonah and Aaron, they made Brayden come to apologize for last night. I told him I wanted an apology for everything."

"You slapped him!"

"Because he tried to brush off what he did in high school as nothing. So, I told him how far from nothing it was."

She put her arms around me like I was one of Cinderella's glass slippers. "Is there anything you need?"

"Ice. And maybe five minutes to pull myself together."

"Anything else?" When I shook my head, she nodded. "I'll cover your tables. We aren't very busy anyway."

I was a little shaky as I made my way back to Cecille's office. I grabbed my phone on the way and sent Jonah a quick text.

H: *Whatever you said to Brayden and Aaron, thanks. Brayden came by today saying he was told he had to apologize.*

Jonah's response was immediate.

J: *And did he?*

H: *Not very well… but I got some things off my chest that have needed to be said for a long time. And I slapped his face. My hand hurts.*

J: *You slapped him. Seriously?*

H: *Yeah.*

H: *Also, I didn't realize your catering company was large enough to affect other companies. He was pretty upset they lost your business.*

J: *I don't deal with assholes. Seeley's isn't so large, but we have earned respect over the years. Our headquarters are here in California. I started it here before moving back to Wisconsin to help Cecille.*

H: *Nephew of the year award?*

J: *I was going for the decade, but I'd settle for the year too.*

H: Hahaha. I think you've won both. Kevin isn't nearly as fun as you.

H: When will you be back?

J: Hopefully a few more days.

H: Before I leave for my trip?

J: If not, I'll find you out here before you leave.

H: I should probably get back to work. Text me later if you aren't busy.

J: Later, Kitten.

"Kitten," I chuckled, returning my phone to my pocket. Maybe next time we saw each other, we could go out on an official date. My stomach flip-flopped at the word. *Was I really ready for dating again? Maybe. With Jonah.*

Seven

As with all vacations, excitement and anticipation made the days until departure drag. What was worse, Jonah said he was busy with his catering business and rarely texted. Abby and I went on our final grocery run the day before my flight, and I packed, repacked, and repacked my bags, still unsure if I had everything I would need.

Abby disagreed. "You have your phone, your camera, your swimsuit, and aloe. You're good."

Finally, the day came for Abby to drive me to the airport. My nerves were fried, as I had never traveled much before and never alone. To my surprise, however, it was Abby that burst into tears.

"I'm so, so, so excited for you," she sobbed on my shoulder. "I'm going to miss the crap out of you, but I'm so excited."

"And you want to go away to college," I chuckled, fighting my tears.

"I'm rethinking all of it!" she wailed.

"No, you're not. We both need this trip to learn how to be on our own. I need to let go, and you need to fly." I squeezed her tighter. "Thank you for making me take this trip. I love you so much."

"You've loved me more than yourself for all this time. And I basked in it when I should have—"

"No. No 'should haves.' It's in the past."

"I love you, Holly."

"Love you, too. I'll text you when I land." With one more hug, I wheeled my suitcase to security, wiping away tears. While I waited in line, I sent a quick text to Jonah.

H: Boarding the plane shortly. Should be landing around 6. Will you be around? Dinner?

I did not get an answer before turning my phone off for the flight and settled in for the ride with a homemade sandwich. I had spent the better part of my limited free time before the trip scouring the internet for Hawaii landscape photography ideas. My entry for the contest had been in the woods not far from our apartment. I had been taking pictures of a client and her family when the sun shone between the trees, turning everything to emerald and creating a beautiful, haunting picture. Wisconsin was one of the few states where you could capture all four seasons, each amazing in their own right. I loved landscape photography, but it was a niche without a guaranteed profit. I had much better luck with portraits and families, editing a handful before selling all the rights to the client. Hawaii would be a fun change to Wisconsin.

Leaning back in my seat, I closed my eyes, my thoughts drifting to Jonah. Abby was right, I had put him in the friendzone, not realizing he wanted more. He had waited so patiently to make a move. And when he had, he had made it seem like the most natural thing in the world. With a smile, I relived our night at Hog's Head, and the kiss, and Jonah. He was so tall, easily six inches taller than me, and his biceps and forearms were corded with muscle, displaying the tattoos on his arms perfectly. The designs were a mix of blacks and grays and blues, all ocean scenes. When I asked him a few months after I started at Cecille's, he'd simply told me that water was life. I was still curious, but he didn't share more. Were there more tattoos? Was the rest of his body covered as well? What would he look like—

My eyes shot open as I blushed furiously. Picturing Jonah naked had *not* been on my list of things to keep me busy on the flight. I dug through my bag, deciding on a good romance novel instead.

ooooo

A few hours later, we landed safely in San Francisco. I fought the achy tired feeling of sitting too long as I gathered up my bag and filed out of the plane. I turned my phone back on to text Abby, a little disappointed Jonah still hadn't responded.

Abby called while I was waiting for my luggage. "You'll never believe this."

"What's up?"

"Jonah is sending a car to pick you up from the airport to take you to his place. He wants you to cancel your hotel reservations."

Her squeal had me pulling the earbuds from my ears with a wince. "Why did he call you?"

"Because you were on the plane. And he said he had a business meeting tonight that he wouldn't be able to call you when you landed."

"He couldn't have texted me?" I asked.

"Oh my goodness, Holly, molehills and mountains. He called me. I promised I would call you. I already canceled the hotel—"

"What!"

"All you have to do is go out to the pickup area, and Jonah said someone would be there to pick you up."

"Abby, I—"

"Live a little! Plus, it saves you money—no expensive hotel room, no transportation costs. And you get to hang out with your *boyfriend*."

"Not my boyfriend."

"Yet. Anyway, I have to get a swim in quick, but I'll text you when I'm done. Also, I'm dying to see his place. Send pictures."

"I'm not sending pictures of his apartment."

"I'm debating between urban modern—all metal and glass, immaculately kept—or rustic simple, all wood and plaid. Either way, I must know."

"You have had too much time to think about this."

Abby laughed. "Come on, you're going to tell me you aren't the least bit curious?"

I was, but I was not going to admit it.

"Oh, and one more thing," Abby added. "We got a letter in the mail today. Our lovely landlord is no more."

"Louis? He's dead?" I gasped.

"No!" Abby said, barking a laugh. "No, sorry, I meant he's no longer our landlord. The letter was vague, but the apartment was purchased by another company. Rent will stay the same."

"Oh."

Abby heard my relief. "One less thing to worry about on your trip."

"Yeah. That's great." Finally, the luggage conveyor belt began to move. "I have to go. I'll talk to you later."

"Love you. Send pictures."

I took several deep breaths against the panic rising in my chest. I was a planner. I organized my schedules and memorized them. Changes did not sit well. Add in the fact that I was two thousand miles from home, in a place I had never been before, and it was a recipe for mental disaster.

Jonah, I reminded myself. *Jonah knows this city. He will help.*

Jonah's apartment.

Jonah's help.

Jonah's company this evening.

One more deep breath, and some of the calm returned. I caught my bag and wheeled it outside. Cars and taxis filled the spaces in front of the doors. The weather was mild, comfortably warmer than the air-conditioned airport.

I moved to one side, debating the best way to go about finding my ride. Luckily, I did not have to wonder for long.

"Miss Douglas?" a man called a few cars down. I turned to see a tall guy in dark wash jeans and a white dress shirt rolled to the elbows. He had elbow length dreadlocks, and tattoos covered the bare skin on his arms. "You're Holly Douglas?" he asked when I approached. At my nod, he extended a hand. "My name is Max. I'm Jonah's… well, I'm a jack of all trades. His assistant is probably my best title."

"Nice to meet you."

His grin was wide. "First time in California?"

"First time on a plane. First time west of the Mississippi. First time being picked up by a total stranger." I shrugged. "It's been a big day."

His laugh was hearty. "Big day, indeed. Well, welcome to San Francisco." He pulled a letter from his back pocket. "As far as being picked up by a stranger, this is from Jonah. You can read it while I put your suitcase in the trunk so that you'll know I am not a serial killer or a kidnapper." He lifted my massive suitcase as though it weighed nothing while I opened the letter.

Holly,

Hope you don't mind the change in plans. I wasn't sure I'd still be out here, so I couldn't plan it for you sooner. I wanted to meet you at the airport myself, but an emergency meeting came up. Max will get you to my place, and I'll be home as soon as I can.

Jonah

I smiled at the handwriting. I knew it was Jonah's— all sticks, hardly any curves, tolerably legible. Max was who he said he was, and it was official, I was going to see where Jonah lived. Butterflies flitted through my stomach as I turned back to the cobalt Mustang.

"Ready?" Max asked, opening the door for me.

I shrugged again. "I hope it beats eating sandwiches in a hotel room."

Max's jaw dropped. "You're kidding, right? You were going to eat sandwiches in your hotel room? Instead of going out and seeing the town, and sampling our delicious food? No," he said, vigorously shaking his head. "No. No, uh-uh. I'm going to feed you. Get in."

It was increasingly hard not to like the man. I climbed into the car and buckled while Max moved to the driver's side. Once buckled, he hit the gas like he was being chased by the mafia.

"Who are you, Mario Andretti?" I squealed, gripping my seat.

Max laughed, completely at ease as he maneuvered the car through traffic. "Just an expert at navigating."

"I hope Jonah pays you well."

"Maybe you could put in a good word for me."

I wanted to enjoy it, truly. I wanted to enjoy the city's vast skyline. I wanted to enjoy the immaculate vehicle, all leather seats and smooth ride. I wanted to enjoy Max, as he turned up the radio and belted various pop songs, only some of which I knew.

Unfortunately, I couldn't. I could only grasp the door and my seat and pray.

Eight

We arrived in front of a massive white building sometime later. Max double-parked and exited, tossing the keys to an approaching valet before opening my door.

"Are you alright?" he asked. "You're a bit pale."

"I'll be fine," I muttered, moving to the sidewalk while he grabbed my suitcase. The building was all windows and white siding with black accents. Through the windows, I could see a lobby, with more sleek white marble.

"Come with me, Ms. Douglas," Max said, offering me his arm and guiding me inside.

Jonah was living a double life, I decided, as we stepped into the lobby. Max left me to ogle the pristine lobby while he spoke with the lady at the desk. The last of the evening's light reflected off the glass coffee tables, and the stuffed white chairs held not a speck of dust. Three massive chandeliers hung from the high ceilings, and the shiny marble floors reflected their soft glow.

"Miss Douglas?"

"Holly," I corrected, following Max to the elevator wall. "This place is beautiful."

"Very. And since Jonah owns the place, he gets the best apartment too."

"Jonah owns this building?"

Max's eyebrows rose. "You didn't know?" I shook my head. "He is a busy man with his fingers in many pies. The catering business, a landlord, and a few other smaller entrepreneurial endeavors."

"And a measly chef at his aunt's café," I mumbled, feeling very small suddenly.

Max laughed. "I asked him one time, and he said that was his favorite job. He said he liked the ease of it, the simplicity of life, not being pulled in a hundred directions at once."

Simplicity. My heart prickled at that. Did he think his coworkers were simple too? Compared to what California was offering, probably.

We traveled to the fifteenth floor where Max had to insert a key in the elevator before the door would open. We stepped into a short hallway and Max opened the next door to the apartment. Abby had been close. His place was all industrial—glass and metal and leather, white walls with chocolate and silver decor. A short hallway opened to the kitchen and then a massive living room. The far wall and one of the side walls in the living room were floor to ceiling windows. The kitchen was set beneath a loft, which was where I assumed the bedrooms were.

The kitchen… oh. I supposed, as a chef, it would be the most utilized room in the home. It certainly lived up to its expectations. White cabinets with dark brown quartz countertops. A large butcher block island, complete with a sink, sat beneath unique industrial lighting. Add in stainless steel appliances, and my jealousy reached contemplating-murder status.

"I ordered out at the lobby," Max said, moving to the fridge. "In the meantime, would you like a beer? Wine? Soda?"

"Water, please."

I set my carry-on bag and purse against the wall and moved into the living room, which alone was the size of my apartment. A beige leather sectional was positioned facing the street and the wall with no windows. A massive television hung on the wall decked out with speakers and several gadgets that screamed "bachelor pad."

In the end, though, it was the view that stole the show. San Francisco and its bright skyline unfolded before me in all its glory. The apartment buildings around Jonah's were tall, but his apartment sat just above those across the street, avoiding any obstructions to the view.

Max presented a glass of water with lemon. "Thanks. This place is incredible." I turned, noting a small seating area on the loft above. I had told Abby I wouldn't send pictures but found myself seriously reconsidering. "It's like something out of a magazine."

Max laughed. "You will not find this place in any magazine. Jonah does not allow pictures in here. He hardly allows anyone in here at all. I'll admit, I am a bit surprised you're here."

"He doesn't bring women up here?"

"He always says he doesn't have time for women."

"Perhaps he does when they're simple," I retorted, flinching. I had not meant to voice my thoughts. My cheeks flared.

"Ah, yes. I felt your demeanor change when I said that," Max said gently. "I apologize. It was my poor choice of words. I meant—and he did too—that here, he is under a lot of stress. Deadlines, expectations, paperwork, long hours. When Cecille offered him the job, he took it, knowing he needed a break from all the stress. He works that job Wednesday through Saturday and then comes out here for the rest of the weekend to clean up our messes. I am sorry, Holly—it wasn't meant to be an insult, to you or Cecille. He really does enjoy being a workaholic, but his favorite work is with you all."

It made me feel a little better... a little. I still felt like a fish out of water. "He never told us about this. I-I knew he had a catering company, but that's all. This... this is... a lot."

He put an arm around my shoulder and guided me back to the kitchen. "You know what soothes frayed, travel-exhausted nerves? Wine." The doorbell chimed. "And food! Excellent timing."

I washed my hands while he answered the door and then moved to a barstool while he unloaded the bags. "How many people are you planning on feeding?" I laughed when four large boxes were pulled from one bag and three smaller ones from a second.

"Just us, and Jonah when he gets back. Plus, it's his credit card," Max added with a wink. "I'll have lunch for tomorrow."

"So, are you a cook as well?" My mouth watered as each box opened held different stir-fries.

"I make a mean mac and cheese. Out of the box. If I follow the directions." He laughed with me as he rummaged through the cupboard for plates and utensils. "No, I leave the cooking to Jonah and his employees at the catering company. I keep the gears running in the machine that is Jonah."

"Did you grow up here?"

Max produced three glasses and poured two, handing one to me. "Not far from here. I grew up with Jonah, and we went to school together. He hired me as his business endeavors grew, oh, about eight years ago now. Okay, if you like spicy, you'll want the shrimp curry. Mild is the beef and broccoli or the chicken. There's a veggie-only one here that is good with soy sauce or wasabi, if you dare."

"I don't dare," I decided, helping myself to the less spicy items. "I will be confined to a small cabin tomorrow. I'm going on a cruise," I said when Max gave me a blank look.

"Cool! Just a spontaneous trip?"

"Ah, no." I told him about the contest and its components.

These cruises must have been well-known in San Francisco because Max hardly batted an eye before moving on. "What kind of photography are you into?"

"I like playing with light. And landscapes. And macro photography. I do family portraits on the side of working at Cecille's."

"Do you have any samples?"

I hopped off the stool and retrieved the binder I had assembled of my favorite and best photographs. I then ate while Max paged through. "Wow," he breathed when he was done. "These are amazing, Holly."

I chuckled. "You sound surprised."

"I am. Not because I didn't think you could do it. These are better than what usually comes out of that contest. You work magic with light."

I tipped my head, studying him. "You don't strike me as one to follow photo and writing contests."

"I'll bet Jonah doesn't either," Max grinned. "But here we are, keeping ourselves informed."

An easy silence passed between us. "This food is amazing."

"I hope it beats a standard PB and J."

I gasped. "Standard? I'll have you know my sandwiches are much better than standard. I am a sandwich master."

"What sort of training does one need to become a sandwich master?"

"A lifetime of too many things to do and not enough time to make dinner."

"Ah," Max nodded seriously. "Yes, I believe I am taking advanced courses."

I giggled. "But you have your boss's credit card. That's cheating."

He raised a fork full of food and toasted me. "Maybe, but it tastes so good." Max laughed with me. "So, Holly, tell me about yourself. Jonah mentioned his awesome coworkers in Wisconsin, but for the most part, he's kept his two worlds very separate."

"There isn't much to tell, really," I said with a shrug. "I've been working for Cecille for two years now since we moved to Hartford from Ohio."

"We? Family?"

"My sister, Abby. She will be a senior in high school this year. What about you? Tell me about life here."

"Life here is… busy. Jonah runs a tight ship and expects the best from his employees. He lets very few people into his private life, so consider yourself very special."

"Are you his personal assistant or his business assistant?"

"Whatever Jonah needs. Usually both."

"And you said he runs several companies?"

Max shook his head. "He only heads his catering company, Seeley's Catering. He owns stock in others and owns a few real estate properties."

I sighed, pushing broccoli around on my plate. "I didn't even know he had a place out here, let alone a small empire."

"He did not want anyone in Wisconsin to know. I'm not even sure Cecille knows how successful he is out here."

"Why? Why keep it so secret?"

He shrugged. "Jonah has always been a very private person, almost to a fault. I think part of it is that here, he assumes celebrity status, though he doesn't care for it. In Wisconsin, he could just be Jonah."

Just Jonah. The thought that I was one of the few who knew the real Jonah made me warm to my toes, but I sighed. "I wish he would have told me."

"Would it have changed your opinion of him?"

I considered this a moment. "No, I don't think so."

"Well, then, it doesn't matter too much, does it?"

"It doesn't matter that my friend is rich and successful and decided not to tell me? That he wanted to keep life simple?"

Max cocked his head, his green eyes piercing. "There's that word again. Holly, I didn't mean—"

"I know." I set my fork down, my appetite fading. "I know you didn't."

"Holly." He came around the table and put his hands on my shoulders. "I want you to listen to me, very carefully. You are *not* simple. Your life is *not* simple. If Jonah kept his life here under wraps from his friends, it was only to protect himself from gold diggers and to protect you from the crazy bullshit called publicity. And I do believe the term 'friend' is incorrect where you're concerned. And for what it's worth, I am pleasantly surprised by his choice."

My cheeks burned. "Oh no, we're not—"

Max's vibrating phone interrupted us. "And just like that, he calls," he said, holding it up to show Jonah's name. "Yes, sir what can I do for you?" I heard Jonah's voice through the speaker, but I couldn't make out the words. "Yes, Holly is safely holed up in your apartment with an entire table full of Dolche's slowly going cold. Yes, we have some for you too. Of course, I used your credit card—you think I'd use my own money? Fine, see you later." He hung up the phone, cracking a wide grin. "He'll be home shortly. He drives like me."

"You two don't act like boss and assistant," I remarked. "More like… brothers."

"Jonah *is* more like my brother than my boss," Max shrugged. "We grew up together, attended most of the same business classes in college, and we were even roommates for a while. I guess I know him the best. Out here, that is."

"Probably best overall. He has an excellent way of… deflecting personal questions."

"That he does."

"What do I need to know?"

Max considered my question a moment before answering. "Jonah is a very private person, but he is as loyal and protective as they come."

"I believe it. When he closes himself off, what do you do to help him?"

"I don't. You can help him, though."

"Me?"

Max grinned. "Anytime life gets too crazy out here, he stays in Wisconsin instead of coming back. I don't have the answer to your question."

I thought of the times he had worked the weekend shifts with me and shook my head slowly. "It wasn't anything I did. Nothing stands out."

"Perhaps he sought your company."

My cheeks flushed as I sipped my wine. Little butterflies flitted through my stomach. Secretly, I wanted what Max had said to be true. We had never really hung out together outside of work, though we did bump into each other occasionally. Jonah attended a few of Abby's plays and her swim meets, but that was all. How sweet indeed, the knowledge that Jonah wanted to be with me when times were tough. "I would have helped more if I had known."

"As I said, Jonah is private. I've known him most of my life, and sometimes, I still have to pull teeth for information. You've only had two years of practice. A piece of advice?" he asked. At my nod, he held up the plate he was about to load into the dishwasher. "The way to that man's heart is through his stomach."

I rolled my eyes. "I already told you. I only make sandwiches."

"Make them with love, then, and hope for the best." His smile turned sassy. "Perhaps, being a woman, you might have a few more tricks up your sleeve."

My face burned as I tossed a rogue chopstick at him. It ricocheted off his hand and landed in the wasabi, sending green chunks splattering.

Max's mouth formed an 'o'. "I'm telling Jonah you tried to start a food fight in his kitchen."

"You do, and I'll tell him you ordered tomorrow's lunch with the meal tonight. And-and that you were late picking me up from the airport because you crashed the Mustang."

He gasped. "You play dirty!"

The warmth from the wine had created a little buzz, making me cocky. "I play to win."

"And here I heard mid-westerners were so nice."

"Whoever told you that was likely charmed by brandy old-fashions."

"And saucy, beautiful women." Max chuckled. "Guess I'm due for a trip out to Cecille's."

I poured another glass of wine, my last if I was going to get to the ship in the morning. "You've never been there?"

The massive man shook his head. "I have seen pictures, though. Seems like a fun place."

"If you're going to Wisconsin, don't come just for Cecille's. Hartford is a truck stop town, good for just passing through."

While he finished cleaning up, we discussed the best places in Wisconsin to visit. He wasn't a cook, but Max admitted he dabbled in bartending and enjoyed creating and trying new drinks. He suggested making a rum and coke float with ice cream and wrote down a few names of drinks to try on the cruise.

I laughed when he listed the ingredients in each. "Those all sound delicious, but I'm going to be a hot mess if I try them all."

"Cruises are for drinking and having fun. Who cares if you get a little snookered?"

"Cecille would appreciate that." I told him about her dirty suggestions for the cruise.

Max howled with laughter. "She sounds exactly like a person I need in my life."

"Who?"

I jumped at Jonah's voice as he came in from the hallway. Without missing a beat, he wrapped his arms around me in a hug, dropping a kiss on my head. His touch affected my nerve endings from head to toe.

"Cecille, your aunt," Max supplied, grinning at our exchange. "Holly was just telling me about what Cecille recommended for the cruise."

Jonah lifted an eyebrow at me. "Cabin boys?"

"And drinking." I gulped my wine, trying to alleviate my shock. Jonah in jeans and a t-shirt was good. Jonah in perfectly fitted slacks, a white dress shirt rolled to the elbows, and a loosened tie was mouthwatering. *Clearly, the state of California knew how to grow her men.*

"How was the meeting?" Max was asking. "Was an agreement reached?"

"No."

Max's jaw tightened. "You're kidding."

"I wish I was. It's been a very long day."

"I should get back there and see what I can do, then," he decided. His face brightened significantly as he came around the island. "Holly, I have to go. It has been wonderful getting to know you. I hope we will see each other again soon."

"Thank you for the ride, and the food, and the drink suggestions," I told him.

"I look forward to hearing your thoughts on them. See you later. Jonah, I'll see you… well, I'll see you."

"Bye," I called, as he left, confused by his goodbye to Jonah. I turned back, tossing a thumb over my shoulder. "He's your assistant. Won't you see him tomorrow?"

"Ah, no, I won't," Jonah admitted.

"But… oh, are you headed back to Wisconsin, then?"

"No."

Private, almost to a fault. "Oh," I said quietly, finishing my glass.

"Holly."

I raised my eyes to find that his mouth held the hint of a smile. "I'm taking you to the cruise ship tomorrow."

My face heated. "Oh."

His smile was slow and sweet. "Relax, Holly. It's all good. How was your flight? I hope you didn't mind changing your plans."

"I-I have a hard time when it's big things that change," I admitted.

His brows furrowed. "Big things?"

I offered him an apologetic smile. "I may have nearly had a panic attack in the airport when Abby called me. I planned everything out. It just caught me by surprise, that's all."

Jonah grinned between bites. "It was supposed to be a good surprise."

"It was! Oh, Jonah, I'm sorry. I don't mean to sound ungrateful. This place is better than any hotel, and Max's food choices easily beat a room temperature, squashed sandwich. And I would much rather be with you than by myself," I admitted. "I was just worrying something would go wrong on my way out here."

"But nothing did?"

"No."

"Are you still worried?"

I considered his question. "No, I guess not. As long as I make it to the ship on time tomorrow."

"You will, I promise."

"I don't know. Max gave me a lot of wine," I snickered.

"I noticed," Jonah chuckled, holding up the two bottles Max had pulled out. One was empty, and the other had less than a glass left.

"Sorry."

"It's fine," he laughed. "Whatever helps you relax."

I was relaxed, mostly. "Your apartment took me by complete surprise. How long have you called this place home?"

"This isn't my home."

"It isn't?"

"I reside here sometimes, just like I reside in Wisconsin sometimes. But my home is elsewhere."

"Jonah," I sighed. "If… If we are going to make a relationship work in the future, I need you to know that sometimes your privacy borders on secrecy, and… and I'm struggling with it."

"Holly, I—"

Holding up my hands, I continued. "Look, finding out you're richer than Midas is by no means a terrible secret to discover. That you dabble in several businesses at the same time is admirable. Your stamina and ability to manage all that while traveling back and forth across the country seems almost impossible. It just makes me wonder what else I don't know."

"Trusting comes… difficult to me."

"I understand that on a deeper level than most, but it is part of being in a relationship. Even a friendship."

Jonah studied me a moment before responding. "You're right, of course. I'm sorry, I will try to do better."

"Me too," I promised. "Let's give it a shot. How was work today? You told Max an agreement was not reached? What happened?"

He chewed slowly, as though he was buying time to find a suitable answer. "It's… complicated."

I shrugged. "Fresh pair of eyes?"

He took several bites more in the silence that followed. "All right. Let's say you… you manage a company… under a board of directors. The company is *very* large, and you serve as… manager, human resources, and sometimes even security as needed."

"Right. A manager trying to be eight people at the same time. Got it. Keep going."

Jonah chuckled. "So then, one of the board members comes to you with a problem. He wants out because he… he starts his own smaller company." He became more animated then, embracing the story. "Shortly afterward, the larger company gets… blown apart, separated into tiny little pieces. The tiny company disappears. As you help to put the company back together, the board member who wanted to leave finds his little company. He asks you to look into it, as he has to be a… a ghost owner. He gives you the job of protecting this company, very hush-hush."

"Why hush-hush?"

"The board members have an agreement. The company that you manage is the only organization they will own. It is for… strength in numbers, for lack of a better explanation. Separately, the board members' companies are… well, killed off. Obliterated by another company that wreaks havoc on the business world."

"Glad I'm not in this business world," I decided. "What next?"

Jonah rubbed the back of his neck. "This board member, he… he has the option to let it go, but he doesn't. So, he asks you to look into it, protect it. Fast forward a few years and the opposing company discovers it. A few times, the little company nearly breaks, but it hangs on. The board member exposes his secret to the other members, who are… beyond furious, but they agree to help when they can. A few of the problems are diverted or avoided with their help, and you can prevent a few as well. All the while, the board members have been attempting to create agreements with the outside forces, but they have all been rejected. They simply want this company *gone*. Or to absorb it into their own, which would prove equally disastrous."

"So, today was another attempt at an agreement?"

Jonah nodded, resting his palms on the island, his shoulders hunched in frustration. "Again. Meanwhile, the little company is just starting to heal from past damage, starting to flourish and prosper. But the opposition is coming, and there *will* come a time when I cannot protect it anymore. I want to, as I've… I have come to love the company, but I can only do so much."

"What about the board member? If he owns it, can't he take over for you?"

"He has to remain a ghost owner. His hands are tied."

"So… what are your choices?"

His smile was sad, never meeting his eyes as he looked up at me. "Let it go or absorb it into one of my own companies."

"Absorbing would save it? Seems like a logical answer."

"Logical, yes, but this company is… independent, and takes much pride in being so. It would also need to be relocated, which would not go over well. Plus, there is a smaller company tied to it."

"Would the smaller company be at risk, too?"

"I don't know, but I fear it will be. I can't let either of them go. They… they have become incredibly important to me. And the one won't willingly go without the other."

He spoke as though these companies were family members he was afraid of betraying. "It's clear you care for them, Jonah. Whatever you decide, hopefully, they can see your love as clearly as I can. I don't have any advice for you. Only to keep trying. You're doing a good job." I moved around the island to wrap my arms around his waist, resting my cheek on his chest. "I hope it all works itself out soon."

"Me too, Kitten." His arms came around me, and I felt my cheeks heat as he dropped more kisses in my hair. "What's so funny?" he asked when he heard me giggle.

I leaned back to look up at him. "I never thought I'd enjoy any pet names. When you say it, I don't mind. It makes me laugh."

His grin was wide, and it seemed to banish some of the stress from his body. "I know it's late, but we still have a little more time before bed. What would you like to do?"

I shrugged. "None of this was on my itinerary when I left Wisconsin."

"Does that mean you're up for anything?" an eyebrow rose, challenging me.

"Within reason."

"This apartment building has a pool and a hot tub."

My cheeks bloomed once again. Jonah, seeing me in my swimsuit, unable to hide my body's imperfections? A swim and a soak after a long day sounded wonderful, but I wasn't sure Jonah needed to be my partner for that endeavor yet. "I-I don't know…" I said, searching for an excuse. "I can't pack a wet swimsuit in my suitcase tomorrow."

"We will make sure it's dry by the time we leave."

"I don't know…"

"Aw, come on, Holly, I know how much you like swimming after long days. What is it again? A swim, ice cream, and Netflix?" He left my arms to rummage through the freezer. "I have cookie dough and chocolate caramel."

"You play dirty."

"I play to win. What?" he asked when I burst out laughing.

"I said the same thing to Max earlier tonight. He said that made us two peas in a pod. Guess he's right."

"So, is that a yes I'm hearing?"

"Jonah, I just ate a ton of food! And I've been drinking."

"I'll be your lifeguard." He put his hand to his ear. "Is that a yes I'm hearing?"

I threw up my hands, out of excuses. "Fine!"

"Haha!" he cried, throwing a fist in the air victoriously. "You can use the bathroom down here to change. There's another bathroom upstairs."

Nine

With a sigh, I wheeled my suitcase into a bathroom that was as large as my bedroom, and as pristine as the rest of his apartment. Nerves warred with excitement as I considered my options. I had brought along three suits—one was a competition suit that Abby made me promise to only use when I was working out. The next was olive green with white polka dots, complete with halter top and rouching and gathering to even out my wide hips and smaller chest, all while conveniently sucking in my stomach. The third suit was an Abby-insisted splurge, strapless, deep blue, with mesh decoration to expose more of my middle. Privately, I loved it, but in public, it would take a bit more courage and a lot less eating to display. In the end, polka dots won. I checked my phone when I was changed.

A: I need an update, STAT!

I snickered at Abby's text and typed a quick message back.

H: The apartment is incredible. Very modern and classy bachelor pad. Awesome view of the city.

A: PICTURES PLEASE

I looked around and snapped a shot of the bathroom.

H: Sorry, we are getting ready to go for a quick swim before bed.

I received a series of emojis that made me laugh. Abby only did that when she was feeling big feelings. They were followed by a series of rapid-fire texts.

A: ARE YOU SERIOUS RIGHT NOW?! I need more pictures.

A: Also, you're going for a late-night swim with a hot guy? Get it, girl.

A: Don't do anything I wouldn't do.

A: Or do.

A: Maybe you can waste him in a swim race too, just like darts.

H: I'll text you later tonight. Love you!

I pulled on my wrap and opened the door just as Jonah appeared in the hallway. *Cheese and rice, was there anything the man wore that didn't make him look like a god?* Long legs beneath a gray suit and a black t-shirt leaving little to the imagination. I turned back to the bathroom to hide my burning cheeks. "Do you have an extra towel?" I asked.

"They have some downstairs."

"Okay." With a deep breath, I followed him to the elevator.

"Have you talked to Abby since you got to California?" Jonah asked.

"She called when I was at the airport. And she has been texting since I've been here. She's dying of curiosity to see what your apartment looks like."

Jonah chuckled. "Did you send her any pictures?"

"Max said you rarely let people into your apartment."

"I make exceptions for those closest to me."

I took the opportunity to probe for information. "Max, me, Abby in spirit. What about your family?"

"My mother is not a large part of my life—never has been," Jonah said with a surprisingly nonchalant shrug. "My father has been… all over the world on business since I moved here. He's never had time to come. In truth, Cecille is the closest family I have, besides Max."

"I'm sorry," I said quietly, reaching out to squeeze his hand.

Before I could let go, he wove his fingers through mine. "I'm good, Holly. It's complicated, but I'm good."

I gave him a shy smile, my heart pounding at the skin contact. "Sounds like a motto to adopt."

"Feel free."

The elevator doors opened to a glass wall overlooking the pool. Jonah swiped his key card and held the door open for me. I grinned. It was a swimmer's paradise, complete with four lanes, diving blocks, and a wall of paddles, kickboards, weights, and every other piece of equipment one might need in the pool. The pool also had an attached diving well, two separate hot tubs, a sauna, and a set of bathrooms.

"I don't know why you ever want to leave this place," I chuckled. "This is awesome."

"There's also a gym one level above us. It's a great place to live."

"And you don't call this place home?" I asked.

"No, but it's a close second."

I shrugged out of my coverup and smothered a gasp with a cough as I turned. Jonah had also shed his shirt and was making his way to the diving blocks. Not an ounce of fat on him, making me all too aware of my bloated stomach, lack of a thigh gap, wingy arms—

"Well, Douglas, are you going to show me what you've got?"

"Seriously?" I demanded.

"Yeah, seriously. Get up here. I know you know how." He stepped onto the block, cocking an eyebrow. "What's wrong? Scared?"

"Yeah, I'm scared!" I snapped. "I'm bloated. I've had a long day. I've been drinking. And you're standing there like a dang Olympian, ready for war."

"Aw, come on. I'll go easy on you."

"Oh, no, you don't." His jabs spurred me into action. I stormed over to the wall to find a pair of goggles before stepping up onto the block. "I already know who is going to lose. I can't streamline very well in this suit. And yet, here I am. I don't like you."

Jonah was chuckling as he crouched down. "Sounds like a lot of excuses."

"I'll give you a lot of excuses," I grumbled. When my goggles were adjusted, I bent down, my mind frantically trying to come up with a distraction. "Wait, wait, wait," I said, starting to stand. As Jonah moved to do the same, I quickly bent back down. "Go!" I shouted, launching myself off the block. Thankfully, my boobs stayed inside my suit as I hustled toward the other side. We had not decided how long the race would be, and after I dove in and started, I decided one length was enough. I did not look over to see where Jonah was, but I could feel him approaching. Our hands hit the wall at the same time.

I turned to find him grinning, and glared at him. "You're hardly out of breath!"

Jonah shrugged. "Care to go again?"

"No!" I cried. I was the sprinter, but not right after I had eaten. To slow my breathing, I did another length, slower this time. Jonah came too, sans goggles, swimming close to the bottom for long stretches before surfacing. *Olympic swimmer indeed.*

When we reached the other side, I glared at him. "This was payback for darts, wasn't it?"

Jonah's grin was wide. "Not intentionally, but I won't apologize."

"Were you on the swim team, then?"

"No."

I snorted. "Could've fooled me."

Jonah vaulted out of the pool. "Come on. Nights like tonight call for the hot tub, not laps."

I followed him into the warm water, sighing contentedly as I sank next to him, letting the jets do their thing. Most of the buzz I had been feeling at dinner had worn off, leaving me relaxed and lethargic beneath the swirling water. "If you didn't swim, what sports *did* you do in school?"

"None."

I glanced up at him. "Really?"

"I went to an… alternative school that didn't offer sports teams."

"Like… homeschooling?"

"Something like that."

"It's been two years, and I hardly know anything about you, Jonah. Why is that?" I realized, voicing the thought aloud.

Jonah shrugged. "I don't like talking about myself much."

"And so, we've always talked about me. That's terrible!"

"No, it's not. I like talking about you." He found my hand beneath the water and threaded his fingers through mine again.

"Jonah," I sighed, feeling awful.

"Holly," he mimicked.

His smile faded when I met his gaze. "Please, tell me something… something not many people know. Make me feel like I'm an insider, rather than at arm's length like everyone else."

He considered my question for a few moments, studying my face in the silence. "Cecille's is my favorite place to work. You have made Cecille's my favorite place to work."

My cheeks heated as I smiled. "Sweet words, but Max knows that already. He told me so earlier."

He sighed, looking down as he shifted his free fingers through the bubbles from the jets. "More often than not, I hate my job here."

"Which one?"

His voice was soft when he spoke, as though he had never said the words aloud before. "Most of them, but especially the one I told you about before."

"Why not walk away?"

He shook his head. "I'm under contract. Certain rules and regulations have kept me there all these years. And besides, I can't leave the inherited company."

"You're a manager, though. Isn't there anything you can do?"

"Being in charge of so many people comes with its own set of problems. It requires you to act and make decisions for the good of all, not for yourself. And besides, the inherited company thinks it's just me, not all the board members behind me. It... it will not go well if they become known." His hand tightened on mine as his brows knitted together. "Forgive me?"

I chuckled. "For what? I'm glad you're letting me in! Although, you do need some cheering up."

His expression lightened a fraction. "What did you have in mind?"

"Tell me something awesome."

"Well," he said carefully, "I do have news. I think it's awesome. I hope you do too."

"What is it?"

"You know I head a catering business."

"Yes."

"And that we have a lot of big clients."

"Mmhmm."

"Well, one of them is the *American Voyage* magazine. They've asked me to come on the cruise."

"What?" I shrieked.

"As one of the board members, I've helped with a lot of the—"

"Wait!" I cried, my heart pounding. "You're a board member? Does that mean—did you have a hand in my being a finalist for this contest?"

Jonah's eyes went wide, realizing how it sounded. "No! No, Holly, I promise I didn't. I have not seen any of the submissions. Truly."

"Why didn't you say anything? You knew I applied!"

"I did know, but I didn't say anything because… Well, number one, I didn't want you not to apply. And number two, because I didn't think it was necessary, since I didn't have any say in the decision."

My mind moved to my next question. "What about Cecille?"

"I did not know I was going on this cruise until yesterday. As soon as I did, I called Kevin. He will be happy to fill in for me with the monetary bonus I provided."

"What about Abby and—"

"I asked Kevin to keep an eye on her."

"But—"

"Holly, everything will be fine. I promise. You have a phone. You'll be able to contact Abby whenever you want. It's not like you'll be gone for a month."

I pulled my hand from his, hurt by the bite in his tone.

"Holly, I'm sorry, that came out harsh."

"Why didn't you tell me right away? You know, like when I asked you what you were doing tomorrow? That would have been an excellent opportunity."

"Yes, it would have, but it would have also killed the mood that Max and the food and the wine had created for you. I wanted to be a part of that, Holly, just for a little while. I wanted to put off your worrying for just a bit longer. It is a short trip, even if it is the longest time you two have been apart. You are going to be fine. Abby is going to be fine. Cecille will be fine."

More secrets. Always more secrets with this man. I stood, hugging myself, trying to find my inner calm.

"Holly." Jonah stood as well, turning me back to face him. His expression was desperate, worry creasing his brows and tightening his jaw. "I thought you would be happy. If it bothers you this much, I can try to get out of it. The board uses the trips as an opportunity to touch base and plan for next year. Plus, we get to meet the finalists. I thought you'd be excited that you knew someone else on the trip. I can cancel my plans and stay behind. Just say the word."

His hands were on my shoulders, his thumbs tracing little circles on my collar bone. His eyes searched mine for answers. "I want to go back upstairs. Please," I whispered. I felt close to bursting with the strong emotions racing through my body. I just needed a moment by myself to collect my thoughts.

"Sure, yeah," Jonah said gently. Putting a hand at the small of my back, he guided me out of the hot tub, grabbing a towel to wrap around my shoulders before grabbing one for himself. He did not say anything, just held doors open and guided me back to his apartment.

I was about to close the bathroom door when Jonah finally spoke, catching the door with his palm. His voice was soft, with a hint of desperation. "Holly, please, talk to me."

I did not have any words. I just needed to be alone. However, one look at his face, and I realized he was struggling nearly as much as I, for different reasons entirely. I reached for his hand, squeezing it. "Let me shower and change and then we'll talk."

Inside the bathroom, I reached for my phone, thinking to call Abby. With a sigh, I put it back. Abby had been my social cane, always processing my feelings for me, and often swaying them. It was time I took charge of my chaos and figured things out myself. I stripped and stepped into the glorious shower for some major steam therapy.

Ten

I spent nearly an hour in the bathroom before emerging in pajama shorts and a tank top. Jonah was standing at the window in gray sweatpants, arms crossed over his bare chest as he looked out across the city. Piano music was playing softly in the surround speakers. I moved quietly across the room, but he heard me and turned, watching carefully as I came to stand beside him.

"If this place has an incredible view and you don't call it home, I can only imagine what your home looks like," I said quietly.

Jonah chuckled. While he was looking out at the skyline, his mind was far away. "Words can't describe it."

"How often do you get there?"

"Enough, though it hasn't been as enjoyable lately."

I glanced up at him. "Surely you can afford a few days off."

"Financially, yes, but at work, everything falls apart."

"So, why leave? Why go to Cecille's every week if you're needed here?"

"Because Cecille asked me to help."

"You're too nice."

He shrugged. "Probably."

I sighed, nudging his shoulder. "I'm sorry about before. I struggle with anxiety on certain things. Some of it I've grown out of, and some I need a few minutes to process. It's been a long day with lots of unexpected changes. I wish you would have told me right away."

"Holly, if you don't want me to go—"

"No," I said firmly. "It's okay. For one, it sounds like your presence is needed by the board, and two, it also sounds like you could use a little vacation after your meeting today."

"Are you sure?"

I smiled up at him. "Yeah. And it *will* be nice to know someone else on the cruise. Even if everyone will think I'm there because of your sway."

"The people who make the final judgments will know you aren't. And besides, they will not be seen on the cruise by anyone in the competition. That way entries are kept completely anonymous."

"You'd know better than me, I guess."

He moved to stand in front of me, studying my face closely. "So, you're okay with this, for sure?"

"For sure. I've had a long day, and I'm tired. Exhaustion often makes the anxiety worse, blowing things way out of proportion. I was worrying more about Abby and Cecille than anything else."

"Cecille has gone without me before, longer than this trip. Kevin has her covered. And Abby—"

"Abby will be fine."

"She will," Jonah said with a nod. "I could even send Max to check in on her if you'd like."

I snorted. "So that he can get her into trouble?"

"Max is harmless."

"To a seventeen-year-old girl easily swayed by a cute face and smooth words?"

"You think Max is cute?" Jonah returned.

"Abby will think so."

Jonah's grin was infectious. "You think Max is cute?"

I patted his cheek. "Focus."

He was laughing then. "Right, Max and Abby in the same room, not a good idea."

"No."

"You will be able to reach her, though. Pretty much at any point during your trip. They have internet access on the ship. If you can't get it, come find me. I will see that you have it. Really, Holly, anything you need. Ask and it's yours." Gone was the humor from his voice. Only the sweet, soft-spoken words.

"Thank you." I reached out to him then, wrapping my arms around his waist and resting my cheek on his warm chest. This level of comfort, with so much skin contact and Jonah's arms wrapped around me, was new and incredibly relaxing. I felt the last of my anxiety dissolve.

I had always been the comforter. My grandma needed pillows and blankets when she was too hungover to leave the bathroom or too high to stumble to her room. Abby had needed hugs and kisses—for scrapes and bruises, and then grief, and then a shoulder to cry on as she entered the harsh realities of teenage years. As she grew, she had begun to recognize when I needed help. I had accepted that help but always with a twinge of guilt. Still a teenager, I was exposing her to so many problems that I should not have. It had forced her to grow up too fast.

A tear slipped out, soaking into Jonah's skin. My cheeks heated as he held me at arm's length. "What's wrong?"

I tried to laugh as another tear escaped. "Nothing. I'm okay."

He brushed the tear with his thumb. "Tell me. Please."

I shrugged. "It's… It was a moment of guilt. I… I don't know. It's hard to talk about."

"Guilt?"

"I'm in new territory here, Jonah. In my life, *I* am the soother. Now that Abby is getting older, she's picking up on my problems, getting upset *with* me, sometimes even *for* me. I'm forcing her to grow up too soon."

"You're thinking about Abby right now?"

"Yes—no! Ugh!" I groaned, covering my face with my hands. "I don't know."

Jonah pulled them away gently, tilting my chin so I had to look up at him. "I'm here for you, Holly."

"I know. That's just it. I've not had that before… Ever. It's new."

"Bad new?"

I giggled at his continued confusion. "No. Good new. Too-good-to-be-true new."

"Oh."

"Could we just… just… yeah," I said, lifting his arms and snuggling back into him. "Just a few more minutes." I leaned into him with a sigh, grinning as his chest rumbled with laughter. He still smelled faintly of chlorine, as any swimmer did, but it was well masked by a delicious guy-soap smell.

We stood like that for a long time before Jonah began gently swaying to the background music. "Hey, look, our first dance," I said, leaning back to look up at him.

"First of many, I hope."

"Smooth."

Jonah smirked at me. "I try."

"Have you been on a cruise before?"

"Not this one, but I have attended meetings on other trips. The board likes to get together every other year, or every year, if possible. I went on the one to Alaska two years ago. Right before you started at Cecille's, I think."

I grinned. "That feels like forever ago. But I remember the first time I met you."

"You thought I was tall, dark, and handsome?"

More like sexy as hell. "I recognized you as a person I could truly be myself around. A safe person, and a good friend."

Jonah winced. "I want to take that as a compliment, but my ego just took a major blow. You friend-zoned me? Just like that?"

"It was the only space I had open for relationships at the time."

"And now?"

I sighed. "And now, I've had two years to evaluate my self-worth and my needs. Maybe it took seeing Brayden again to fully bury the past. I finally feel like I can start moving on from that. There's still fear, apprehension, anxiety. But… but it's different now. Less… consuming."

"I will never hurt you intentionally, Holly."

"I know. Maybe that's why I did friend-zone you so quickly. I recognized that."

Jonah shook his head, his shoulders drooping. "Too nice, that's me." He leaned in conspiratorially. "You aren't going to ask me what I thought of you?" When I shook my head, he began making little chicken clucks. "Come on, Kitten. Join me on the wild side."

"Fine. What did you think when you first met me?"

"I thought you were ridiculously beautiful. Not pretty like a magazine model—"

"Hey!"

"More like a seashell. One that is beautiful despite years of being thrashed around and pounded on by the ocean waves. The shell that stands out as resilient, scared, and damned determined. One you'd never find for sale at any store, but authentic, straight out of the salty water."

My face flamed. "Smooth," I said, clearing my throat.

Jonah laughed. "I do my best." We danced a few more minutes before he spoke again. "Have you reached out to any of the finalists yet?"

I rolled my eyes. "No. Abby has been reading me all the bios as they come in. I didn't put one up. They all sound like dating profiles. Abby wrote one up for me, but I didn't submit it. I will meet them all on the boat. I think we will be dining or at least having social hours most of the evenings."

"Last time, the board members also mingled with the finalists, too."

I snorted. "Who needs a dating profile when I'll be standing next to you?"

"Smooth." His phone buzzed, killing the moment when he excused himself.

I moved to sit on the couch. Leather was neither my cup of tea nor in my budget, but it was surprisingly comfortable as I tucked my feet up under my knees to relax.

ooooo

"Holly?"

I opened my eyes to light streaming in the windows.

"It's eight o'clock. I wasn't sure when you wanted to be up. We will need to leave by about eight forty-five."

I sat up groggily, mumbling my thanks at the cup of coffee placed in my hands. I was in the loft in the bedroom. Behind the headboard was all shelving, a combination of metal and glass, filled with books and water-related knick-knacks. Above me, a vaulted ceiling with exposed metal beams, and the wall of windows from the lower floor continued, presenting yet another view of an amazing city. The bed was large, covered with a blue and white striped comforter and a four-poster of etched metal.

My cheeks heated as I realized both sides of the bed had been slept in.

Jonah saw me blush. "I hope you don't mind. You fell asleep on the couch while I was on the phone, so I carried you up here. I figured you'd be more comfortable. Nothing happened."

I stood and moved to the stairs, sipping my coffee. The couch had been comfortable, but I was glad for a bed. It had been a late night, and a bed-sleep was always more restful. Still, I blushed furiously, having never shared a bed with anyone except Abby.

Jonah, however, did not appear to feel any of the awkwardness. Instead, he was as giddy as a kid on Christmas. Waving to usher me downstairs, his grin was wide. "Come on! We've got a boat to catch, a vacation to enjoy, and you have a competition to win."

Eleven

An hour and a half later, Jonah guided me to the elevator of the ship, pulling both of our bags. A hot guy carrying my bags, on my way up to my cabin on a cruise. Giddiness threatened to overtake me as I entered the elevator behind him, suppressing the need to skip.

Jonah chuckled as the doors closed. "I can feel your excitement."

"This place is amazing."

"Wait until we get to Hawaii."

I snorted. "Well, of course, you've been *there,* too."

We traveled in silence the rest of the way up. When the doors opened again, the hallway was long and narrow. I double-checked my ticket and gave him the cabin number. Jonah wheeled the bags down the hall, pausing while I opened the door. It was like a tiny hotel room—a queen size bed, nightstands, desk, small closet, bathroom. The shades were pulled, but I peeked out to find a view of the interior of the ship.

"Seriously?" Jonah muttered at my shoulder.

"What?" I asked.

"Come with me." He grabbed my hand and his suitcase.

"My stuff—"

"It will be here." He dragged me back to the elevators. "They want you to take pictures and capture life on a cruise ship, and they can't even give you a decent view."

We went up further to the eighth floor. He pulled out the key and opened the door. The differences were staggering. His room was several times larger than mine with a nice sitting area nearest the door and a half wall separating the bed space. Beyond that, a wall of windows looking over the ocean, complete with a deck and an outdoor hot tub.

"No way," I breathed.

"Yes, way. This is where you should be," Jonah said, as I moved out to the deck. My camera was still stored in my carry-on, but I hoped Jonah would let me come back on the next sunny day, to capture some more pictures. To the right, the San Francisco skyline was shrinking, and to the left, nothing but water, stretching out to the horizon.

"Here." I turned to find Jonah with a glass of champagne in each hand. "Cheers," he said, tipping his drink to mine. "To an excellent vacation."

"Cheers." I took a sip and grinned. "A girl could get used to these luxuries."

"I hope she does. That means I'll see more of her."

I turned to look back out to the water, resting my arms on the railing. Jonah did the same, close enough that our arms were touching. A little shiver slid up my back, remembering the skin contact from the night before.

"Tell me something," Jonah said quietly. When I looked up at him, his smile was sweet. "This morning, you seemed upset that I slept in the same bed as you. And last night, you were upset at my news that I was coming with you today. I know I said I would wait until after the cruise, but I can't help feeling that you're having second thoughts. I—"

Interrupting him, I leaned over and kissed him. Surprised by my actions, I started to pull away, but he came with me, wrapping an arm around my waist. In a matter of seconds, I was relieved of my glass of champagne and turned so my back was against the railing. My whole body sizzled in response to Jonah's lips, and his hands as they traveled around my back and up my arms.

"Holly," he breathed, breaking the kiss and putting his forehead to mine. "I just want to know you're sure about this."

"I'm sure." And I was. My healing journey began the day I met Jonah two years ago. His gentle kindness had pushed me to open up. His sarcasm and humor had reminded me how to laugh and enjoy life's little amusements. He was always there, boosting my mood, my confidence, and my self-worth. His kiss at the bar had only accelerated the process so that I walked onto the ship feeling like an entirely new person. Someday, I would tell him all that, but not yet. At that moment, I wanted nothing more than to be in his arms and be kissed to my heart's content.

He didn't kiss me right away. Simply stared down at me with an expression between surprise and excitement. "What?" I asked, blushing furiously when a slow smile lifted his lips.

"I can't believe you're finally mine."

"Me?" I giggled. "I'm nothing special."

"You are *my* everything." And then he lowered his lips to mine once more. His fingers were on my neck, in my hair, tracing my jaw. My hands fisted in the fabric at his waist. I could not help the whimper that escaped when his tongue flicked out, caressing my lip. Jonah reacted as well, snaking an arm around my waist, pulling me closer still.

I wanted to ignore the knocking on the door, lost in the ecstasy of Jonah's touch, but when it began a third time, I pulled away reluctantly. "You should probably get that," I said with a sigh.

Putting his forehead to mine, he ran a thumb down my jaw. "To be continued," he said softly before releasing me. I straightened my shirt as he moved away, willing my cheeks to pale again.

"Mr. Seeley, I was asked to deliver this to you."

"Thanks." Jonah fished out his wallet and handed the attendant a tip before closing the door. "The board wants to meet this evening," he told me after reading the note.

I nodded. "I should probably head back to my room. We have our first meeting tonight too, and I need to unpack my stuff."

"You could stay here."

Would I ever stop blushing around this man? I should have said no. I could have listed a million reasons why staying in his cabin was not a good idea. And yet, whether it was the kiss or the excitement or the positive energy oozing from this man, I found myself nodding. "Okay," I said quietly.

"Okay," Jonah repeated, a brilliant smile spreading across his face. He kissed the tip of my nose. "Why don't you run down and grab your things? I have a few phone calls to make. And then let's tour the ship."

Ten minutes later, I had returned to the cabin to find Jonah agitated and practically growling into the phone. He stepped out onto the deck, closing the glass door behind him. Not exactly the way I wanted to start living with him, but I remembered his quiet admission about not liking his job in California. I unpacked what I could, taking a few minutes in the bathroom to freshen up, pausing at the mirror, trying to see what Jonah saw.

I had always believed my best features were my eyes, a bright hazel color, wide-set with heavy lashes. Beyond that, ordinary. A long straight nose with a spattering of freckles. Long, narrow lips that were always too red, lipstick or not. Fair skin that was prone to furious coloring when embarrassed or angry. Mousy brown hair, with lazy curls that did what they wished, especially in humidity. A body heavy in the butt and thighs, a stomach that never tightened completely, broad swimmer shoulders over arms that still jiggled traitorously. This time they were hidden by a short sleeve jean shirt and white shorts. Anything but perfection.

This is what Jonah wants. The reminder made me smile at the girl in the mirror, a smile that lit up her features. Not one to take selfies, I snapped one with my camera anyway, wanting to preserve the moment. I then bent to adjust a small mirror. It reflected the beautiful assortment of soaps and perfumes, all blue and green pastels with burlap and white ribbons. The flash of my camera on my shiny little subjects captured the colors beautifully.

With my camera around my neck, I emerged from the bathroom, letting out a squeal. Jonah was there, his hand raised about to knock. Though his body was tense, the smile he gave me was sweet. "Ready to go exploring?"

I nodded enthusiastically. Lacing his fingers through mine, we headed out to the hallway. "Everything okay with work?"

"No, but they have to figure it out without me this time. Max will do well enough until I get back."

"Still no agreement?"

"No."

"I'm sorry."

Jonah shook his head. "I'm not worrying about it today. Your choices today have made me happier than a thousand business agreements."

ooooo

We spent the day exploring the ship, which was like a city on water. Anything I could think of, they had it. Movie theater, exercise facilities, pools, surfing, ziplining, bars and clubs, a doctor's office, a pharmacy, clothing stores, sports equipment, and scuba stores, literally *everything*. Together, we located the breakfast area, the dining room where the contestants would be gathering, and the private room where Jonah was meeting with the other board members. Jonah bought us sandwiches for lunch, and we found a pair of chairs on one of the upper decks to eat in the shade. A few people stared as they passed, though I was not sure if it was because they knew Jonah or because he was devastatingly attractive.

"May I?" he asked, gesturing to my camera. I nodded, and he lifted it carefully. "How long have you had this?"

"A while. My high school photography teacher, Mr. Hockenstad, left it to me when he passed away. I was only a year out of college then."

"Your teacher gave you this?"

I smiled, remembering the older man fondly. "He had collected several different cameras throughout his lifetime and often took the older models the school replaced. When he found out he had brain cancer, he tracked down the alumni he thought deserved one of his cameras. His wife distributed them as part of his eulogy. I doubt there was a dry eye in the room."

"He sounds like a great man."

"He was. He was my biggest help in getting a full-ride scholarship to college."

"I don't think I knew you went to college on a full-ride."

I nodded. "If it wasn't for Mr. Hockenstad, I wouldn't have been able to go at all. If it wasn't for him, I wouldn't have *wanted* to go at all. He made me believe in myself." None of the school staff had known what had happened, but Mr. Hockenstad had reached through the darkness of those days and helped me see the light. He knew something was wrong but never asked. Instead, he created a sanctuary in his classroom. Spending lunch and study hall in his room, using his darkroom to develop photos, and soaking in all the knowledge he had to offer. It was a sort of therapy. The calm, quiet space allowed me to work out my pain by creating routines and schedules to follow. In that room, I could block out the bad in my life and see the beauty instead.

Jonah reached out to squeeze my hand. "May I?" he asked again, his thumb on the review button.

I nodded, trying not to squirm as he flipped through. He had seen a few of my photos over the years, mostly the family portraits I took and an occasional one or two when I had felt particularly extroverted. However, the unedited, raw pictures on my camera were a different matter. They were personal, my creative dumpster, some good, some abysmal. I had a general rule to never delete from the camera. Even if it was a bad photo, sometimes editing on the computer could do wondrous things to save it. Jonah, on the other hand, seemed engrossed, occasionally zooming in to inspect something closer. When I couldn't handle it anymore, I spoke. "Well?"

Jonah held up the camera, showing me a photo I had taken a few weeks ago. While walking around the apartment during a particularly beautiful sunset, I had laid down in the grass and taken a picture with the sun behind the seedy sphere of a dandelion, angling the shot so that the sun sat on the stem.

I grinned. "I blew the seeds in the next burst."

He flipped through the next series of pictures. The seeds had blown off the plant from the top to the bottom, creating some really neat photos. "Holly. These are incredible." When I blushed in response, he continued. "No, I'm serious. Holly, why are you here?"

"What?" I squeaked.

Jonah laughed, holding up a hand. "No, I mean I've seen the winners' photographs from past years. You are so far beyond what they are doing here. Wh—I—How—"

I laughed with him. "Jonah Seeley speechless? I never thought I'd see the day."

"Holly, these *are* incredible. Why aren't you selling these? You'd be a damn zillionaire if the world could see what you can do behind a camera."

"I thought this would be a bigger, easier break than trying to branch out on my own," I said with a shrug. I did not want to admit how poor my business class grades had been.

Jonah was still struggling with his emotions. "Holly… you could do this," he said, holding up the camera. You could sell these for enough to live off comfortably. You need to do this. Let me help you do this."

"If I win this competition, I will be able to start my own business, after I get Abby through college."

"No."

"What?" my voice came out in an exasperated laugh. "What do you mean, no?"

"I'm going to make a deal with you, Holly Douglas." He handed the camera back to me and leaned forward, elbows on knees, hands clasped. "As a… well, a rather business-savvy guy, I'd like to invest in your business. I'm going to put in a call to my lawyer. When we get back to California, there will be a business contract waiting for us to sign. Regardless of whether or not you win this competition, I will put Abby through college so that you can focus on your craft."

His words knocked the air from my lungs. "Jonah, that's very nice of you—"

"Pay me back if you want, but I'm serious, Holly. You need to do this. Please."

"I can't accept that." After waiting for him to look through my camera, his push toward my dream left me antsy. I stood and moved to the railing, looking out over the water. Sure, having a studio with all kinds of lighting to play with, it all sounded amazing. That had always been the ultimate goal, the someday dream. The idea of taking that final leap, making it a career…

"Talk to me," Jonah said quietly, turning my shoulders so he could drop the camera strap around my neck.

I shrugged. "I love photography. I do. I like playing with light and colors, to show the world through your eyes."

"But?"

"To just jump in headfirst and pray for the best is… scary. I need to be able to support myself and Abby. I don't understand the business end of things."

"You need a business advisor. I have a few of those. I would be happy to lend you one until you get on your feet."

"Jonah, you can't do that. You have so much on your plate as it is. You said so yourself."

Jonah closed the space between us, running a hand up my arm. "Don't worry about me. Don't worry about Abby or Cecille or anyone else but you. If *you* want to do this, let me help you."

My heart leaped at his words. *Let me help you.* "What happens if… if we don't work out?"

Jonah shook his head. "No matter what happens between us, I will always want you to do this. The world needs to see life through the lens of your camera."

I scoffed. "If we were to break up, there is no way I could keep accepting your money. I'm struggling to accept even the *idea* of it now."

"Fine. I'll deposit it into a bank account for you now. An advance."

"Jonah. Thank you, but you can't do that."

"I can, and I'm going to. You deserve this, Holly." His grin turned mischievous. "How does one hundred thousand sound?"

"Jonah—"

Jonah chuckled, pulling me into a hug. "I'll have my lawyers write up the documents."

"Jonah, I feel… dirty for taking your money. It isn't right."

"How about this: we will put this conversation on hold until after the photo contest. If you win, which you will, we will talk. If you don't win, we will talk about getting you the money."

"Why are you doing all this? Do you do this for everyone you have relationships with? Give them a crap ton of money to pursue their dreams?" I asked, leaning back to look up at him.

He winced. "I've had a few girlfriends over the years," he said, his voice soft. "None of them lasted. Probably in part because I didn't make time for relationships. There was always more work to be done, and I'm used to doing it at any time of day. The women I met did not like that and wanted me at their beck and call. They also knew how much I was worth and *expected* me to give them expensive gifts."

My heart ached for him. "I'm so sorry, Jonah."

He shrugged. "It wasn't the money I missed. I don't mind spending it on others, but they knew when they met me. That's what makes you different. You didn't know. The anonymity Hartford provides me is my lifeline. No one tracks my every move for the tabloids or wonders how much I have in my wallet at any one time. In Hartford, I can be my truest self. You know me better than anyone. And you have never once asked for anything for yourself. *That's* why I want to give you this gift. It isn't a gift of money, Holly. It's a gift of freedom."

Twelve

I entered the large dining room two hours later and grabbed a space at one of the back tables. About half the chairs were filled. The email had only said an informational dinner. I did not know exactly what that meant for the dress code, so I wore a soft cobalt blue wrap dress with nude heels. Having taken the extra time on my hair, taming it to display the soft curls, and applying a little makeup, I felt like my best self. Jonah had knocked on the door before I was finished getting ready, saying he would see me later that evening.

"Is this seat taken?" a short, impossibly thin woman in a black polka dot dress asked. She had golden blonde hair, brown eyes, and perfect white teeth as she smiled down at me.

"No."

She sat with a grin. "I'm Isla Young."

"Holly Douglas," I said, shaking her hand.

"Writer or photographer?"

"Photographer."

"Oh, good," she said with a grin and a wink. "I can be friends with you, then. I'm on team writer." We shared a laugh at her sarcasm.

"Have you met any of the other contestants?" I asked.

"A couple, yeah. Several of us were on the same flight last night from Texas. Some of them seemed great. Others… Well, they weren't. Have you met anyone else?"

"No. I spent the afternoon with my… friend."

Catching my blush, she raised her eyebrows. "Guy friend?"

I shrugged. "Yeah. It's new."

"Got it." She glanced around and spotted the bar. "I'm a southern girl in need of a drink. Two drinks, if it's an open bar. What can I order for you?"

I considered how alcohol would affect my evening before answering. "Beam and Coke. Don't let me have more than one."

"No promises," she said with a wink, jumping up from her seat.

I checked my phone for the time. There were still ten more minutes before the dinner was to start. Nerves tightened my belly as I flipped my phone in my hands. *Why was I so edgy?* I glanced up at the stage area. *Would the board of people Jonah talked about be there? Would he single me out? Would the others think I had an advantage?* That would eliminate my opportunity to make friends.

Isla returned with three others, laughing as she set my glass down. "Holly, this is Isaac, Layla, and Creed. They were all on my flight from Dallas. This is my new friend, Holly."

"Hi," I said, reaching across the table to shake their hands. "And thanks," I told Isla, sipping at the drink.

"Where are you from, Doll?" Creed asked, sitting on my other side and draping an arm over the back of my seat. He was good looking in a rugged cowboy way with his cotton beige shirt, jeans, boots, and cowboy hat. He reminded me of one of those guys from the old cigarette magazine ads. Classy with a little badass and a lot of ego.

"Wisconsin," I said, discreetly scooting closer to Isla. "You?"

"We're all from Texas," Layla replied coolly, echoing the same drawl as the other three seated at my table. "Isaac and I are writers, and Creed is a photographer."

"I don't remember seeing your bio on the website," Creed commented.

"I didn't write one. I am better with photography than with words."

"Did they all sound like… I don't know. Personal ads?" Isla asked.

"Dating profiles," I agreed.

Isla laughed. "Yes! I guess if you're single, a cruise is a great place to have a good time, but this is a competition, not a reality show."

"Did you guys hear who is all on the board of directors?" Layla asked, leaning in conspiratorially. She was a tall blonde, her low-cut white dress amplifying her cleavage.

Isla leaned in as well. "Jonah Seeley? Yes!"

"Who is Jonah Seeley?" Isaac asked.

"Only California's most eligible bachelor," Isla supplied. "He's the head of a national catering business, owns a ton of real estate, and invests in dang near everything he can."

"I heard he's on track to be in the top ten grossing entrepreneurs by the end of the year," Layla added. "And he's gorgeous."

While my cheeks heated, I grasped for a subject change. "Are you all full-time artists?" I asked.

"I'm finishing journalism school," Layla said proudly. "I'll be done with classes in December. I just snagged an internship at the *Dallas Observer* and then I graduate in the spring."

Isaac was markedly younger too. "I just finished college, and I am currently working on a memoir about my father, grandfather, and two uncles who all served together in the Vietnam War."

"I'm an elementary school teacher. I'm writing a series of children's books," Isla said.

"I specialize in fine art photography, but I make a living with portraits and boudoir photography," Creed said.

"What about you, Holly?"

"I-I dabble in all areas of photography. Currently, I'm a waitress."

We exchanged another minute or two of small talk before our attention was drawn to the front of the room. An older gentleman had just walked in, clapping his hands for attention. "Ladies and gentlemen! I'd like to say a few words before dinner if you could all find your seats, please."

The room quieted quickly, excitement buzzing through the air.

"First of all, I'd like to say congratulations to you, the finalists of the New Writers and Photographers of America competition. You have all earned your place here with your talents, and we commend you for your efforts. We would like to thank you for not only submitting your work but also for taking time out of your busy lives to join us on this adventure." A light spattering of clapping crossed the room. "My name is Bob Vaughn. I am the head of *American Voyage* magazine, as well as a chairman of this competition. Before dinner is served, I wanted to go over a few things to help you better understand what is in store for you.

"Over the last few weeks, we have been distributing emails regarding your time in Hawaii. Upon arrival, writers and photographers will be split in the mornings for various excursions and then you will be able to recongregate in the evenings. On day four, you will submit a final entry piece in the category of either food, tradition, landscape, or other. The winners of each category in photography or written work will receive five thousand dollars. From those, we will choose one overall winner in photography and one in writing. They will each win a one-hundred-thousand-dollar prize.

"We have joined forces with Southern California University to provide several classes on the cruise. Business, photography, writing, technology, and many others. Please see the brochures at the doors for the full list and times. In the meantime, we will also be emailing a few daily contests on various cruise-themed items. You have all signed waivers that any photographs or essays will be the property of *American Voyage* upon submission. They will be used to promote the cruise line, as well as Hawaii tourism. All submissions must be entered by five p.m. each day, and winners will be announced by seven. Winners will receive two hundred dollars to use as they wish.

"I was also asked earlier who will be making the decisions on the winners and I wish to reiterate that it is not the board. We have chosen three very distinguished professors in the areas of art, photography, and journalism who will be reviewing all entries. They will not be accessible to any contestant for the duration of this trip, and your names will not be submitted to them with your entry. You will meet the judges at the final presentations in Hawaii."

"I wonder who the judges are," Isaac said quietly. "I did some research—they never have the same judges two years in a row."

"I wonder if any of the board members will be teaching classes," Layla gushed. "I would *love* to take a business class with Jonah Seeley."

Isla snorted. "What kind of business?"

"Any kind," Layla said with a wink.

I turned back to Mr. Vaughn, my cheeks flaming.

"We, the board, will be hosting another dinner party tomorrow evening to answer any further questions. We wish to be transparent in our goals, for us and you on this trip. We sincerely hope for an enjoyable trip and a most pleasant experience aboard *Cali Cruise Lines*. Thank you."

There was more clapping as he stepped from the podium. On that cue, waiters suddenly swarmed the room with carts full of delicious food.

"Is this catered by Seeley Catering?" Layla asked the waiter who stopped at our table. A mountain of crab legs, a mammoth bowl of shrimp, and large plates of some sort of filleted fish were set before us.

"Yes, ma'am," the waiter said quickly, adding an enormous salad bowl, melted butter in a bowl, and steaming biscuits before moving to the next table.

"Hopefully no one has seafood allergies," Creed muttered, as he helped himself to the nearest dish.

"Forget business classes," Isaac said with a grin. "If Jonah Seeley is hosting cooking classes, that is where you'll find me."

"There's no way he can cook," Creed practically spat. "Chances are the man never cooked a day in his life. Everything handed to him on a silver platter."

"He doesn't come from old money," Isla said, helping herself to a crab leg. "I researched some of the board members, and I could not find anything on his family."

Layla was laughing. "You researched them too? Too bad they aren't the judges."

"I did not research them for bribery purposes! I was curious about what their ties were to this contest, and or *American Voyage*. That way I had a face and a background for small talk if needed."

"What about you, Doll?" Creed said, nudging my elbow. "Did you research everyone like these ladies?"

I shook my head. *Doll*...ugh.

"I would like to pick Bob Vaughn's mind about how he started the magazine," Isaac admitted. "What a career he has had."

The three writers dove into a discussion comparing notes on some of the board members. Which ones had made money, who had been born into or married into money, marital status, families, biggest accomplishments. I had not done any of the research—I didn't even know all their names. It was both enlightening and daunting, my competition knowing their facts while I did not.

I didn't think it mattered and told Isla so quietly while the other three were debating one of Bob Vaughn's merits. "I thought this competition was about our skills and creativity."

"It is, but it never hurts to come to the fight ring prepared," Isla replied with a shrug. "People are petty."

I listened quietly, wondering how I would present the new piece of evidence that Jonah Seeley was, in fact, my boyfriend, would not sit well with people like Layla, who wanted him for herself. I wanted to make friends on this trip and network. Would I be shunned for exactly what I feared Jonah had done—pulling strings to get me in?

Isla seemed nice enough, carefree, and fun. Layla quickly became Isla's partner-in-crime, the two of them piggy-backing off each other's jokes until both of them were wiping tears of laughter from their faces. Isaac was young and intelligent, all wide eyes and brilliant smiles. I liked him because he reminded me of Abby.

Creed, on the other hand, was a self-certified G.G.W.—God's Gift to Women. When he had nothing else to contribute to a conversation, he was all smoldering looks and flexed muscles. He reminded me of the boys in high school, the ones too horny to see the woman beyond the boobs and ass. I found myself fighting against a brewing anxiety attack when dinner was over, as each of his movements invaded more of my personal bubble.

When I was practically in Isla's lap from avoiding him, I stood abruptly. "I—um, it has been very nice meeting all of you. I am pretty tired, so I think I am going to call it a night."

"See you tomorrow?" Isla asked. At my nod, she smiled. "Have a good night, then. Let's chat more in the morning."

I nodded again and made a break for the door, hoping Creed would not follow. Grabbing a brochure, I hurried to the elevator, digging Jonah's key card out of my wallet, and clutching it in my fist like a weapon. My sigh of relief came only when I was safely enclosed in Jonah's suite, completely alone.

"Jonah?" I called, dropping my wallet on the bed and checking my phone. There were two messages. One from Abby, and one from Jonah.

A: Call me soon! I want to hear all about your first day on a cruise!

J: Have a great time tonight. Love the blue dress.

I grinned, responding to Jonah's message first.

H: When did you see me?

J: I was passing by the dining room and I saw you sitting at a table with a tiny brunette woman.

H: That was Isla. She's a writer from Texas. How's your party?

J: Long-winded speeches. Rich guys who know everything. Lots of small talk. Good to catch up with a few of them, though.

H: I look forward to meeting them tomorrow night.

J: My turn for a long-winded speech. Later, Kitten.

With a smile, I grabbed my suit. Nothing like a late-night soak. On a cruise. In a suite. Waiting for a hot guy who was my boyfriend. "Boyfriend," I whispered, unable to keep a grin off my face. How could one simple word feel so good to say out loud? "My boyfriend." Two words—even better.

Thirteen

Sinking into the hot tub with a sigh, I looked over the brochure and then the emails on my phone, reviewing the side contests. I had taken a few pictures earlier with Jonah that might work, but I would need to do some more exploring tomorrow.

"I got your picture," Abby said without preamble when I called her. "Smokin'. Hot. Just like I knew that dress would be. Did you draw every eye in the room when you entered?"

"Cheese and rice, Abby, my life is not a *Hallmark* movie."

I could hear the eyeroll in her tone. "Well, did you at least have a good day? Wait, why are you calling me so early? Shouldn't you still be at the reception dinner?"

"Did you memorize my itinerary?"

"Of course, I did." My phone pinged, and I found the video call waiting. I hit accept and her face popped up, happy and then curious. "Are you in a hot tub right now?"

"Yeah."

"Jealous."

My heart fluttered as I prepared my next few words. "A lot has happened today, Abby. I am not sure I've even fully processed it."

Her brows furrowed. "Bad happenings?"

"No." I flipped the camera, giving her a panoramic view of the suite.

"Wow… Are all the rooms like that?" Abby asked incredulously.

"Nope. Just Jonah's."

I couldn't help the giggle as Abby processed my words. "Are you staying with Jonah?" She asked in a screech. When I nodded, she flailed her arms, sending her camera down the crack between the wall and bed. "Holly!!!! What? What does this mean? Why? I— eeeeeeeeeek!"

Self-conscious of the noise, I looked around. No one was in the room, and the ocean stretched for miles. "Abby! Calm down."

"How can I calm down? You're staying with Jonah! Does this mean you guys are together? I only saw one bed!"

"Abby!"

She pulled her phone closer to her face. "I need answers, Holly! I'm dying!"

"Yes, we are *trying* this boyfriend and girlfriend thing. I have been thinking about it a lot and… I don't know. It just feels right. Jonah makes me happy. And he makes me feel whole, and-and safe. I like how confident he makes me." Tears filled my eyes, taking me by surprise.

"Holly," she whispered, all giddiness gone.

"I'm good," I said with a chuckle, quickly wiping at my face. "These are happy tears."

"I know." She sniffed a few times, wiping at her face. "I'm so happy for you."

"Thank you for making me do this. The trip, I mean. Thank you for pushing me."

"Oh jeez, stop it!" she cried, laughing. "I would have stayed on call if I knew we were going to be this sappy!"

We talked a few more minutes about our plans for the following day before hanging up.

"Holly?"

I yelped, nearly dropping my phone into the tub. Jonah stepped from the shadows, dressed in a cotton blue dress shirt rolled to his elbows and gray slacks. Impossibly attractive, I decided, made better by the fact that he was oblivious of his good looks. He approached slowly, resting his elbows on the edge of the tub near me. "I thought you'd be at the party."

I shrugged. "It was a bit of a bust, so I left early."

"A bust? Why?"

I didn't want to tell him about Creed, or that I felt like a fish out of water. I didn't want to tell him that every girl I heard was buzzing that he was there. Instead, I just shrugged and smiled at him. "The food was spectacular, though."

The distraction proved effective. "I am glad you liked it."

"Not just me—everyone. There was a request for you to teach a cooking class while we are on the cruise."

Jonah laughed. "Maybe I'll volunteer for a class next year."

"Was your meeting done for the night too?"

"No, but my part was. I thought I'd come up here and drop off my paperwork and then go find you. But I like this idea much better. Can I join you?"

"Sure."

He leaned over, kissing my forehead. "I'll be right back."

My cheeks flared as I thought about my conversation with Abby. "Jonah?" I asked before he passed the bed. He paused to look back at me. "How much of my phone call did you hear?"

His grin was wide. "Enough," he said simply.

I squirmed while he was gone, mortified. Eventually, I would have told him all those things, but not yet. It was too early. What if he thought I was clingy? If he did think that, there was no way he would want to stay with me. Flashbacks came then, unwanted and horrendous.

Boys in high school and college asking me out on dates.

Forcing themselves on me and making me do things that were neither comfortable nor enjoyable. Things I wasn't ready for.

And then seeing them again in the days following, comparing notes with others, and brushing off my attempts to stop them.

Humiliation.

Pain.

Rumors.

Judgment.

Mortification.

"Holly?" Jonah was there, practically vaulting into the water and pulling me to my feet and into his embrace. "Holly, talk to me."

I gasped in a breath, followed by another, and another. "I'm sorry," I wheezed. "I'm sorry."

He moved back and cupped my cheeks. His eyes were wide with concern. "Breathe, Holly. With me. In, out. In, out."

"I'm sorry." I clutched at his forearms, trying to do as he asked.

"Don't apologize. Just focus on your breathing. In, out. In, out."

We stayed like that for a long time, me breathing on his command. As my body began to relax, tears spilled down my cheeks.

"Holly," he said in a sad sigh. "What happened?"

"I'm sorry," I whispered.

He sat down and pulled me into his lap. For a moment, I froze, past demons threatening to consume me once more. But then he nestled me into him, my head tucked into his collar bone, an arm around my back, and another running up and down my shins. There were no sexual advances, just the intimate touch of a trusted, comforting man. The gentle movement helped, and I felt my body start to relax. Exhaustion crept in on a wave.

"Are you all right?"

I smiled, liking the way his chest vibrated when he spoke. "Better. Thank you for helping me. I haven't had an attack to that degree in a long time."

"What triggered it?"

"Fear. Embarrassment. Facing the unknown."

He was quiet a moment before asking, "Why now? What happened?"

"I just… I scared myself. You said you heard what I told Abby. I started worrying about what you would think and how you'd react if you knew what I was feeling."

"How I'd react…" Jonah moved me to look at him. "Holly, you're wrong. All wrong. I am *glad* I make you feel that way. Safe, confident, protected, happy, whole. I *want* you to feel all those things, when you are with me and when I'm elsewhere. Everyone deserves that, but especially you. I just… I don't understand. Why did you think I would be upset?"

I leaned back to look up at him. "I thought if you heard me having such deep feelings, so soon, that you'd… be a little freaked out."

"Freaked out? Holly…" he laughed, exasperation seeping out. "Holly, I am over the moon to hear you feel the way you are. That means I'm accomplishing what I've set out to do since the day I met you."

His words caressed my soul, kissing my broken spirit. Self-confidence, however, came slower. "Why me? You could have had anyone, but you picked me. Why?"

Jonah was quiet for a moment. Fearing I had put him on the spot, I rested my head back on his chest. *Maybe he will tell me someday.* In the silence, my eyes drifted shut.

"The day I met you, I saw a beautiful woman, scared but strong beyond measure. I recognized your capacity to love others, in the way you cared for your sister. I admired you for your dedication to make ends meet, even at the cost of your dreams. You're a hard worker and loyal, funny and kind, and as humble as they come. Your blush at nearly everything I say tells me you don't always believe my compliments, but I wish you would." He tipped my chin up to look at him. "You make me feel loved, Holly. You make *me* feel confident, and I happen to enjoy making you feel all those good things too."

Well… apparently, the emotional rollercoaster wasn't finished yet. "Smooth," I whispered, smiling through my tears.

"I try." He kissed the tip of my nose before snuggling me back into his chest.

I looked out over the ocean and marveled at the stars. Wisconsin had a lovely night sky, but it was nothing in comparison to a night over the Pacific. "I don't think I have ever seen so many stars," I said quietly. "It's beautiful." Already my mind was wandering, trying to come up with a way to capture the amazing horizon with the camera.

"There is no place I would rather be right now," Jonah said, hugging me closer.

"Thank you for being my peace," I whispered, letting my eyes drift closed again.

"Thank you for trusting me with the job. Come on," he said, nudging me from my seat. Chuckling at my irritated groan, Jonah stood behind me, guiding me to the steps, and helping me out. Wrapping me in a towel, he then shepherded me into the bathroom with a robe and waited patiently while I showered. I dressed while he took his turn in the bathroom, pulling on a t-shirt and shorts, and brushing my hair before returning to the deck with my camera. A few shooting stars raced across the sky, so I tried a few burst sessions, as well as some long exposure shots. With a smile, I returned to the room. Just like old school film development days, I did not hit the review button on my camera. Instead, I would wait until the morning to see what my camera had captured.

I paused for only a moment before climbing into the bed. Jonah was a safe person, one who would not take advantage of the sleeping arrangements. He had had an opportunity the night before, as well as earlier when I had dozed against his chest in the hot tub. I knew in my heart that nothing would go wrong overnight.

Thank you for trusting me with the job. With a smile, my eyes drifted shut.

Fourteen

The next morning, I awoke with a jolt. In the process of flinging the blanket off of my body, I whacked Jonah in the face. He rolled over with a groan of pain as I yelped in surprise.

"Jonah! Oh, I am *so* sorry. Are you okay?"

He laughed groggily. "Well, that's an interesting way to wake up on the first day of vacation."

"Are you okay?"

He wrapped an arm around me, pulling me back to his side. "I'm fine, Holly. Come here."

Warmth and a delightful woodsy-man smell surrounded me. "How do you smell so good?" I asked with a giggle, self-conscious of my messy hair and probably horrid breath.

"Mm… you smell good too," he mumbled, kissing the back of my head. "You okay?"

"Yeah," I laughed. "I just forgot where I was for a minute. Deep sleep and traumatic high school experiences will do that."

He pulled me closer, his breath making my hair tickle my face. "That bad?" At my nod, he asked, "Why?"

I shrugged and then sighed. "The guys I went to school with, they were awful. Thank goodness Abby found me before—" I froze, realizing what I had been about to say. "Well, thank goodness for Abby."

"Found you before what?" When I didn't answer, he scooted back and rolled me over to face him. "Found you before what?"

"It doesn't matter." I reached up to smooth his bed head, hoping to distract him with a smile.

"Found you before what, Holly?" he asked again.

Closing my eyes, I sighed, consciously out my nose to avoid sharing my breath. "It was a long time ago, Jonah. I was in a bad, dark place." When I opened my eyes, he was still studying me. Under his gaze, the words just tumbled out. "I tried to commit suicide."

I felt the sheets scrunch under his fist near my head, but his face remained passive beyond the tightening of his jaw. "What happened, Holly?"

"Do we have to?"

"Please tell me."

I squirmed away from him and stood. I had ruined the tranquil morning with a slap to the face, but this conversation certainly was not going to clear the air. One look back at the man on the bed, however, and I was reminded of all the things Jonah had whispered to me the night before. The lovely, beautiful things. The things that made me feel whole again.

Returning to the bed, I perched on the edge, staring down at my hands. "About three weeks before my senior year, things had reached a breaking point. I didn't want to go back to school, and Gram refused to consider online schooling to get my diploma. I had just found out that morning that I was pregnant. The guy who knocked me up denied any involvement, calling me all sorts of terrible, terrible things. I didn't want to have sex in the first place. There was alcohol… a-and drugs, I think. It wasn't consensual. The only reason I knew it was him was because somebody had taken a video of him bragging about it. It was shared with everyone."

I kept my eyes on my hands because I didn't want to see the pity or disgust or anger in Jonah's eyes. I powered through the rest of the story quickly.

"When I found out I was pregnant, I wrote a note for Abby, put all my money under her pillow. On a day that my grandma was out, I filled the tub with water and brought the toaster up from the kitchen. I was naked, in the tub, and ready when Abby walked in. She was so young, but she knew what was happening." I closed my eyes as tears streamed down my cheeks. "Sh-she knew what was happening. She unplugged the toaster and took it out of my shaking hands. She climbed into that tub, fully clothed, and hugged me. 'Don't go yet,' she said. 'I still need you.'" Finally, I looked up at him, though he was blurry through my tears. "She found my note before I finished what I had set out to do and walked with me to the abortion clinic, helped me fill out the paperwork, a-and held my hand while they prescribed… medicine. She held me when it was over and never breathed a word of it to anyone. All of that, and she wasn't even ten years old."

Slowly, Jonah stood and came around the bed. Pulling me into his arms and whispering my name, he hugged me as I sobbed. I clung to him, thankful for his touch. After so many years of silence, sharing my secret came with mixed feelings. I didn't want pity, anger, or sadness. I didn't want him to tell me everything would be all right. There would be good days and bad days, and I had long since accepted that. I only wanted him to listen.

"And so you've dedicated yourself to loving Abby the way she loves you," Jonah said softly. I nodded into his chest. "You've nailed that, Holly."

"She is so much stronger than me. When she started middle school that year, she was a straight-A student, and more than one guy walked away from trying to harass her with a black eye or a bruised groin." I choked out a laugh as his chest rumbled. "She didn't put up with anyone's crap. Some tactics I picked up from her along the way, but she had thicker skin from the start."

"Don't compare yourself to anyone else. No one— *no one*—has lived the same life as you."

"You're wrong," I said, pulling myself away from him, wiping furiously at my eyes. "There are so many people who have lived through what I have and have come out stronger than I am. I want to help them, but I don't know how."

Jonah spread his hands with an ambitious look. It was almost silly—him standing there in a pair of gym shorts, hair mussed from sleep, and ready to conquer the world. "What do you have in mind?"

"I don't know!" I cried. "I'm not ready to volunteer in a shelter, and I certainly cannot give any inspiring speeches at charitable events. I have my camera and a dream. That's all."

"And me. Now, you have me too." He held his arms out again, this time waiting for me to come to him.

I did, wrapping my arms around him and resting my cheek on his chest. "Thank you, Jonah."

"No, thank you for telling me. We will find a way to help you help others."

"We can help together."

"No. This is going to be all in your name. I will help *you* find a way."

ooooo

An hour later, I emerged from the shower to find Jonah had ordered breakfast. "I didn't know what you wanted," he said with a sheepish grin when I gaped at the amount of food. "I am hungry."

I pulled the silver covers off the dishes. Eggs, pancakes, bagels with cream cheese, and a pair of delicious-looking fruit crepes. "I'm guessing you are one of those people who shouldn't grocery shop when you're hungry either."

"I try not to do that. Max often takes it upon himself to keep my fridge stocked," Jonah admitted, scooping a huge pile of eggs onto his plate. "They only served breakfast until ten, and I did not want you to miss it. I had my guys whip something up for us."

I had slept later than I had in a long time. In the shower, I wondered if I'd make it for breakfast. "Seeley's Catering this morning too? I feel spoiled."

"You should. That's how vacations are supposed to work."

I had a feeling vacations with Jonah would take me well beyond spoiled. Grabbing a plate of eggs and one of the crepes, I took my breakfast out to the balcony. It was still new—the pain of remembering and telling Jonah one of my deepest secrets. I felt torn. On the one hand, I was glad he knew. On the other hand, I had just exposed a wound, deep and painful. Giving him my trust, it was up to him not to stab a knife into it and twist.

The morning was bright and magnificent, and the waters calm and cool. Abby had kept tabs on the weather and reported a possible storm coming overnight about halfway through our trip. I was curious about what a lightning storm looked like over the ocean and looked forward to capturing what I could. There weren't any classes that day, but the first contest had a "water fun" theme. That was all. Just "water fun." I considered the possibilities as Jonah sat down beside me. The awkwardness returned, and we ate in silence.

"I don't want to brush this morning under the rug," Jonah said after a few bites. "What happened was a very big deal. I mean, both your suicide attempt and your decision to tell me about it. Know that I'm not taking this lightly. I have questions, though, if you don't mind. What about the photography teacher you raved about last night? Did you reach out to anyone for help?"

I shook my head. "Everything happened right before school started. And then, when school did start, I avoided everyone. If the teachers knew, they didn't do anything to help. Mr. Hockenstad started receiving chemo that fall, so he was in and out throughout the year. He knew something was up, but I didn't let him in."

"Where did you—I mean, did you seek any…
help?"

"You mean therapy?" I shrugged. "Gran had only
the most basic medical insurance, and her plan only
allowed so many therapy sessions. I did go, as well as
calling the free numbers. They gave me a few coping
mechanisms, but that's about all. And then Gran died,
and life got crazy. Focusing all my attention on Abby,
work, and school removed me from the toxic social
environments that surrounded me. It was enough until
we moved to Hartford. I thought about going to
therapy, but Cecille's insurance isn't the best, so I always
figured I'd only use it if it was absolutely necessary."

Jonah nodded, though the clenching and
unclenching of his fists on the table gave away his
feelings. "I'll admit, the anger I feel for the asshole who
caused you this pain is… well, beyond words. I want to
know his name and then I want to destroy him."

"Jonah," I sighed.

"That isn't the answer right now, though," he
continued, the bite leaving his tone. "Right now, just
know that as long as I am with you, I will never, *ever*
push you to do anything you don't want to do or aren't
ready for. As long as I can be near you, that will be
enough, until you are ready. That I can promise you."
He reached over and squeezed my hand. "It's all good,
Holly. I am not going anywhere."

"Thank you," I whispered, squeezing his hand back.

He allowed a short silence to pass before smiling.
"Okay, back to vacation-mode. What are we doing
today?"

I considered a moment, remembering the previous night's conversations at the dinner. "Um, well…"

"What's up?"

I squirmed a few moments before it burst out of me. "All the lady contestants want in your pants, and I think I will ostracize myself if I'm seen with you. I mean, I'm not embarrassed to be with you, I just… I just want to make some friends before they all hate me because they're jealous."

Jonah stared at me a moment before he burst out laughing. "'They all want in my pants'?"

With a burning face, I nodded, sharing some of the comments I had heard the night before. Jonah was still chuckling, shaking his head as he leaned back and stretched in his chair. "Jonah," I whined. "Be serious."

"I'd like to tell you this is the first time that people are curious about me, but it isn't. People ogle over large bank accounts—I never asked for that, but it is what happens." I started to protest but he spoke again. "If you want me to keep my distance, I will. I understand. I mean, I would love to keep you all to myself, but that isn't fair to you. Get out there, meet people, network, make friends. I'm not offended that you're not ready for others to know about us."

I stared at him. "How did I get so lucky finding someone like you?"

He leaned over, touching his nose to mine. "I'm the lucky one."

I kissed him with a smile, loving the little butterflies in my stomach. "I have a little money to win today."

"Oh?" I told him about the daily contests. "Ah, yes, Bob mentioned something about that. I dislike the idea."

"Why?"

Jonah shrugged. "It's a cheap way for Bob to get some free advertising. You all signed waivers that anything submitted would be the property of the magazine. It seems selfish to try and weasel more out of you guys."

"But he is paying us for it," I replied.

"Wrong. He is paying one of you for it. The rest are freebies."

"Our cruises, meals, and lodging have all been paid for! It seems only fair that we give him a few 'free' things in reciprocation."

He shrugged. "You can do what you want, Douglas. Believe me when I say that the deal he worked out with the cruise for lodging and meals is cheaper than what he'd have to pay otherwise."

"Do you not like Bob, then?"

"I like Bob a lot. He took a crumbling magazine and made it more prosperous than anyone expected. His heart is in the right place, as he was a struggling journalist too, once upon a time. He wants new voices to be heard, new perspectives to be seen, and has striven to ensure that others are presented with the opportunity to shine. I just don't like how he ends up benefitting so heavily from this competition, for so little."

"A free cruise and a possibility of a hundred thousand dollars are more than beneficial for us struggling artists," I laughed. "I take thousands of pictures every year. I'm happy to sacrifice a few, in exchange for a trip and a little recognition."

"Agree to disagree, Kitten." I chuckled as I stood, gathering our plates. Jonah jumped up, grabbing them from me. "I'll get them. You get your camera."

I did as I was told, digging through my bag for several different lenses. Pushing the table on the deck out to the railing, I returned to the room and took two champagne flutes from the cabinet. Filling them with different amounts I took several shots, trying to catch the various shades of light on the metal tabletop. The shadows reflected perfectly with a crystalline light in the center where the sun touched the liquid. I then moved them to the edge of the hot tub, where condensation formed quickly on the cool glasses. I snapped a few more, already planning a black and white shot or two later while I edited.

Engrossed as I was, I didn't notice that Jonah had returned to the doorway to watch me work. When I finally looked up, he grinned, producing a bottle of orange juice from behind his back. "Mimosas?"

Laughing, I handed him one of the glasses and held mine out. "I think I've had more alcohol with you than I've ever drank in my life."

"Is that a bad thing?"

"Ask me again after I finish this. I feel like I'm drinking on the job."

"Badass Douglas," he remarked, wiggling his eyebrows.

I snorted. "Keep going and it will be Drunk-ass Douglas."

"Like Hog's Head? Oh, yes, let's do that again." I swung my open hand to slap his arm playfully, but he jumped out of the way with a laugh. "Whatever it takes you to loosen up and relax, I'm all for that."

Before I could respond, he reacted to a vibrating noise coming from the table by his bed. His face darkened. I caught his arm before he could turn away. "This is your vacation, too," I said quietly. "You said Max could hold everything down while you're gone."

He smiled, leaning to kiss my forehead. "Some things have to be handled by the boss himself."

I let go and saluted, extracting a short chuckle from him before he moved to retrieve his phone.

"What's up, Max?" Jonah began as a greeting. I watched as his face darkened further. "They did *what?* Hang on a second."

Uh oh. As he glanced around the room to excuse himself, I caught his attention with a wave. Finishing my mimosa, I gathered my phone and camera and left quietly.

Fifteen

I stumbled upon Isla and Layla poolside, watching Creed, Isaac, and a few of the other guys from the contest playing a violent game of water polo.

"Holly! Come join us!" Isla cried, flagging me down to sit on the lounge chair beside her. Both women had their computers out. "How's it going? The boys are busy showing off. It's ridiculous, really. After you left last night, a bunch of us decided to meet here for the day. I wasn't sure if we would see you or not. You should give me your room number, so I know where to find you next time."

"Did you get the email about the water-themed submissions?" Layla asked.

"Yeah, I did," I replied, grateful I did not have to drop the information that I was not on the same floor as the other contestants. "I took a few this morning, but I decided to wander a bit and see what else I could find."

Layla huffed. "It's so vague," she cried. "What about water?"

I shrugged, nodding to the pool. "Anything. You're watching water fun right now."

Layla rolled her eyes. "Darlin', what I'm watching is a bunch of grown men acting like boys."

"Maybe that's what you could write about," I said, watching two guys dunk another, the ball popping out of the water like a rocket. "Water is a natural element that makes us remember the innocent fun of our childhood."

"That was anything but innocent," Isla shouted to the men who had done the dunking. "Foul!"

Layla's eyes lit up, however. "Do you mind if I use that line?"

"All yours."

"Thanks," she said, and began pecking furiously at the keyboard.

"You coming in, Doll?" Creed called from the side of the pool.

I shook my head. "I didn't bring my suit."

"You play water polo?" Isla asked.

"Goodness, no."

"I didn't do sports. Still don't. No hand-eye coordination. Yoga and Pilates are more my speed."

"I am not nearly flexible enough for either of those things."

"If you want to join me tomorrow, I joined one of the group classes in the dance studio. This morning was Zumba, and it was really fun."

I smirked at her. The idea of shaking my butt in a room full of strangers was not on my bucket list. "I'll think about it," I said.

Isaac vaulted out of the pool, grabbing the towel from my chair. "I'm getting another drink. You ladies want anything?"

"Piña colada," Layla asked without looking up.

"I'll take one, too," Isla decided.

"Water, please."

"Water," Isla repeated when Isaac walked away. "You do know we are on vacation, right?"

I chuckled, nodding. "I have already had a mimosa this morning."

Isla set her computer aside, leaning in conspiratorially. "Is this with New Guy? Was this a breakfast in bed mimosa, then?"

"No! I was actually taking pictures of champagne in the glass. He suggested mimosas when I was done," I replied, blushing furiously.

"I like this man already. And it's very clear you're head over heels in love."

Love was a hard concept, to define, to identify, and to use with anyone beyond Abby. I loved Jonah as a friend, but platonic and romantic love were vastly different. A history of broken relationships left me wary of dropping the term lightly. "It's new," I repeated quietly.

After a few minutes, the pool emptied, and I studied it, wondering what I could try. I always liked finding ways to capture ripples and waves. I switched out my lenses before turning back to Isla. "Can I borrow you for a minute?" I asked her.

"As your model? Absolutely." She fixed her impossibly large beach hat and laid back on the chair, striking a pose, bikini model perfection.

Grinning, I snapped a few shots. "Actually, I wanted to try something by the pool. You do not have to get in the water."

"I want copies," she decided, standing gracefully.

"Sure." I had brought a small printer along with me, not high quality, but it worked in a pinch.

She followed me to the edge, and we both knelt together. "I want you to just reach out, about here, and just touch the water with a fingertip. Extend your fingers a little. No, just the pad of your finger touches the water. I want to catch the ripples." We did a few tries with me taking burst sessions at different angles and distances. I couldn't wait to see how they turned out.

"I think you've given me something to write about too," Isla decided when I lowered my camera.

"Thank you for your help."

"I love this idea, Holly. I can't wait to see how they turn out."

"Me too. I'll probably head—"

With a shout, someone entered the water in front of us with a massive splash. Isla and I jumped back, but it was too late. We were both doused with water. Isla shrieked as I scraped the back of my leg on the ground.

"Not cool, man," Isaac growled, helping me to my feet. "Are you all right?" He offered his towel when we both looked down at my camera.

"I'm fine, thanks."

"Of course, she's fine," Creed crowed. "Right, Doll?"

"Jackass," Isla spat at him, only making him laugh more.

I did not give Creed the time of day and followed Isla back to the lounge chairs, still wiping my camera. Having been hunched over, most of the water had landed on my back and shoulders. Luckily, I had chosen a peach top rather than white. And my camera would be okay too.

"Aw, come on, Doll. The water's fine," Creed persisted.

"Back off, Creed," Isaac said. When he continued to pester me, Isaac jumped into the water in front of him, drawing his attention away from me. The two engaged in a vicious splashing fight before more guys returned to the pool and the volleyball net was raised.

I borrowed Isla's fruity drink to snap a few close-up photos before returning it to her. Grabbing my water, I excused myself, excited to examine and edit my photos before submitting, plus I needed to get ready for the party.

"Wait," Isla said before I left. She gave me her phone number and told me to text if I needed anything. I sent her a message so she would have mine too. She replied with *have fun with New Guy* along with several saucy emojis.

"Jonah?" I asked, letting myself into the room. Gone were the trays of food, and gone the man who ordered it. I moved about the room, retrieving my computer, camera, and phone. With the soundtrack of Cecille's café filling the room, I curled up on the couch to edit.

ooooo

My alarm went off at four-thirty, forcing me to make my final decisions and submit them. I decided on one of the champagne glass photos with the condensation, and a few of the ocean I had taken earlier. Next, I printed two photos Isla had helped me create. One was a very flattering photo of her, stretched out on the deck chair. She looked like a pin-up model from the fifties with her huge hat and polka dot suit. The other was one of the ripple photos in black and white. They had turned out awesome. Isla's perfect French-manicured hand had created the delicacy and grace I was hoping for, and several images had captured not only the ripples, but a drip from the pad of her finger. However, I remembered Jonah's concern over losing ownership of the photos, so I kept them out of the competition.

I sent Jonah a text message asking where he was before turning the music up and hunting through my clothing for something to wear to dinner. The winning garment was a pretty silvery-gray halter wrap dress that flattered my figure. My hair was curling wildly, so I set to work taming it. Eye liner, mascara, pink lipstick, and perfume. I had enough sun so far throughout the summer to darken my cheeks and set off my freckles. Most people hated their freckles, but I was not among them. Abby, as a child, had once called them my sun sparkles, and as an adult, the memory had become a treasured one.

My phone pinged again.

J: I got held up with work stuff. Will probably miss the start of the party.

H: Is everything okay?

I did not get a response to that, which probably meant his meetings had continued to go poorly. I thought about sending him another message but decided against it. He had enough on his plate without my text messages. My job later would be remaining chipper and happy after the party to boost his mood.

Abby had imparted the wisdom of fashion on me, ensuring I would look inches thinner with heels. I did as I was told, donning a pair of stilettos. Snapping a picture for Abby, I gathered my phone and wallet.

Ping.

A: You look smokin' hot. I showed Cecille—she spouted off some Shakespeare quote about love and the voice of gods speaking.

A: She also says, 'Get it, girl!'

I giggled over Abby's text for most of the walk to the party. It was in the same room as the previous night's dinner, but the bright meeting room lights were replaced with dimmed purple bulbs. They had a band playing current pop songs and had added a second full bar. The previous night, long curtains hung against one wall which were pulled back, showing a wall of windows with a beautiful scene of ocean and stars. One look at the beautiful chandelier, lit with hundreds of tiny twinkling lights, made me wish I had brought my camera. Settling, I tried to snap a few pictures with my phone.

Along the window, a table was set up with several framed photos and sheet protected papers. They were the entries from the day's contest. The other photographers' work was amazing—they were all very talented. A few of the stories from the writers kept my expectations high as well. The note on the end of the table said winners would be announced over dinner.

"Holly!" Isla cried, appearing at my side and looping an arm through mine. She was in a barely-there red sequined dress that accentuated her narrow waist. "Did you submit a photo?"

I pointed to the two I had submitted. "What about you?"

She shook her head. "I did come up with a good idea, but I just couldn't perfect it in time. I figured I would scope out the winners tonight to try and figure out how to best persuade the judges for tomorrow."

"Here," I said with a smile, handing her the photos I had printed.

"Oh, Holly! These are incredible. Thank you, I love them. You'll have to sign the backs, in case you ever become famous. Come on, we have a table already."

She led me to the back of the room, a table perfectly situated to everything going on—not too close to the front where a head table was reserved for the board members, and not too close to the band or the speakers, so that we could hear each other over the music. Layla, Isaac, and a few others stood near the table, talking and laughing amongst each other. Creed, thankfully, was not among them.

"Are any of the board members here?" I asked Isla.

She shook her head. "Someone said they had a meeting before dinner and that they were going to make some grand entrance."

"That seems excessive."

"Maybe it is so they can all sit down for the meal without being bombarded by questions," she said with a shrug.

I glanced again at the door, willing Jonah to enter. Though I had been busy that afternoon, I had missed his company. I was worried, I realized. Worried he was not okay, worried that he would come back so stressed, and then have to deal with a party on top of it. I glanced again at my phone, hoping for a response.

Isla caught me. "What's the matter, Holly?"

"Nothing," I said, forcing a smile. "I wonder what the meal will be tonight."

"Someone said pasta, I think."

Layla plopped down beside me, still giggling at something from the other conversation. She was immaculate in a white halter dress. Her bronze legs, and golden hair reminded me of a Greek goddess. "Was the champagne picture yours? I loved the magnification on it. Who knew condensation could be so pretty?"

"Look what else she did," Isla chimed in, presenting the pictures I'd taken. She ran her finger over the photo of the ripples. "This one needs a title I think."

We all considered a moment before Isaac chimed in behind us. "Spreading Kindness," he suggested.

"Ooh, I like that," Isla cooed. "Holly? What do you think?"

"I was thinking of New Beginnings," I said.

"Oooh," Isla and Layla responded together, their matching awed tone making us all laugh.

"Here," Isla said, producing a pen from her wristlet. "Sign it."

I carefully wrote the name of the photo and signed the bottom corner before handing it back to her.

"Do you have a watermark or a logo yet, Holly?" Isaac asked.

I shook my head. "I don't even have a company name yet." When eyebrows rose, I hurried to explain, blushing fiercely. "I have a degree, but after college, I had—I had expenses, and photography became a side gig. Someday, I'd like to pursue full-time, but it hasn't worked out yet."

"If you would like some help on a logo design, I dabble," Isaac said with a shrug. "You wouldn't have to pay me. I like media design as a hobby."

I gawked at him. "That would be *great*. Thank you." I never had the extra income to hire anyone to design a logo, and I never could decide on what I wanted.

"I'll work on it tomorrow," Isaac said. "Let's meet around one. Maybe poolside, like today? I'll throw together a few ideas tonight, and we can perfect it."

"Thank you, Isaac. Thank you." I stood to hug him. It was definitely not customary for me to hug virtual strangers, but this was something I had been looking forward to for so long. My dreams were starting to feel like a reality, thanks to the help of some great new friends.

"What'd I miss?" Creed asked, appearing at my shoulder when Isaac stepped away. With an arm around my waist, too low for comfort, Creed leaned past me to grab Isla's photo. The way our bodies grazed, I knew the intimate contact was not an accident. "Nice picture. Whose is it?"

"Mine," Isla said, snatching it back from him. "Holly gave it to me."

"You took that?" he asked.

"Yeah." Stuck between Isaac and Creed, I had nowhere to go, no way to escape his roaming hand. My face began to burn as I reached back and pushed his hand away as discreetly as possible.

"I didn't enter the contest today," Creed announced. "I did take some photos, though. Boudoir photos, poolside, and then my room. Very sexy."

I suppressed a cringe and caught Isla doing the same. "That sounds… no, man. Just no." Isaac finally moved, and I sank into my chair, wishing I could wipe away the feeling of ick off my skin.

"Oh, it was awesome," Creed laughed, punching Isaac's shoulder as he passed. "Twin sisters!" Isaac was still shaking his head, walking away. Creed followed, still trying to argue his case.

"It was disgusting," Layla said quietly. "They were practically naked by the pool, and he walked off with a hand on each woman's ass."

"Why does he think we are all friends?" Isla asked. "Just because we all rode on a plane together? We talked, but that was all."

"Unfortunately, he seems to have his eyes set on you, Holly," Layla commented.

"He's not the only one. Look," Isla said, nodding toward the front of the room. We all turned to see the board members filing in, each finding a seat at the head table. "That's Jonah Seeley eyeing you up, Holly."

I turned to find Jonah across the room. His jaw had dropped a fraction, and I caught the surprise on his face. My face burned.

"Oh my goodness, he's checking you out," Isla squealed.

"Give him a wink," Layla hissed, wiggling her fingers at Jonah with a grin. Isla was also waving.

I looked back to Jonah, chuckling as I gave him a little wave and a wink. When he overcame his surprise at my bold gesture, he grinned back.

Layla clutched my arm, squealing again excitedly. "Oh my god, Holly!"

The poor man was going to be swarmed after dinner, I realized with a chuckle. Jonah made it sound like it was something he dealt with regularly, but I had never seen it in Wisconsin. Tonight would be interesting, to say the least.

We smelled the food long before it appeared. Waiters circled with colorful salads and then delicious broccoli alfredo. Isaac, Layla, Isla, and I sat together on one side of the large table, joking and laughing throughout the meal. It was the most fun I had had with others beyond my tiny inner circle of friends at home, and I came to love each person for their unique qualities. Isla was a tiny ball of fun with a knack for people-watching and creating wild stories. Layla was very *Legally Blonde*, a social genius to go with a beautiful face. And Isaac proved to be a computer nerd, quiet and kind, and sweet.

Though my chair was facing away from the head table, I kept taking glances over my shoulder, checking on Jonah. He was going through drinks faster than I had ever seen him, but I hoped with the meal that he would not get too drunk. More than once I caught him staring into his glass, as though the amber liquid held the answers he needed.

I pulled out my phone and sent him a quick text and then watched to see if he would answer. He pulled out his phone almost immediately and looked up when he read it. With a quick half-smile, he responded.

J: I'm fine. Enjoy your friends.

H: It's hard to enjoy myself when I can tell you're not 'fine.' And besides, you're my friend, too. It's my job to check up on you. Do we need to bail on this party early, like last night?

J: I was hoping there would be dancing. Me. You.

I snorted, looking up at him to shake my head.

J: Also, what are you drinking?

H: A Max-recommended delight. Blood orange vodka with white soda. It's delicious.

J: Cheers.

I looked up at him, raising my glass in his direction, my cheeks heating at the intimate moment. He did the same, and we drank together before I was drawn back to the table's conversation.

"Holly, maybe you can settle this for us," Isaac said. "Wisconsin: best scenery or best urban nightlife?"

"It depends where you are. If you're in a bigger city, the nightlife is pretty great," I said with a shrug. "But when you get out in the rural areas, it is very beautiful."

"Best of both worlds," Isaac grinned at me. "Plus, all four seasons. You said yesterday you like to do scenery and light pictures. I would love to see some of your work."

"I'll bring my computer tomorrow."

"Great! I'm very much a visual writer. Scenery inspires me. My fiancée's family is from the Chicago area. Despite an overbearing mom and an impossibly stubborn dad, I always look forward to visiting them."

My brows raised, remembering he hailed from Texas. "Chicago? Did you guys meet in college?"

"Yeah." His smile was sheepish and adorable. "She helped me get through my business classes. I proof-read and edited her papers."

"Aww," Layla sighed. "Match made in heaven."

"Have you set a date yet?"

"Valentine's Day."

Isla nudged me with an elbow. "Are you looking for a photographer?" she asked him.

Isaac grinned. "We are. We are getting married in Chicago, so we wouldn't be quite so far from you, Holly. Have you done any weddings before?"

"A couple," I said, my stomach doing happy little flip flops.

"If you have some samples, I'd love to see them. We are looking for a natural, earthy style."

"I'll bring them tomorrow."

Isaac laughed. "At this rate, maybe you should just bring everything. I'll bring my phone, so we can video chat with Amanda."

Sixteen

"Excuse me, miss." A waiter appeared at my shoulder, placing a drink in front of me. "I was asked to bring this to you."

"From who?" Isla said, grabbing my hand. "If it's from Creed, don't drink it."

"I was asked to keep it anonymous."

"What is it?" I asked, sniffing at the drink, before grinning. "Never mind, I know. Thank you." The waiter disappeared with a nod. I moved to sip from it, but Isla stopped me. "It's okay. I know it isn't from Creed."

"Who is it from?" Isla asked, as she and Layla looked around curiously. Isla gasped. "Is it from New Guy'?"

"New guy? Who is New Guy?" Layla squealed.

"She has a new boyfriend," Isla said without looking at her. "Spill it, sugar."

My face was on fire, as I sipped at my drink. When I realized they wouldn't give up, I sighed. "Yes, it is from my boyfriend." Goosebumps prickled deliciously my skin at Jonah's new title.

"Why did he want to remain anonymous?"

"Because we were worried that…. We worried that if people knew we were a thing that it would put a damper on the contest."

"Is it a judge?" Layla hissed.

"What? No," I cried. "I don't know who the judges are, just like you guys."

"Who is it? Who is your boyfriend?" Isla asked again.

"I'm going to go get a drink while you ladies sort this out," Isaac said with an eye roll. "Does anyone else need a drink?" When the girls shook their heads, he got up.

"Holly," Isla begged when he was gone.

"I'd rather not say."

"Please?"

I shook my head, purposely not looking anywhere but my drink, making lines in the condensation with my thumb.

"Killjoy," Layla grumbled.

"It seems we have a mystery on our hands," Isla decided, rubbing her hands together conspiratorially. "If she isn't going to tell us, we will have to figure it out on our own. Now, where do we start?"

Layla looked around with a giggle before pointing discreetly. "Mediterranean hottie, two tables over."

We both turned to see a man in a white cotton shirt and blue cotton lounge pants. He reclined back in his seat, arms crossed over his chest, laughing with the others at his table.

"Oh," Isla grinned, nodding. "I'll bet he's romantic and excellent in bed."

"If he isn't yours, I'll take him."

Before I could respond, Isla was shaking her head. "He's too… intense. Holly needs a down-home good boy, kind and sweet and funny." She tapped a finger to her cheek, looking around before her eyes lit up. "That one. The tall blond by the bar, white shirt, khakis, flip flops."

I turned to see a younger guy who bore an uncanny resemblance to Ryan Gosling.

"Oh, nope. I will take that one instead," Layla decided. "If he isn't yours, that is."

"He isn't."

"Holly," Isla pleaded. "Give us something to go off. You're adorable and awesome, and you deserve someone who respects that. Who is it?"

I was saved by Isaac's return. "The band is getting ready to start. One of the guys said they do a little of everything, but they prefer oldies."

A grin spread across my face, and it took everything not to look back at Jonah. I wondered if he had a hand in choosing the entertainment. Waiters came to clear everything, and I snuck a peek at the head table as I thanked the man who took my plate. Jonah's space was empty. My heart fluttered as I then scanned the rest of the room. I spotted him at the table with the contest entries, discussing something with Bob Vaughn and two other board members I had seen at the head table earlier. Bob took two pieces from the table, and they all moved back to the stage. Bob walked back to the podium alone.

"Ladies and gentlemen," he said cheerfully. "I would like to take a moment to thank you for your beautiful submissions to today's contest. We were blown away by the talent presented, and I can tell you the judges had a very difficult decision to make. Before the band starts up, I wanted to announce the winner of today's contest, so you know who will be buying the next round." Chuckles circulated the room. "Barry Sandson, photography, and Layla Hendricks, writer."

Isla, Isaac, and I cheered louder than the others as Layla sashayed up to the front of the room to collect her prize. She returned with a grin. "Guess I owe you a drink," she told me. "After all, you gave me the idea."

I slurped the last drops from my glass. "I accept," I replied with a grin.

Who was this new woman, I wondered. Giggly, confident, willing to speak her mind… It could be the result of the drinks, but I didn't think so. Since my run-in with Brayden, I had felt something blooming in my soul. It was not the drink—it was me. The new me. The *real* me. Crawling out from beneath years of damage and scars and emerging victorious. And it felt good.

We all went to the bar while the staff moved the tables. Some of the contestants had flocked to the head table, bombarding several members. Jonah, I noticed, had mostly women around him.

"Gosh, look at him," Layla sighed, following my gaze. "He's just gorgeous, isn't he?"

I nodded, grinning when I saw him slam the rest of his drink. Turning back to the bar, I leaned across to speak to the waiter over the first notes of the band's song. "Could I have one of whatever Jonah Seeley is drinking and three shots of rum, please?" He nodded and moved away to fill my order.

"What are you doing?" Layla asked. She had not heard what I ordered.

My grin widened. "Something I should have done earlier." When the shots came, I handed one to her and one to Isla, who had just returned from the bathroom.

"What's this for?" she asked.

"New beginnings," I decided. "Friendships, vacations, and freedom."

"Cheers to that!" Isla cried, and we all tipped the tiny glasses back.

"Now, if you'll excuse me, I need to go save my *boyfriend* from the clutches of desperate women." I grabbed the whiskey drink and made my way through the crowd toward Jonah.

When he saw me approaching, Jonah's eyes widened and a slow smile spread across his face. The reaction made my entire body tingle. I waited on the outskirts of the group while he made his excuses to the disappointed ladies around him.

"Hey," I said, holding out the glass.

"Hey, yourself. Thanks." He studied me over the glass as he took a drink. "I thought we weren't doing this."

I shrugged. "I'm certainly not going to make out with you like Cecille and Number Six, but this will likely be the only time I see most of these people. I know I'm not cheating at this contest. You know I'm not cheating. What do I care what anyone else thinks?"

Jonah's grin made his eyes crinkle. "That's my girl."

I glanced over my shoulder to where Layla and Isla were watching me with eyes wide and dropped jaws. I wished I had brought my camera to capture their expressions. "Would you like to meet some of my friends?"

"The ones flirting with me during dinner? Absolutely."

He followed me back to the bar, though our progress was hindered by people stopping Jonah on the way. I waited patiently, trying not to notice the curious looks I was drawing. When I was close enough, I went to Isla and Layla while Jonah finished speaking with two older gentlemen about stocks and business theories.

Both women were still processing this new information. "New Guy is Jonah Seeley?" Isla screeched.

"Wh-how… Are you kidding me?" Layla stammered.

"Jonah and I have known each other for two years. We work together."

"I thought you said you lived in Wisconsin."

"I do." My face heated when I remembered that Jonah's time in Wisconsin was not public knowledge. "It's a long story."

"I bet it is," Isla said with a wink.

"The tabloids all say he's single," Layla cried. "And clearly, I'm not the only one who reads them. Most of the women here have been drooling over him tonight. You lucky little—"

An arm wrapped around my waist, and I turned to find Jonah at my shoulder. "Hey," I said, still blushing fiercely. "Jonah, these are my friends, Isla and Layla. Oh, and here's Isaac."

"Nice to meet you, sir," Isaac said, leaning past me to shake Jonah's free hand.

"Isaac," Jonah said curtly. "Nice to meet you all. Are you in photography or journalism?"

"They are all writers," I told him.

"She didn't want to fraternize with the enemy," Isaac said. "Not that it's much of a competition."

"Have you seen her work, Jonah?" Layla asked.

Jonah's hand on my hip tightened. "I've seen a few, yeah."

"Look at this!" Isla cried, bringing out the picture again, laughing with me. "I have been showing everyone—I feel like a model."

Jonah cocked an eyebrow at me. "You did this?" I nodded, smiling at the pride on his face. "It's very good."

"Thanks," I said quietly.

"She even signed the back, if she ever becomes famous."

"When. When she becomes famous."

"Agreed," Isla grinned at him. "*When* she becomes famous."

"Anyone can be famous if you have the right friends." Creed had sauntered over to the group, catching the tail end of the conversation.

"Dude, shut up," Isaac replied, exasperated.

"Sorry? Don't believe I caught your name." Jonah's tone was icy calm. "I'm Jonah."

Creed rolled his eyes, and his voice dripped with sarcasm. "Of course. How very silly of me. My name is Creed. Charmed."

I looked back and forth between the two of them. "Do you know each other?"

Several things happened at the same time. Creed began to answer with a "Funny you should—" while Isaac took a threatening step forward, and Jonah's arm tightened around me. Over our conversation, one of the band members called over the loudspeaker. "Ladies and gentlemen, *The Cupid Shuffle*."

Isla and Layla effectively herded me away from the group, Layla grabbing Isaac's hand. "Let them grumble out whatever beef they have," Isla said when we were out of earshot. "We are here to have fun."

I glanced over my shoulder to find both men still glaring at each other, speaking in angry, hushed tones. Something was up, judging by Jonah's fisted hands and rigid jaw, and my instinct was to go back and to protect him from whatever Creed was dishing out.

"He's a grown man," Isaac said, throwing an arm over my shoulder. "The real question is how are y'all gonna teach me to do this?"

With me on his left and Layla on his right, it took most of the song to get Isaac on track to do the line dance. Whether it was the alcohol inhibiting his ability to follow the directions or a deliberate attempt to distract me from Jonah and Creed's exchange, by the end of the song, he was holding me up. I was laughing too hard to handle his two left feet. And since the line dance had brought so many people to the floor, they followed with two more line dances.

When the first lines of *Footloose* began, Isla threw up her hands. "I don't know this one!"

I fanned my face. "Let's go get a drink." Turning, I collided with a large wall of a man.

"Come on, Douglas. I'll bet any money you know this one," Jonah said, a mischievous grin on his face.

"I'm not very good."

He tipped his head so that his lips were deliciously close to my ear. "That was a dare, Kitten. Take it."

Butterflies flitted through my stomach as he reached up to loosen his tie, already bouncing on his heels to the music. I turned to Isla to distract myself from the sexy man beside me. "I'll teach you."

The truth of it was, when Abby and I had no extra money to spend on fun things, which was more often than not, we practiced different line dances. When I was finished with work or school, we would watch videos online to learn the dances. Anytime a new one came out, we would practice until we had it. Abby took them out into the community with her theater classes and swing choir. Or late nights at Cecille's. I kept my skills more lowkey.

I gave Isla a quick overview as we started. A few others around us knew the dance as well, so Isla had several examples around her and picked it up quickly. I turned my attention back to Jonah, who was watching me with a broad smile. Remembering how he had surprised Abby with his moves, I threw my head back laughing. How had I found someone so amazing, I wondered for the thousandth time. As the song drew to a close, he reached for my hand. After spinning several times, I ended up in his arms for the final notes before being dipped low.

"Smooth," I giggled.

"I try."

"Ladies and gents, let's slow things down for a song or two," the band announced.

"Guess I could get that dance now, huh?" Jonah asked. "You know, since you're already here."

"Guess so," I decided. I secretly gushed again to discover he danced the old-school way, hand in hand, and my other hand on his shoulder, his on my waist. The arms around the neck, boy's arms around the waist had always seemed so… middle school. This way was grown up and hopelessly romantic.

"Have I told you that you look incredible tonight?" he asked softly.

I remembered his surprised look before dinner. "You looked like you didn't recognize me earlier."

"I wasn't sure," he chuckled. "I mean, you always look beautiful, but this dress? Wow."

"Abby picked it out."

"Did she pick out other items in your luggage?" At my nod, he grinned like a cat in milk. "I can't wait."

I was aware of a lot of eyes on us around the dance circle. A few people had come onto the dance floor for the slow song, but being that everyone had come without their families, Jonah and I were one of the few couples there.

"What happened with Creed?" I asked, not seeing him on my first sweep of the room.

"He decided it was best to leave."

"Oh?" I asked.

"I'd advise you to steer clear of him, Holly. He is bad news."

"I've already learned that." I gave him a quick overview of the events by the pool. "He creeps me out."

"I told him to leave you alone, not that he'll follow my orders." One look at Jonah, and I realized I wouldn't get anything more from him on the topic.

"You were gone a long time today."

This topic, I realized, wasn't going to get far either. "I was. Things at work have… reached a breaking point."

"What does that mean?"

His scowl darkened. "It means the competing company is going to catch up with us, soon."

"That's not good."

"No. No, it isn't."

"Is there anything I can do?"

"Keep massaging my shoulder," he mumbled, closing his eyes. I hadn't realized I was. Grinning, I increased the pressure. He put his forehead to mine. "Never stop being you."

There seemed to be a hidden message in his words, but I wasn't sure where it had come from. "That's all I can be," I said with a shrug.

The song ended, and he kissed my forehead. "Come on, I'd like to buy you a drink."

"I'll let you." I followed him to the bar, aware that there were still more eyes on me than before.

"Jonah!" We were waved over by Bob Vaughn himself, who was at the bar surrounded by some of the other board members. "What are you two drinking?"

When we told him, he passed our orders to the bartender and smiled at me. "Are you going to introduce me to your pretty dancing partner?"

"Holly, this is Bob Vaughn, Brad Phillips, and Jordan Davies. This is my girlfriend, Holly."

"Nice to meet you." Each of the men shook my hand before Bob spoke again. "How long have you guys been together? You know I'll need to tell Edith. My wife," he told me with a wink, "loves Jonah like another son. I don't think she knows about you yet."

"It's new," I said quickly.

"We've known each other for a couple of years. She is my coworker in Wisconsin."

Jordan laughed. "You have coworkers? I thought everyone worked below you."

"Don't be an asshole," Jonah growled.

Jordan shrugged, sipping his drink. "When you choose not to share anything about your life in Wisconsin, pardon us for jumping to conclusions." His flippant attitude made me uncomfortable.

Jonah's arm tightened around me. "I choose to keep intrusive noses out of my life in Wisconsin."

"What do you do there, Holly?" Jordan asked, ignoring Jonah's comments. "Maybe you can give us some intel."

"Why?" I asked incredulously. "If someone asks you what you do behind closed doors, you wouldn't tell them, would you? Wisconsin is Jonah's closed doors."

"Well said," Bob muttered.

"You realize if we want to figure out, all we need to do is look at your application, right?" Jordan replied.

I stared at him, my jaw dropped open. Everything had happened so quickly that I had not even thought about how Jonah's private life would be affected by my presence. After the wave of shock came anger. "I cannot believe—"

"Holly, why don't you head back to the dance floor with your friends," Bob suggested, patting the backside of my arm.

I moved out of reach of all the men in the conversation, including Jonah, who had not heard Bob. *Because I wasn't a business mogul or otherwise rich and worldly person, I wasn't welcome to their conversation.* Of all insults, condescension was one of the worst, and Bob had just dismissed me like a child. Fuming, I spun on my heel and exited the room as quickly as possible.

"Holly!" Layla and Isla were on my heels. "What's going on?"

"Oh, you know, I just met some of Jonah's *friends*," I said, throwing up my arms.

"The board members? You didn't like them?"

"They are jackasses!" I relayed the conversation to them, and both women saw red, just as I had. "I'm sorry. I'm just going to go back to my room and—"

"No! No, you can't," Layla cried, clutching my arm. "Stewing in your anger is bad for your health. No, stick with us, and we will make sure you forget everything they said."

"We were just discussing our options," Isla agreed. "What good is a dance party if you don't know anyone? Most of the guys in that room are wearing wedding rings. We need to find out where the single guys are."

"I have a boyfriend."

"They don't need to know that. They just need to think we might be interested, and we can drink for free all night."

This wasn't on the agenda for the night. However, Layla was right—pacing in our room, waiting for Jonah to return just to argue with him would not end well. "What did you have in mind?"

Seventeen

"Holly?"

I opened my eyes and shut them immediately. Light, sound, nausea, headache. Rapid, awful succession.

"Holly?" The bed flexed, and a hand smoothed the hair from my face. "Are you awake?"

I groaned, pulling a pillow over my face.

"That good, huh?" When I did not answer, Jonah lifted the pillow. "Your phone just went off. It says 'meeting with Isaac at one.' I figured you would need a little extra time to get ready."

I just growled at him again.

He chuckled. "I have ibuprofen and water waiting for you. I tried to get you to take some last night, but you… well, you weren't having it."

In the silence that followed, I tried to piece together what had happened the night before.

Dancing.

Laughter.

Alcohol.

So much alcohol.

"Come on, Holly," he said, trying to ease me into a sitting position, wrapping a robe around my shoulders.

"I'm naked," I mumbled. "And I'm going to throw up."

Jonah reached for the trash can, holding my hair out of the way while I dry-heaved. Though he spoke quietly, his voice made my head roar. "When I tracked you down last night, I ended up having to carry you back here. As soon as you were here, you yelled at me about… well, I'm not even sure what it was for. You threw your shoes at me. And then you took off your dress, climbed into bed, and passed out."

"I'm never drinking ever again."

Jonah laughed again. He smelled freshly showered and wore a thin black t-shirt and khaki shorts. "Probably a good idea. You and your friends were about to get tattoos when I found you."

"*What?*"

"Don't worry—the place was already closed for the night. Isaac and I managed to pull the three of you apart and get you back to your rooms safely."

I took several slow breaths as the last of the nausea passed. Bits and pieces of the previous night were coming back to me. Isla, Layla, and I hit various bars on the ship. The three of us flirted with men to get free drinks. Dancing and karaoke—*had I really sung in front of a huge room of people? Yes. Yes, I had.* Wham, Shania Twain, and… cheese and rice. I sang Disney songs with Isla and Layla. I danced and drank until I could not walk straight. After that, I could not remember anything.

I thought back to earlier in the night, and the anger returned. Pulling the robe around me, I leaned out of Jonah's arms. When I was mostly sure my legs would hold me up, I stood, moving away from Jonah when he stood to try to continue helping. "Thank you for taking care of me, and thank you for waking me up."

"But?"

I glared at him. "But you and your friends pissed me off last night."

His eyebrows rose in surprise. "Why?"

"Why? Jonah, they made me feel about *this* big when you introduced me last night," I cried, holding up my thumb and forefinger an inch apart. "Why did you even bother introducing me to them? They are the type who will never accept anyone lacking a six-figure bank account."

"Holly, I—"

"If you're going to defend them, forget it. Jonah, I will *never* fit into your circle of people. In Wisconsin, sure. But California? If that's the way it's going to be, I don't want to—I can't—"

"Holly, can we talk about this?"

"Sure," I snapped, crossing my arms over my chest.

He pulled a hand across the back of his neck, trying to look anywhere but me. "Holly, look I am sorry about them. They can be jerks. None of them can understand that I do not want to be Mr. Forbes five-hundred all the time. They do. They love the limelight, and the-the fame, and everything that comes with it. I…" He grinned at me helplessly. "I'm having a hard time arguing with a beautiful, half-naked woman."

My embarrassment and frustration and hangover accumulated and erupted in a growl. I snatched clothes out of the closet and stormed into the bathroom. Luckily, the queasiness passed, and besides tired, I was feeling mostly like myself by the time I got out of the shower. I dressed in a pink tank and white shorts, steeling myself for what was going to be Jonah and I's first argument.

Only to find an empty room, with a text on my phone.

J: I had an emergency work meeting. Can we please continue this discussion tonight over dinner? I will order in. Whatever you'd like. I'm so sorry—I will make it up to you, I promise.

I started typing several messages but felt guilty with the amount of passive-aggressiveness in them.

H: Sure.

J: What would you like to eat?

I did not respond. I grudgingly admitted that I liked everything Jonah cooked, but it was the discussion that would be more important. What we ate for dinner was not.

ooooo

"Hey, Holly," Isaac said when I showed up at the pool a half-hour later. "How are you feeling?"

"I've been better. Currently, I am grateful to whoever invented sunglasses." I dropped into the lounge chair next to him. Thankfully, he had chosen a table beneath a large umbrella. "How did you fare last night?"

"Better than you. Jonah and I had to divide and conquer to find you three. It took a while." He laughed helplessly. "Isla was shoeless and crying about losing her earrings, Layla gave away her bra and undies to some stranger, and you were raging mad at Jonah. It was quite a spectacle."

"How are they this morning?"

"I checked on them about an hour ago. By all accounts, you are probably in the best shape, being that you are out of bed and functioning. The other two will not be coming out anytime soon."

"I will not be accompanying those two on any more magical mystery tours."

"Magical mystery tours. That's a great name for it." He was still laughing as he pulled out his notebook. "Are you okay enough to get a little work done, or do you want to reschedule?"

"I'm good. I'll take a nap later."

We spent the next two hours discussing the logistics of my logo. Once upon a time, I wanted Holly Douglas Photography. Abby, however, had convinced me otherwise. If I got married, she reasoned, what if I would want to use my married name? That would mean a lot of branding issues. So, I had chosen the name New Beginnings Photography from the photograph I had given Isla. Isaac put the name into the ripples of the water in an italic breezy font that made it seem as though the letters had been there in the original image. He then took the time to show me how to use the logo, making it into a header for paperwork, as well as how to put it on my photos. Despite my headache, I absorbed the information, and the excitement in my heart grew ten-fold. It was another step toward making my photography skills a business.

"Thank you, Isaac. I *really* appreciate all your help with this. How much do I owe you for this?"

"I think I have a way for you to pay me back," Isaac said, pulling his phone from his pocket. "Do you mind if we call Amanda?"

I pulled myself up straighter, removing off my sunglasses, and running a hand through my hair. "Does it look like I'm hungover?"

Isaac laughed. "No. You look great."

"Let me just pull up my photos while you call her."

He hit send and she answered on the second ring. "Hi," she gushed.

"Hey. How's it going?"

I heard her sigh. "Fine. Just got home from work. How are you?"

"Great," Isaac said. "I think I have news that will make you very happy. I am ninety-nine percent sure I found our wedding photographer."

"Really? I mean, I was hoping, but—oh, that was so fast!"

"I asked her to bring a few of her wedding shots, and I have seen some of her other photos. She's amazingly talented."

"Did you tell her about…"

"Amanda, it doesn't matter."

"Yes, it does!"

"Amanda…" Isaac began. "You are beautiful, just the way you are. Everyone thinks that." I looked up when I had the files open, and he abandoned the argument. "Okay, Amanda, this is Holly Douglas. Holly, meet Amanda, my fiancée."

He turned the phone to show a beautiful young woman with voluptuous black hair, dark eyes, and deep bronze skin. Her smile was hesitant, and she subtly turned her head. I had seen it, though. Long angry scars stretching from her ear down her jaw and neck. "Hi," I said with a wave.

"Hi, how's the cruise?"

"It's been great."

"I wish I could have gotten off of work to come along."

"Amanda works for a domestic violence center," Isaac supplied.

My heart squeezed. "That's amazing. If there is anything I can do to help remotely, please let me know."

"I just run the business end, but thanks."

"Okay, I owe Isaac a favor because he just helped me design my logo. So, I will be offering a discount if you choose to use my services, but we can work that out later. I will be honest—I haven't done a lot of weddings but not because I don't want to. It's because life has prevented me from pursuing photography full-time."

"She needs to do this full-time," Isaac said, turning the camera to himself. "Seriously."

"How are you with editing and covering things up?" Amanda asked.

"Amanda, please."

"Isaac, I want to look amazing. And I need a photographer who can capture more good qualities than bad."

Isaac looked at me with pleading eyes. "I don't want her to look like someone else in the pictures. I want to see the woman I married."

"May I ask what happened?" I said softly when he turned the phone back to me.

She shook her head, waving her free hand. "I was seventeen and stupid. My friend got in an accident, and three of us were stuck in the car when it started on fire."

"I'm so sorry."

She lifted a shoulder, trying to brush off the weight of the memory. "It sucks."

"I don't care about the scars," Isaac insisted.

"I do!"

I put my hand on his arm, shaking my head sadly. "I think it's different for boys. They don't understand. We grew up with Barbies and other dolls, planning our perfect wedding from young ages. We want it to be perfect—we want to *look* perfect and *feel* perfect," I told him gently. "But Amanda, Isaac is right too, in a way. I can change the way you look in the photos, but do you *really* want me to make you look like someone else? Isaac doesn't want that, and I am not sure I can do it with a clear conscience. I will do my very best to make you feel beautiful. That I can promise."

Amanda's eyes were filled with tears. "I have to live with these scars for the rest of my life. I just want to have one more day without them."

I gave her a warm smile. "Some of us wear our scars on the outside, and some bear them on the inside. We all want one more day without them."

"Why don't you show her some of your work?" Isaac suggested, clearing his throat a couple of times.

"Sure." Over the next half hour, I went through several pictures of the six weddings I had done previously. Isaac asked a question here and there, but Amanda stayed quiet. I could not gauge either of their feelings, but I was proud of my work and tried to let that be all that mattered. Finally, I closed my files and shut down my computer. "You two can talk it over and let me know. I'll give you my phone number."

"Sounds good. Would you be willing, if Amanda agreed, to do our engagement photos without the wedding photos? It's not that we don't want you. It might help us make our final decisions."

"The engagement and wedding photos don't have to be a package deal. I mean, that would be great, but I can do separate contracts for each." I looked back and forth between the two. "Any other questions for me?"

Isaac looked to Amanda, who shook her head. "I think we are good. Thanks, Holly."

"Thank you for helping me with my logo," I replied. "Amanda, it was so nice to meet you." With a wave, I gathered my belongings and headed back to the hotel room. My head was still pounding, and all I wanted to do was crawl in bed and take a nap.

I had purposely ignored my phone while meeting with Isaac but dug it out of my bag on my walk back. Nothing from Jonah. A couple of texts from Abby. I called her as I flopped into bed. "Hey," I said after the voicemail beeped. "Sorry I've been M.I.A. Last night, we had a dinner party and, well, I had a lot of fun—mostly. Drank a little too much. Very hungover today, but I might have gotten a wedding booked for next year. Hopefully—fingers crossed. Anyway, I'm supposed to be having dinner with Jonah tonight. If I don't answer, I will give you a call tomorrow morning. Love you."

I set my phone down on the table and snuggled into bed. We had received our next contest, titled 'cruise days,' but after the condescension I had experienced from the board, I had no desire to contribute any more of my material than was absolutely necessary. Just thinking about the conversation made me angry all over again. Why did people think they had the right to speak down to others? Why did money make the difference between them and I?

Letting my eyes drift closed, I focused on my breathing, willing the anger to leave.

Eighteen

A knock on the door woke me. The evening had arrived while I slept, but my hangover was gone. Groggy and disoriented, I stumbled to the door.

"Mr. Seeley asked me to deliver this," the man in the white coat said when I opened the door. "He told me to tell you he would be arriving within the hour."

"Oh. Um, thanks," I said, watching him wheel a cart of drinks into the center of the room before leaving with a nod and a kind smile. No more alcohol, I decided, no matter how good the champagne tasted. Grabbing a bottle of water from the cart, I stepped into the bathroom to freshen up, exchanging the yoga shorts and tank for a pretty blue sundress. Since dinner was coming to us, I didn't worry about shoes or accessories, but I also didn't want to look like a bum. My headache was gone, and after finishing the water, I felt almost back to normal.

There was a message from Isaac on my phone when I returned to the couch.

I: Amanda and I would like to take you up on your offer. One contract for engagement photos. Hopefully, when Amanda sees them and sees how beautiful she is, we can make another contract for our wedding day.

H: I will do what I can! Amanda is so beautiful, but in the end, we are our own worst critics.

I: I hope she can move past this someday…

H: Four years is not that long to come to terms with what happened. She needs a strong support group around her to learn to see past the scars.

I: You sound like you speak from experience.

H: I do.

I: Are you coming to dinner tonight?

I sent him a picture of the beverage cart.

H: Eating in.

I: Classy. Have fun.

H: You too—see you tomorrow.

I set my phone aside and curled my legs up under me, turning to look out the window. The cruise ship absorbed the sway of the waves, which had gotten progressively larger throughout the day. A storm was brewing, judging by the large gray clouds in the distance. The weather report had given the possibility of a storm tonight, but I had remained cautiously optimistic. Abby had panicked when she first saw it, worrying that this cruise ship would be like others that had capsized or gotten stuck in the middle of the ocean without power or resources. I laughed at her worrying, reminding her that she was the one who had convinced me to go in the first place.

"You had better get some spectacular pictures, then," she growled, fists on hips. That was an easy promise to make and keep.

I rested my chin on my arm on the back of the couch with a sigh. Watching the waves was so mesmerizing and relaxing that my eyes drifted closed. My thoughts turned to Jonah, and I realized that much of my anger had gone. His friends had hurt me. Not him, I reminded myself. He had tried to defend me, but the others were not having it and had simply ignored his angry comment of *don't be an asshole.*

No, I decided, my anger stemmed from fear. Fear that I would not be enough for Jonah. Fear that, if things continued, I would have to interact with those uptight, awful people all the time. *Would those types of dinner parties become part of our regular schedule? Would Jonah want to stay in California or Wisconsin? Or would he continue to—*

"Whoa," I whispered, my face flushing. That was too far into the future. There was no reason why things couldn't stay just the way they were with a few extra dates thrown in. The little *what if* voice in my brain was trying to intrude, presenting all sorts of scenarios in my head. She was a tough little broad to ignore, but I tried.

"I wish I had your camera."

I screeched in fright. "Cheese and rice, Jonah, you—oh my goodness, what happened?" Leaping off the couch, I hurried across the room, taking his forearms and guiding him toward the nearest chair. His arm was bleeding, and he had a bruise on his cheek.

He smiled down at me, cupping my cheek and kissing my forehead before sitting. "I'm fine."

"You are not fine." I had seen a first aid kit in the desk drawer the day before and ran to retrieve it. "What happened?"

"Work got… a little ugly."

My pulse raced. "Did they come to the cruise ship?"

"No, I had a helicopter take me back to California."

Swallowing hard, I tried not to think about the amount of money that must have cost. And for Jonah to just *go*? Richer than Midas, indeed. "Jonah, I thought you were in business. You're going to tell me a bunch of middle-aged, balding, fat rich guys resorted to fisticuffs over a business deal?"

Jonah held up a finger, chuckling. "What makes you think they were middle-aged and fat? And follow up question, you don't think I could hold up against that?"

"You need to wash this first," I decided before adding any bandages. "What happened?"

"I'm fine. You look beautiful. Let me go shower and change my clothes, dinner will be here in about twenty minutes." He kissed me again before he left.

When he was gone, I rifled through the pathetic contents of the kit, hoping there would be enough to clean him up. I pulled the map of the cruise ship up on my phone, locating the twenty-four-hour pharmacy, just in case. Then there was nothing left to do but pace the room. Not only was he going to work when he was supposed to be on vacation, but he was getting into fights too? He had said work was bad, but I thought it was just an expression of mental exhaustion. I did not realize that there were punches being thrown as well. The mama bear inside me hated it. I needed Jonah to be safe, for himself as much as for me.

He emerged from a steamy bathroom with a towel around his waist. Only slightly sheepish, he grinned. "I forgot to grab clothes."

I swallowed hard. His body never ceased to amaze me. The enjoyment was fleeting, though, because when he turned to the closet, there was another large bloody streak across his back. "Jonah!" I cried.

"What?"

"You're seriously going to tell me you don't feel that?" I approached, preventing him from moving any more than necessary. "Sit," I demanded.

"Yes, ma'am."

He did as he was told, and I gently wiped down the wounds on his back and arm before covering them both with bandages. Neither was as bad as I had originally thought, but they were still serious. "You should probably go see the cruise's doctor," I told him. "These might need a little glue, maybe even a stitch or two."

Jonah stood and grabbed a black polo and khaki shorts before heading back to the bathroom. "I'm fine, Holly. Thank you for taking care of me." Someone knocked on the door. "That's probably dinner. I didn't know what you wanted, so I guessed. Could you grab it please?"

"I still think we should take a quick trip to go see the doctor," I said on my way to the door.

He winked. "When I have a great nurse right here to care for me?"

"Miss," the waiter said politely when I opened the door. He wheeled in a small mountain of food.

"Thank you," I called, as he walked away. I could not help peeking beneath the covers. Caesar salad, bruschetta, grilled chicken, a beautiful fruit tray, and cheesecake for dessert. I snapped a few pictures as the last of the evening sunlight glared across the round metal covers.

Jonah emerged a few minutes later, his hair tied back. He lifted his brows when he saw me replace the bruschetta cover. "How'd I do?"

"Good," I replied with a shrug. "It just isn't the same as your cooking at Cecille's."

My comment confused him. "What do you mean? Most of those recipes are mine."

"Yeah, but it isn't the same. For me, your food goes beyond taste. It's about the process of you and I working together." My face burned as I spoke. "It's peaceful, comforting. Safe." I sighed as the rest of my thoughts spilled out. "That was why I was so angry last night. I don't know if I can handle dealing with people like Bob Vaughn on a regular basis. Those holier-than-thou people who think the world bows to them. They were awful last night! I can't—"

He crossed the room in two strides, wrapping me in a hug. "I'm sorry," he said quietly. "You're right—they weren't being fair."

"Why do you associate with people like that?"

He smiled down at me. "Unfortunately, there are people like that in the world—well, my world. Would you believe me if I told you that the people on this board were not like that?"

"No," I admitted.

"They aren't. Bob is… well, he is a dick to protect us. That was an… initiation of sorts. He keeps tabs on the rest of the board, in part because we are the financials behind his mission, but also because he understands the challenges fame and fortune can bring. When they grilled you about Wisconsin, they were testing you. They wanted to make sure you can be trusted. When Jordan brought his—well, now she's his wife—to a fundraiser, I did the same thing."

"That's horrible."

"No…" Jonah began, and then his shoulders sagged. "Well, yes, a little, but it's meant to help each other."

"While belittling the woman."

Jonah sighed. "I'm sorry. I know what you're made of. They don't. Or didn't." He sighed again. "What I'm trying to say is that what happened last night won't happen again."

"Promise me *you* won't do that again. Promise you won't interrogate and deprecate the next woman. If the others do it, that can't be helped, but you won't."

He studied me a moment before replying. "Okay. The next woman who joins the group will not hear a peep from me. I promise."

"Thank you," I said, reaching up to kiss his cheek.

At the last moment, he turned so that our lips met instead. His hands slid up my back into my hair, his thumbs skimming my jaw. Did he understand what his fingers were doing to me? I melted into his embrace, running my hands up his back, causing him to flinch. "Oh, I'm so sorry!" I cried. "Are you okay?"

Jonah closed his eyes, clenching his hands into fists as his jaws tightened. "Holly," he groaned.

"I'm sorry," I repeated. "Please, *please*, let me take you to the doctor, Jonah. Please."

"Holly—"

"Where is your wallet?" I asked, my eyes sweeping the room before spotting it on the desk. "I'll just grab your insurance card and—"

"Holly." He caught my arm as I passed and pulled me back to him. "I'm fine. Stop worrying." He shook his head when I started to argue. "Yes, it hurts a little. Yes, I'm exhausted after a day of dealing with bullshit. Yes, I have been in everything but vacation-mode since we got on the boat. And I'm sorry about that. All I want right now," he said softly, rubbing his knuckles across my cheekbone, "is you."

I swallowed hard, my face turning red. "Smooth."

"I try. Let's get some dinner and then start back up where we left off. Okay? Also, do not make dinner plans tomorrow night," he said, handing me a plate. "I'm taking you on a date."

"Aren't we on a date now?"

Jonah shook his head. "No, this is just eating in. Tomorrow, we are going out."

"What about my friends?"

"You'll be able to visit with them during the day, right?"

I chuckled, thinking of all the places Isla's mind would go when both Jonah and I failed to show up for dinner, two nights in a row. "Yeah, although I'll never hear the end of it."

Jonah laughed with me. "Those two ladies are quite the pair. Last night certainly proved that. Isaac carried Isla over his shoulder and had to stop at almost every garbage can on the way back so Layla could barf."

I flushed crimson. "Bits and pieces have come back to me, though most of the night is still a blur. I'm sorry I threw my shoes at you."

"I'm just glad I know the reason why. You were yelling at me—lots of swearing—but your words were pretty slurred," Jonah said, unable to hide his laughter.

"Sorry."

We sat together on the couch, letting the conversation lull while we ate. As usual, the food was exceptional.

"How was your day?" Jonah asked later.

"Besides being hungover? Great! Not only did Isaac help me make a logo, but through him, I also got a photography gig. I will be taking his engagement photos, and if it goes well, they might even contract me out to do their wedding photos too."

Jonah's brows furrowed. "Why wouldn't they just sign on to do both?"

I told him about Amanda's scars. "One of them wants me to make them disappear, and the other is afraid it will look like he's marrying a stranger. I have to find a happy medium."

"Is that even possible?"

"Anything is possible if you know how to play the light game and edit like a boss."

"Which you have mastered."

I shrugged. "Mastered, no. But I have a few ideas. If Isla is willing to model, I will probably be practicing a little over the next few days."

"I'm sure she will be more than willing."

His comment triggered a memory from the previous night. "Do you and Creed—and Isaac—already know each other? Last night, you—"

"Creed is a first-class dipshit I'd rather not ruin the night talking about." I tried not to flinch under his harsh tone, but he caught it. "Sorry. Yes, I know Creed," he said more gently. "I just don't want to talk about him tonight."

"Okay."

A less easy silence passed between us before Jonah spoke again. "On my way back to the room, I stopped by the board's meeting to check out the entries for today's contest, but I didn't see yours. Did you submit something?"

I shook my head. "I was so angry about what happened last night, I didn't want to share any more of my content than was necessary."

He reached across and gave my knee a gentle squeeze. The skin-on-skin contact sizzled through me. "I hope I changed your mind about Bob. He is a good guy."

"I'll think about it." With a reluctant sigh, I set my plate down. "I want cheesecake, but I am so full."

"Should we walk it off?"

I glanced outside. Night had settled in, but there was lightning on the horizon. "Do you mind if I take my camera?"

Jonah's smile was broad. "Not at all. I look forward to seeing what you can do with a storm."

I gathered my things while Jonah stacked the empty trays and plates, pulled the chairs off the balcony, closed the lid on the hot tub, and slid the glass doors closed. We left hand in hand, my camera around my neck, and my lens bag over Jonah's shoulder.

The wind had picked up since I had been outside that afternoon, and the temperature had dropped. There was something deliciously sensual about the shiver that ripped through me whenever I stepped into that charged environment. My grin only grew when I felt the first few droplets of rain.

"Look," Jonah said, nodding toward the horizon. An epic light show had begun. He followed me to the railing and held the bag open while I dug through my supplies. "Are you worried about anything getting wet?"

"The bag is waterproof. And I have a towel to wrap around my camera. It will last as long as it doesn't start downpouring." I took a few long exposure shots, before digging out my lens ball.

"You don't look at any of your photos," Jonah observed.

I shook my head. "It's more fun to pull them up larger on the computer later."

"Like waiting for the disposable cameras to be developed."

"Exactly—the thrill of the unknown."

Jonah huffed. "Or whether or not a finger was in the way."

I laughed. I held the small glass ball out, considering the different angles before snapping a few more as the wind picked up speed.

"It's going to pour soon," Jonah observed.

I knew it too, but I did not want to go back yet. I wanted to preserve the moment when my soul was so happy. Dropping the ball back into the bag, I changed a few of the settings on my camera. Moving a table, I set my camera down and took the bag from Jonah. Taking his hand, I kicked off my shoes and pulled him back to the railing. "I have the timer set."

"What are we doing?"

"Using our silhouettes." I stood on my tiptoes to kiss him, my arms stretched out behind me, a foot lifted. The flash was dim in comparison to the storm around us. Jonah had not been prepared for the first one, but his hands cupped my cheek as he put his nose to mine, smiling down at me. The camera flashed before he moved again. Taking my hand, he gently pushed me away to spin me around. I threw my head back and laughed as the heavens suddenly opened, and torrents of rain began to pound the deck. Jonah was laughing too, pulling me back to him to dance. It was sheer bliss, especially when he started kissing me.

"Oy—are y'all crazy?" a man in a white uniform shouted over the din. "It's storming out here and y'all are just neckin' on the metal deck. Get inside!"

Jonah led me back beneath the overhang, pausing to kiss me once more before gathering my things. I was still giggling, wringing out my dress. "You're crazy, Miss Douglas," Jonah said, shaking his head.

"You picked me," was my quick retort.

He caught my hand and kissed my knuckles. "Yes. Yes, I did." His soft tone sent a new wave of shivers through me.

My soul was happy, and my heart was giddy as we walked back to the room together. Jonah laughed when I skipped down the hallway ahead of him. I knew those photos were going to be spectacular. It was the first time in a long time that I had modeled for any photos, and the desire to peek at the pictures was nearly overwhelming.

I gasped as the air conditioning in our room hit me like a freight train. My dress and hair were drenched, and one look at Jonah, also dripping like a wet dog, sent me into another fit of giggles. Taking the bag and my camera, I spread the contents across the couch on a bath towel.

"Well, I have to say, that's a first," Jonah said, dropping a towel around my shoulders before stripping off his shirt.

"What's that?"

He ticked reasons off on his fingers. "A legitimately *fun* photoshoot. Dancing in the rain. Getting caught. Hearing the word 'necking' from someone other than Cecille."

Laughter bubbled out of me. "Cecille would be so proud of you."

"Us." He took my towel, gently wringing my hair with it. "She would be proud of us."

"What will she say about the two of us being together?"

"Probably 'About damn time thou cracker-brained guts.'"

"Very nice. What is that from?"

"*Henry IV* maybe?" Jonah shrugged. "I don't know. I've been called it before, and will likely be again."

"For what?"

"Not asking you out sooner." My cheeks flushed as our eyes met. His face held the hint of a smile as he continued. "Cecille knew how I felt. She badgered me incessantly about it too. But I knew… I knew you needed time. Time to find yourself, your strength, your happiness, your confidence. Cecille knew it too, but she was impatient. I think she might love you more than she loves me."

I snorted. "Maybe if you quit making her mad."

"Give up a hobby that completes me? Not a chance." He laughed with me as he moved the towel to my face, his motions slowing. "I have no regrets. You were worth the wait, Holly. This… all of this was worth the wait."

I swallowed hard, my heart melting at the sweetness of his words. "Jonah," I sighed. There were so many things I wanted to say, but forming words was just too hard.

Very slowly, he lowered his lips to mine. I moved closer to him, both to deepen the kiss and to absorb his body heat. The towel dropped from his hands as he explored my skin. "Holly," he murmured when his lips reached my ear. "Do you know what you do to me?"

I pulled back enough to look into Jonah's eyes. His expression was almost pained. It only took a moment to understand his words. I felt my face flush crimson. Part of me wanted to retreat, to move away and end this. And yet, the other, louder part basked in the confidence his words gave me. It put me in complete control of the situation, and I shivered with the thrill of it.

"You're cold," he whispered, bending to get the towel.

I took a step back from him, grinning at his confusion. This inner voice was brazen and wanton, and… Well, she gave me the confidence to look him straight in the eye as I untied my dress and let it fall to the floor. All that was left was my favorite matching blush pink bra and panties. I watched as Jonah's pupils dilated, his jaw tightened, and his throat bobbed several times. His gaze warmed me, traveling down and back up again. He waited so long, that the little voice began to doubt herself.

I felt my smile falter. "I'm—"

"I swear to God, if you apologize, woman," he snarled, scooping me into his arms and devouring my mouth.

I squealed, laughing as he dropped me on the bed, discarding his shorts and climbing into bed in record time. Pulling me into his side, he ran his fingers through my hair, brushing it all away from my face. It slowed the momentum that had been building, taking any self-conscious or embarrassed thoughts with it. Instead, it relaxed me, as it always had when anyone played with my hair.

My eyes dropped to his chest, and I lifted a hand to touch the tattoos where his collarbone met his shoulder. "Did you choose all these?" I asked, tracing my fingers over the waves that lapped onto his collarbone. "When they are sleeves, I don't know how that works."

"Most of it was my idea. The tattoo artist just had to fill in some of the gaps."

"Why did you choose what you did?"

"I grew up near the ocean. The water holds a special place for me. It *is* home. The tattoo artist added some awesome indigenous Hawaiian designs to it."

"So, you were Maui before *Moana* was cool."

Jonah snickered. "Yeah, I guess."

"The other arm is different."

"A world map with little details added in. Travel has been my life as well."

"Land and water. Interesting."

"What about you?"

"I don't have any tattoos."

"You were adamant that you needed one last night." He laughed when I buried my face in his bicep with a groan. "What would you have gotten?"

"I don't know! Thank goodness you found me before I could go through with that. A drunken tattoo would have been a disaster."

"Would you ever get a tattoo?"

I shrugged. "How do you justify putting something on your skin permanently?"

He ran another finger down my face, starting at my temple, down my hairline, and along my jaw to my chin. I felt goosebumps prickle across my skin. "Some people choose a saying they live by. Others pick a representation of who they are and what they do."

We both glanced up as rain loudly pelted the windows. Thinking again of our photoshoot, I smiled. "It might be cliché, but I've always liked the learning to dance in the rain quote. After tonight, it has an extra special place in my heart."

His smile was wide, showing where he would have crow's feet sometime down the road. "That is an excellent description of your life."

"Maybe someday," I sighed. "Abby has been dying to get matching tattoos. I told her not until she was eighteen, to buy myself time."

"Scared?"

"A little." I smiled up at him, trying to combat the small wave of nerves. Where was that little voice in my head now, bringing out that sexy confidence?

"Do me a favor," Jonah whispered, still running a finger along my neck.

"What's that?"

"Don't give those photos to this contest."

This was not what I had expected him to say. "Okay," I replied, more as a question than a statement.

"I don't want to share you, or that moment, with the world."

I pictured the little voice in my head as an *I Dream of Jeannie* woman, scantily clad in light, airy, sexy silks, drinking wine, and eating fruits in a small compartment of my brain. Jonah's soft-spoken words made her leap off her velvet chaise, grinning like a banshee. "Because of the tabloids?" I asked hesitantly, hoping he would say no.

"Because I want to be the sole owner of those photos, Holly," Jonah said, his eyes burning. "I will purchase them from you, edited or not. I want to remember your face, your spontaneity, your vibrance.

No matter how bad life gets, I want to be able to show you how you look to me, every day."

Jeannie fainted. I gently pulled his head down for a kiss, hoping he would not see the happy tears pooling in my eyes.

ᗡᗡᗡᗡᗡ

Later, listening to Jonah's soft snores, his arms wrapped around me protectively, with not a scrap of clothing between us, I let a few tears fall silently. Past demons threatened to destroy the happy feelings.

Once upon a time, a boy had not given me a choice, and it had had disastrous consequences. I had woken up naked, in a bed I did not recognize, sore and bleeding and terrified. Overnight, I had become the laughingstock of the school. The laughingstock first and then the easy girl, just like her mom and grandma.

The tears were more than that, though. There were no words for what had just happened—no words to adequately describe the joy, the love.

Love.

I was hopelessly in love with Jonah. It wasn't the post-sex hormones talking either. It was his reaction to the photo shoot. It was his attention to my emotional well-being, and his unfailing kindness to Abby. He had waited two years for me to acknowledge my feelings, never pushing me to act when I wasn't ready.

"Holly?" Arms tightened around me, and the bed flexed beneath his weight as he shifted. "Are you alright?"

"Yeah," I laughed, hiding my face in my pillow.

He rolled me over and wiped away the tears. "What's wrong?"

"Nothing, I'm good. I just… that was the first time… the first time I *wanted* to… do that. The first time I remembered it. I'm sorry—I didn't mean to wake you up."

"Are you okay? I didn't hurt you, did I?" Confused and disoriented, he was adorable.

"No."

"What do you need?"

I kissed the top of his nose. "Your arms around me, and for you to get some sleep."

"Are you sure?"

"Yes. Go back to sleep." He did as I asked after kissing my forehead. With my tears abated, and Jonah's warmth wrapped around me, I finally drifted asleep too.

Nineteen

The next morning, I awoke to Jonah's kisses, leading to another round of lovemaking in the bed and then the shower. He ordered breakfast, and we ate on the balcony, enjoying the breezy aftermath of the storm. Neither of us spoke much, our occasional touches or gentle kisses saying more than any words could convey. Jonah's phone rang a few times, but he ignored the calls, his face impassive.

"You can take that," I said when his phone rang back-to-back three times.

He shook his head. "I don't feel like ruining my morning."

My cheeks heated, but I still smiled at him. "Are you sure?"

"I slept well for the first time in… I don't know how long. I want to hold on to this feeling of refreshed, energized happiness for a bit longer. Besides," he added with a wink, "this is the first vacation day I haven't been rudely awakened by fists or barf." I swatted at him playfully, but he caught my hand, entwining his fingers with mine and kissing my knuckles.

"Smooth," I chuckled, tipping my face to the sky and closing my eyes. If he was going to bask in the joy of the morning, I certainly could too. My phone rang then, Abby's voice belting out part of "Sisters" from *White Christmas* as the ringtone. I opened my eyes, about to tell Jonah I wouldn't answer it either, but he was already reaching for it.

"Hello, sweetheart," he said when her face came up on the screen, and held it out so we could all see each other. "How are you, my love?"

"Jonah!" Abby cried. "How's the cruise? Are you loving it? Are you getting Holly into all sorts of trouble?"

"Absolutely," he said without skipping a beat, making my face burn. "Are you staying *out* of trouble?"

"Of course, I am. I went for a swim this morning and just got done eating breakfast. Holly, we may or may not be out of Fruity Pebbles."

"What? We just went grocery shopping like four days ago!"

"And I may or may not have become a closet eater in your absence. I don't know, Fred Flintstone was just begging me to open the box."

"Are you flirting with cartoon characters behind my back?" Jonah asked.

Abby's jaw dropped. "I wouldn't dare!" She burst into giggles at Jonah's raised eyebrow. "How's it going? Holly, I'm so sad we kept missing each other."

"I know, I'm sorry." Jonah handed me the phone so he could clear the dishes. I filled her in on Isaac's help and the daily photography contest.

"What is today's contest?"

I paused the video with her so I could pull up the email. "Nightlife on the sea."

"What are you thinking of doing?"

"I took a few pictures last night—we had a spectacular storm. Maybe one of those, if they turned out."

She shook her head. "I'll never understand how you can wait so long to look at them. My curiosity would get the better of me every time."

I peeked back to see that Jonah had gone to the bathroom and turned to whisper to her. "Jonah and I had a mini photoshoot last night. It was so fun."

"That's wonderful. Why are you whispering?" she hissed back.

"He told me I couldn't submit them to the contest. I wouldn't have anyway—they are special to me. I'm almost… I'm almost afraid to look at them because I'm afraid I'll get my hopes up and they will be… not what I'm hoping they will be."

"You could send them to me. I'll give you an honest answer."

"I know you would. But… I don't know. They were so fun. I'm afraid to look. I'm not sure a photograph can capture what I felt last night."

"Holly, they are going to be great. And the more you talk about them, the more I want to see them." My stomach let loose the butterflies as I thought about the developments of the previous night and my cheeks burst into flames again. "What is it?" she asked.

"Huh?"

"That faraway look that tells me your mind is elsewhere. What is going on?"

"Nothing. I'm good." When her eyes narrowed, I peeked around the corner again. Jonah was still in the bathroom. "Abby, I think I'm in love with Jonah."

She burst out laughing. "Of course, you are. I already knew that. I've just been waiting for you to catch up. As soon as you told me how he made you feel the other night, I figured it out."

"Isn't it too soon?"

"Nope."

I grinned. "You seem awfully sure of that."

"I am. He loves you too." She was about to speak again but stopped. "Oh, Cecille is calling. She mentioned possibly needing me early today. Talk later?"

"Sure."

"Okay. Have fun, love you, bye!"

I set my phone back on the table and leaned back to close my eyes. There was no way I could tell Jonah I was in love with him. Not yet. Any mention of it would send him running for the hills. My eyes opened. Or would it? When was the right time to say those three little words? At what point did it stop being scary? I had watched one too many chick-flicks where the words were spoken too soon, and the guy ran. Jonah didn't strike me as the type to run, but it was a big deal.

"Abby had to go?"

I yelped. Jonah had become an expert in startling me out of my head. "She had another call."

"Now what?" When I shrugged, he leaned down to kiss my upturned face. "Pool time?"

"That sounds perfect."

ooooo

"Holly! Over here!"

I waved to Isla and Layla, and Jonah followed me over, raising a hand to Isaac.

"We were just talking about ordering a pizza. You guys want some?"

"Sure," I said with a shrug. After a short discussion about toppings, Layla sauntered over to the poolside bar to place an order.

"We missed you two last night."

I couldn't help the grin that spread across my face. "We ordered in. Jonah had to work all day yesterday, so we didn't have a chance to see each other."

"Too bad. Last night we were each given fifty dollars to see what we could do with it at the casino. Isaac and Layla doubled their money. I made a thousand bucks at blackjack. This cruise is on track to ruin all other cruises for me with the amount of money they are giving away."

"How was the daily contest?"

"None of us won. Frankly, I was too hungover to write anything yesterday. How did you fare?"

"About the same. And I was so angry about the way Mr. Vaughn spoke to me that I didn't even want to contribute anything."

"That's one way to look at it, I guess," she shrugged. "Or you could submit so many things so you can win all his money from him."

I glanced over to Jonah, who was in the pool talking to Isaac and a few other guys. "Jonah said they were testing me. You know, to make sure I wasn't some gold-digging whore."

"Surely you passed that with flying colors?"

I shrugged. "I think so. I mean, until I came out to California, I had no idea how much money Jonah had.

When he… visits Wisconsin, he doesn't—I mean, he just doesn't seem like the millionaire type."

"Which makes you a keeper in their eyes. And his," Isla said with a smile.

"That's kind of you to say."

"Did you get the email about today's contest?"

"Yeah. I took a few pictures last night of the storm. I might submit a couple."

"I can't wait to see them. I might need to order a few—my parents collect storm photographs. They are always looking to add more."

Isla's kindness, and the prospect of possibly selling a few photos made the day brighter. "I'm going to edit later this afternoon. If any of them turn out, I'll let you know."

"Awesome." The pool was abuzz with people, milling about in the water and on the deck. Some of the contest participants had become recognizable after multiple gatherings, and the pool had become an unspoken gathering spot for many of them.

Layla returned to her chair, adjusting her sunglasses and beach hat. I wondered if there was an unspoken competition regarding gigantic hats that I had missed. "What did Jonah say to Creed the other night?" she asked.

"I don't know. We all went out dancing. Why?"

She made a face. "I just saw him at the bar. He was drunk, but I overheard him telling some sob story to a couple of women about how he had been ostracized from the group by Jonah Seeley. I'm just thankful Jonah made Creed leave us alone. That guy is bad news."

"Does anyone else feel like his photography business sounds like porn?" Isla whispered. "I cannot imagine what he submitted to get into the contest."

"He told someone on the plane he knows one of the board members, and they got him in." Layla's eyes went wide and she looked at me. "Jonah wouldn't do that, would he?"

"Jonah said he didn't do it for me. I can't imagine he'd do it for someone he didn't like," I said with a shrug.

"He seemed legitimately pissed when Creed showed up the other night. I don't think it was Jonah," Isla agreed.

I sighed. "I could ask, but he deflected questions about Creed when I brought him up yesterday. It just sucks that someone out there is trying to ruin his reputation."

"Not the first time, honey, and won't be the last," Layla said with a wave of her hand. "Jonah is known to be a business genius, capable of destroying as easily as building small businesses. I've read he's also good at intimidating. He has acquired a few properties and businesses that way too."

"Let's change the subject," Isla said cheerfully when I didn't respond. "Layla, what are you planning on writing about for the nightlife?"

As they launched into discussing the various bars and karaoke options available, I glanced back at Jonah. Something Layla said flagged in my brain. Something I would need to discuss with Jonah.

ooooo

Pizza, surrounded by new friends, proved enough to lighten my dark thoughts. At the center of a group of good-looking guys, Layla and Isla were at their best. With their long drawls and honeyed words, the two southern belles made every man in the group feel like a hero. They even charmed Jonah into boisterous laughter. I laughed along with them, thinking that adding Abby in the mix would have been a lethal concoction.

After lunch, we went separate ways to edit and submit our entries for the evening. As we made our way back to the room, I told Jonah about what the girls had said earlier.

His body stiffened at my mention of Creed. "People will try to make me look bad, but I ignore it. Those are the people who are either jealous or feel they have been wronged by something I've done. In Creed's case, it's the former."

"Is it true you coerce people into doing things you want them to do?"

Jonah shrugged. "Sometimes I simply need to present a person with an option better than what they have."

It was now or never to bring up my suspicion. "Is that what you did with our landlord?"

"That man was a scumbag."

I stopped walking. With Jonah's arm around my shoulders, he was jostled to a stop as well. "Why did you do that?"

"Because you asked me to."

"Jonah, I was kidding!" I squealed.

"All right, then it was because I wanted to protect you. I wanted you to stop worrying about money and bills."

"Jonah, I appreciate the gesture, truly. But that's very… intrusive."

His brows furrowed. "I'm not sure—"

"Look, I appreciate it. Louis was a scumbag. But you can't just barge in and take over my life." I closed my eyes with a sigh. "Sorry. That's not—I mean—"

"Let's continue this in our room?" Jonah suggested.

I noted the two couples who were watching and listening to us. "Yeah."

We walked the rest of the way in silence. When the door was closed, he turned to me. "Okay," he said with a sigh. "Please, explain this to me. I thought you guys couldn't afford the raised payment."

"No, we couldn't have afforded it," I admitted. "But that's not—you can't just swoop in, and take over. That's a lot to digest." I paced back and forth. "You have been my friend for two years, and now we're dating, and it's great. It's great! But the whole… the whole knight in shining armor is… It can be a little overwhelming."

"Knight in shining armor?"

I held up a finger for each item. "Taking over my building, ruining Brayden's business, bringing me to your apartment, bringing me here when I have a room—"

"Do you not want to be here?"

I threw my hands up in frustration. "No, this is wonderful. I just—ugh. You make me feel like I can't take care of myself. I can! I've been caring for myself and Abby for a long time."

Jonah stepped toward me, wrapping his arms around my waist. "I know you can. I'm sorry, Holly. I didn't do it to piss you off. I just wanted to help."

"I'm not angry. I'm just… proud of what I've accomplished. I'm proud that I can make my way. It's hard when someone comes in and says 'here, you did it, but now I'll do it better.'"

His brows rose in surprise. "I never thought about it like that. I'm sorry. That wasn't my intention."

I rested my forehead on his chest with another sigh. "I know it wasn't."

"What can I do?"

I raised my head, wrapping my arms around his waist. "Next time just talk to me. Let me know what your plans are and give me time to adjust. Or ask me first."

"I can do that."

"Thank you."

We stood like that a long time before Jonah asked, "Don't you have pictures to edit?"

"Yeah. I should probably do that."

When I didn't move, he laughed. "You okay?"

"Yeah. I just don't like fighting with you."

"Back at you. It will likely take a few more arguments and discussions to figure out how to communicate best, but it's nothing we can't handle. Now, you get to work. I am going to run downstairs and make sure everything is ready for our date night." He kissed my forehead and moved away, laughing at my groan of protest. "I can't wait to see what you're submitting. I will have to run down to touch base with the board, but then I can get out of dinner with them." He slipped into the bathroom to change, emerging a few minutes later with a white cotton dress shirt and gray cargo pants.

"What are we doing tonight?"

Jonah's grin was infectious as he rolled the sleeves up his arms. "I'm cooking dinner for us. And you're going to help me."

I blushed again. "Jonah! Last night was great. I wasn't complaining about the food—"

"I know. But I thought this would be fun too."

"What time should I be ready?"

He glanced at his phone. "I'll be back here by six to pick you up."

"Okay." Jonah paused at the door, studying me a moment. "What?" I asked.

Crossing the room, he nearly bowled me over, gathering me into his arms to kiss me senseless. My nerve endings tingled as his hands roamed my skin. *Holy crap on a cracker.* I hoped this physical fire between us would never extinguish.

"You have work to do," he said breathlessly, his lips moving on my neck.

"It can wait," I murmured.

He shook his head, extracting his appendages from mine. "Six o'clock."

I glared at him through the closed door, growling at my enraged hormones. How could I possibly get any work done in my current state?

Moving my computer out to the balcony, I began editing the storm photos from the night before. The storm photos were brilliant. The long exposures caught branching lightning rods, reaching from one angry cloud to another. It went beyond the blacks, whites, and grays normally associated with storms. Purple, blue, silver, and gold also made their appearances. Playing with the colors, I finally submitted two to the contest, thrilled with the results. I emailed a few to my phone to forward to Abby, Isla, and Jonah. Isla responded immediately, offering me thirty dollars per photo, printed as an eight by ten. I had brought a small printer with me, but I replied saying I wanted to print them off on better quality paper, especially since she would be paying me. She promised to help me find a print shop when we reached Hawaii. I looked at the thumbnails of the pictures of Jonah and I, but I did not open them. Something was telling me to wait. It just didn't feel right.

Turning up the music on my phone, I started a load of laundry in the tiny washer in the closet before hurrying through the shower. Donning my favorite maxi dress, a black top with a black, white, and pink floral skirt, I applied makeup, pulled my hair into a loose bun at the nape of my neck, and switched the laundry, all between five-thirty and six. I was happily sipping a glass of water on the balcony when Jonah returned.

"You look great," he said softly, leaning in to kiss the nape of my neck.

I turned in his arms. "You left too soon," I said quietly, wrapping myself around him.

"I got your pictures. And you won the contest tonight." He pulled an envelope from his back pocket. "Talent at its finest, Kitten."

"I won?" I grabbed the envelope and looked inside. Two crisp one-hundred-dollar bills.

"Congratulations. Guess you're buying pizza tomorrow for lunch."

"I guess so." Two hundred dollars was a good chunk toward replacing my camera and that was motivation to keep competing. If I could win another round or two, I would be able to purchase my new camera when I got back to Wisconsin. It would also cover all of Abby's college application fees, buying me a little more time to save up for tuition.

"That money is for you, Holly." When I looked up in surprise, his smile was gentle. "Your face was full of excitement and then it dimmed when you started thinking about what you should do with that money. It isn't for *should*, it's for *fun*."

"Get out of my head," I chuckled, giving him a playful push before tucking the money in my purse. "Do I need to bring anything?"

"Only your appetite."

Twenty

With a smile and a hand at the small of my back, Jonah guided me down to the kitchen. The halls were filled with people, lines for the restaurants and bars getting longer by the minute, but as we made our way below the main deck, it became quieter. He stopped me at a door, slid his key in, and held the door open for me. I stepped into a small, private dining room, with a bar and kitchen off to the right. There were only ten tables, all with white tablecloths and gold napkins and candlesticks. The lights were dimmed in the dining room and gold lights on the wall behind the liquor bottles made them sparkle. Super romantic.

"Come on," Jonah said, leading me up to the bar.

"Did you reserve this whole dining room just for us?" I breathed, sliding onto the barstool while he walked around the bar.

"Yes," he said with a shrug.

And I had been debating whether to splurge two hundred dollars. "Jonah."

"Holly." He moved around the bar as though it was a second home, making quick work to pull out various bottles and glasses.

I watched him as he began pouring various items into a shaker. "How is Max managing without you?"

Jonah did not want to react, but I caught the slightest pause in his actions before he resumed. "Max will be fine. He's been wanting to start his own company for a while. He's been watching me move through the ranks, and he's capable. That said, they are putting pressure on him, looking for that little company. And me—they are also looking for me, too."

I smiled. "Afraid to tell them you're on vacation?"

He didn't return the jest. "If they find me, there's a good chance they will find a way onto the boat, if not be waiting for me in Hawaii."

"Seriously?" He nodded, making my stomach drop. "I'm sure your presence here was already noted by somebody. You should be lying low, holed up in the room if you don't want others to know you're here."

"And give up time with you? Not a chance." He leaned across the bar to kiss the tip of my nose. "Although… if you're holed up with me in the room… well…"

I reddened under his sultry gaze but persisted. "I don't understand, Jonah. You seem so worried about this work stuff, but then when we talk, you brush it off like it's no big deal. I don't want to be the reason something happens."

"Holly, relax." He reached out to cover my hands with one of his own. "You'd be surprised how well I can compartmentalize."

Still, my unease lingered. "Jonah, I feel like you're hiding something from me, and I'm glad you want me to be happy, but this-this doesn't feel right."

He placed a pretty red slushie drink in front of me and took both my hands. Slowly, he kissed the knuckles on both before responding. "You're right," he said quietly, his eyes piercing. "There is more. A lot more. And here's the truth: I don't want you involved, in any way. This opposing company is… they have been known to be violent, not playing by the rules. The less you're involved, the better. Truly."

This did nothing to calm my nerves. Instead, I felt close to tears. "Jonah, if you're in danger, please don't do this. Let the small company go. Please don't make me worry whether or not you'll come home safe each night."

"I promise I'm going to come home safe to you, every night."

"How can you know that?"

"I do. Oh, no, no, no." When a traitorous tear slipped down my cheek, he hurried around the bar to gather me in his arms, kissing my face and hair. "No, please. This was supposed to be a fun, happy night."

"You just told me your life is in danger when you go to work!"

He held my shoulders and dipped his head to meet my gaze. "Listen to me, very carefully. I promise I will *always* come home to you. Always. *Always*," he said when I started to protest.

"How can you possibly know that?"

"I will always come back to you because I am hopelessly in love with you, Holly."

My sigh turned into a gasp as I stared at him. "You love me?"

"Yes."

I stared at him for a moment and then burst out laughing. "Oh no," I squealed, burying my face in his chest.

"Holly… Holly, I need you to talk to me because I'm a little confused."

My giggles continued. "I'm so sorry." I wrapped my arms around his waist when he started to back up. I took several deep breaths. "I just—how did you make that so easy?"

"What?"

"Saying that you love me?" He stared at me so long that I began to question my sanity. "I have been struggling with whether or not it's too soon to feel that way, or how to tell you that I love you too, and—"

"You love me?"

"Yes. I've been trying to—"

Jonah's lips were on mine, preventing me from finishing my thought. The thoughts then melted into liquid, rendered unintelligible by Jonah's touch and my own euphoria. To be wanted and cherished was wonderful, but to be loved… bliss. I vaguely registered the sound of Jonah's stomach growling. "We should probably eat," I said against his mouth.

"Mmm," he murmured, nibbling at my bottom lip.

"Food, Jonah."

His grin was full of mischief. "Fine." Reluctantly, he put space between us.

I took a sip from my drink before following him into the kitchen. "I've only ever watched you cook. And tonight, I'm going to particularly enjoy the view. How do you make it look like you belong in any kitchen you enter?"

He paused, his hand on the fridge door. "That would be extremely offensive if I was a woman."

I guffawed. "Good thing you aren't. And besides, it was a compliment."

"What are we having tonight?"

I considered for a moment before shrugging. "Surprise me."

The corner of his mouth twitched. "Don't tempt me, Kitten."

Nearly every appliance known to man was packed into the kitchen space, all spotless white and stainless steel. I peeked over his shoulder into the fridge when he opened it. It was filled to the brim. "Are you craving anything?"

"Yes," he replied, his arm snaking around my waist.

"*Food*, Jonah. Are you craving any food?"

"No. I'm here to be your chef. You get to choose."

I could get used to that, I decided. "What about burgers?"

Jonah threw his head back and laughed. "You have this entire kitchen to make anything, and you choose burgers?"

I turned back to him and glared, my hands on my hips. "I miss Cecille's, okay? I like the burgers the cook makes there."

"Whatever you want, I suppose," Jonah said, still chuckling. "I'll see what I can do to spice them up a bit. Less café lunch, more cruise dinner."

ooooo

Later, we sat at the table closest to the bar. Jonah had made teriyaki burgers on buns he had toasted with

Hawaiian roll-type drizzle. He had even made a batch of french fries and homemade ranch dip. We both dug in, starving.

"Where did you learn to cook?" I asked.

"You mean, before college, when they told me I was doing everything wrong?" Jonah sipped his drink. "I spent a lot of time with Cecille. She taught me as soon as I was old enough to pay attention. Armando, Number Three, started letting me around the grill and oven around sixteen."

"Armando," I repeated, raising my eyebrows.

"Cecille has a type. She likes guys with a Latino background. She told me she liked their… ahem, taste."

I choked on my drink. "Oh no."

"I was young enough that went over my head, but now I'm traumatized."

"I bet."

He ran a finger along the rim of his glass, a far-off smile on his lips. "They were all kind to me, though. I never had an issue with any of them. If there was a boyfriend who wasn't good to me, Cecille always knew and sent him packing. We mourned together when Two, Three, Four, and Five passed away. Like a family. It was good." He sighed as he looked up at me. "I went to culinary school and started my business. The rest is history."

"They didn't like the way you cooked at school?" I remembered a conversation from a few months ago.

"No. They wanted me to follow recipes, techniques in the preliminary classes. I couldn't do it. They didn't like that I went with my gut when they gave me directions. They said I was too 'plain' and rustic.'"

I gestured to my plate. "This isn't plain or rustic."

He laughed. "I've improved with time, and hiring the best chefs in California definitely helped. But it's the history of it for me. Cooking with Cecille and her husbands was fun, and I struggled to create that atmosphere in a classroom kitchen. A few times I thought about giving up."

"I'm glad you didn't. You are an amazing chef."

"Thanks. I also couldn't write a paper to save my life, so my transcripts are less than stellar."

I snorted. "I sucked at papers too. And tests. Just let me show you my skills. Why do I have to follow the teacher's every move?"

"Exactly," he said, raising his glass to mine. An easy silence passed between us before he spoke again. "Since we have discovered that we… feel similarly toward each other, can I ask a personal question?"

"Sure."

"Where do you see yourself in ten years?"

My cheeks heated. "Well, after Abby gets through school… I don't know. A studio, a full-time photography job capturing weddings, babies, families, nature. Some photographers like to specialize in one specific area, but I like all of it."

"While that is all spectacular, I meant your personal life."

"Oh. I-I don't know. I don't!" I cried when his eyes narrowed speculatively. "I have perfected the one-day-at-a-time lifestyle. I don't plan much for the future because I know how uncompromising it can be. I have goals, sure, but I don't have plans. A long-term relationship, a wedding, kids, those are dreams."

"You would do them if the opportunity arose?"

My face was surely crimson as I shrugged. "Sure. I mean, maybe." When he continued to glare at me, I shot the question back at him. "What? You're going to tell me you have all your ducks in a row, and you know exactly what you'll be doing in ten years?"

Jonah laughed. "No, I can't tell you exactly, but I can tell you what I want."

"What do *you* want?"

"I want to sell my businesses and retire. I want to sell all my properties and buy one place. I want to find a mate and have a whole bunch of kids that I can spoil rotten. I want to travel with my family."

"That sounds wonderful."

"Your turn."

I sighed, buying myself a moment to consider. "I want… I want to have a thriving photography business. I want to see where life takes Abby. I want to promote the needs of battered and bruised women and be an example of what perseverance and coping looks like. I want to be a beacon of hope. I want to—what? What's so funny?"

"Beyond the profit from photography, none of those things are for you. What do *you* want?"

I shrugged, sipping my drink. "I just want to be happy."

"With a family? Husband, kids?"

"Maybe someday, sure." I laughed. "Is that what this is all about? Your roundabout way of asking me if I want kids?"

"Yes, although you showed me what I need to do to spoil you over the next few months."

"Spoil me? Aren't you already doing that?"

"Oh, no. I haven't even started yet."

I shook my head. "You don't need to spoil me."

"Again—need verses want, Kitten."

I stood and began gathering plates. "I was spoiled rotten with this delicious meal tonight. Thank you."

Jonah jumped up and took the plates from me. "You should sit at the bar while I do the dishes."

"Are you kidding? Some of our best moments have been while washing dishes at Cecille's. I'm helping."

I followed him back to the kitchen. Jonah loaded all the dishes into the handy dishwashing station, pulled the door down while they sanitized, and then I dried while he put them away. He kept the music on his phone turned up, both of us dancing to the music. Jonah, I discovered, was as good a singer as he was a dancer. His voice was all sultry-deep and unapologetically sexy, leaving me to wonder why I had never heard him sing before.

Taking our drinks, we turned the lights off and left the room. "Did you want to join the party or go back to the room?"

I stood on my tiptoes and kissed him thoroughly, fisting my free hand in his shirt.

"Back to the room, then," he growled, sending shivers through me.

As we crossed the main deck, headed for the elevators, Isla called out to us, flailing wildly. "Thank goodness we found you," she cried breathlessly. "Holly, we need your help."

"What's wrong?"

"Jonah! Come on," Isaac called, clasping his shoulder as he passed us.

"It's a men versus women scavenger hunt," she explained quickly, handing me the list.

I scanned the list with Jonah doing the same over my shoulder. "This sounds fun," I told him, an apologetic smile spreading across my face.

"Good. Come on, we only have two hours! The winning group gets two hundred dollars!"

"Meet you back in the room later?" At my nod, he jogged after Isaac.

My hormones were still in a tizzy, but when Isla put the cheap digital camera in my hands, I couldn't resist. "So far I have three of them done. I was just looking for a ship officer. Oh, there's one! Sir!" Isla bounced off toward the man in the white suit.

The good-looking man paused with an appreciative grin as Isla approached. "What can I do for you?"

Isla turned up her southern charm. "We are doing a photo scavenger hunt, and we need a picture with a ship officer. Can we take a picture with you, honey?"

"Sure."

The artist in me came to light immediately. "Could you pick her up? Let's go for like a 1940s old-time, navy officer-type picture." He did as he was told, Isla squealing in delight.

"Like the photo of the people kissing after D-Day in Times Square?" he asked.

"Yeah. That would be great," I giggled

"As the lady commands," he said, pulling Isla in for a long kiss.

I snapped the picture, laughing. "Got it. Thanks."

The man set Isla back on her feet with a wink. "No, thank you. Have fun ladies."

"Thanks, dear," Isla threw over her shoulder as she caught my elbow and hurried away. "And thank *you!*" she hissed at me.

I laughed all the way to the bar, where we tried to finish the rest of the photos in time. The cameras, I learned from Isla, were scheduled to be turned off by eleven. Entries would be reviewed, and a winner would be announced the next day. Some of the search items were silly, like finding a picture of a fish. Others were more challenging, like finding someone with a seasickness patch. For that one, Isla spotted a nicotine patch on a large man with a handlebar mustache and leather vest. She convinced him to let her write on the patch, snapping a photo of both of them flexing like Rosie the Riveter. By the time eleven came around, my face and sides hurt from laughing.

I could not wait to get back up to the room to share our adventures with Jonah. Much of the sexual urgency was gone, but I still wanted Jonah. Having a quiet dinner with him, laughing, and talking about the future only cemented the fact that I was where I wanted to be: right by his side. Sure, the whole zillionaire thing would take some getting used to, but Jonah had said himself that he did not want his job to be a long-term commitment. He wanted to retire early to focus on his family.

Saying I hadn't thought about my future was not entirely true. I had thought about it, a little. Once Abby was stable on her own, I wanted to settle down with a guy who loved me and a few foster children. With my flexible schedule as a full-time photographer, I would be able to devote time and care and love to them, helping them escape toxic environments. None would share my particular story, but I knew I would be able to relate to them on a level others wouldn't.

With that in mind to discuss with Jonah, I opened the door to our room. The shower was running, I noted, kicking my shoes off by the closet. I started to turn when I saw another pair of shoes not far from mine. A female's flats, smaller than mine. At the same time, there was a sigh behind me.

Twenty-One

I whirled around to find Layla slowly sitting up. In the bed. My bed. Jonah's bed.

And she was naked.

"Oh, hey, Holly," she said sleepily, stretching. "What are you doing here?"

The world fell out from beneath me. "Why are you here?" I whispered. And then I spotted it. There on the floor next to the bed, a condom. Used. Bile rose in my throat. They would have had several hours of alone time while I was off gallivanting with Isla.

Vaguely I registered the shower turning off. I must have made some noise because I heard Jonah say, "Be right out!"

"Holly?" Layla asked again, her face confused as she looked around. "Are you all right?"

"Why are you here?" I asked, my voice coming out in a squeak.

She looked around, running her fingers through her hair. "I must have fallen asleep after we had sex. Oh, but where did he go?" she turned back to me, her brows furrowed. "And how did you get in?"

It was the most ridiculous question I had ever heard. As my breathing rate skyrocketed, I stumbled to the door blindly. Wrenching it open, I ran, anywhere to get some fresh air. I left everything behind, even my shoes. Let Jonah realize I had caught them in the act. I didn't care. All I knew was that I was not ready to face the man I thought I loved.

The deck had cleared considerably since the last time I had passed through, allowing me the freedom to find a place next to the railing to dry heave over the side. When I couldn't anymore, I sank to my knees, letting a ragged sob escape.

And then another.

And another.

Oh, my heart. My mind. My soul. Jonah told me he loved me. He made me feel things I hadn't felt before. He made me believe in love again and to look happily to the future, and promised he would never hurt me.

"Why?" I moaned, wrapping my arms around my stomach, afraid I'd implode at any moment. He knew everything. He knew what had happened to me. He knew my insecurities and had taken great lengths to calm them. *For what? Why? Why wasn't I enough?*

"Holly?" I looked up to find Creed hurrying toward me. "Are you alright, Doll?" When he reached me, I allowed him to pull me to my feet before moving away, my back against the railing. "What is it?"

I shook my head. "P-please, leave me alone."

"I'm afraid I can't do that, Doll." He stepped toward me again, putting his hands on my waist. "I've been waiting to get you alone."

"I said, leave me alone!" I shrieked, shoving at his chest.

"Sorry, Doll. This is for Jonah. You really are better off without him." He lifted up and tossed me over the side of the ship.

I screamed as I fell, managing to get my feet beneath me before I hit the cool water. Clawing for the surface, I watched in horror as Creed disappeared from the main deck. With only seconds, I swam hard, out away from the current of the propellers. By some miracle, I was not pulled under, and swam after it, screaming for help. No one acknowledged me. Aboard the ship, it always felt as though we were only trudging along through the water. From the surface of the water, the cruise ship looked more like a speed boat, putting more and more distance between us. I swam hard after the ship, but it was difficult. The waves that looked so small and serene from the boat were colossal and pushed me in every direction, rendering my efforts futile. Still, I powered on, fighting for my life, screaming for the boat to come back.

As the cruise ship disappeared into the darkness, I began to shiver. If I did not keep moving, hypothermia would set in. I pulled the skirt of my dress up and tied it above my knees, giving my legs more room to move. Swim or stay? Considering my options, I kept swimming in the direction of the ship. We were nearly halfway through our cruise, which meant both directions were a very long swim to land. Creed knew where I was but most likely would not tell anyone. Jonah would know I had been in the room and left, but he wouldn't know where I was. Even if he found out, and cared, there was no way he would be able to get the ship to turn around. Maybe they would call the coast guard to look for me, in which case I needed to still be alive in the morning. *If* Jonah wanted to help me.

I dropped my head beneath the surface, letting out a sob into the salty waters. This wasn't supposed to happen. I should never have taken the cruise. I should never have even entered the contest. Staying home was safe. Working at Cecille's was safe. Caring for Abby was safe.

Abby.

Abby would never know what happened, or why. Or that I loved her so unconditionally. She would wonder if it had been an accident or if I had successfully committed suicide. She would ask Jonah, and Jonah wouldn't know either. I would not get to watch her graduate high school, or college, or get married, or spoil her kids. She would have to go through life alone, the one thing I had striven not to allow happen since that day in the abortion clinic.

And then there was Jonah. Jonah who I foolishly believed had loved me and had made me want to hope and dream. He had built me up only to destroy me. I saw Layla in the bed, disheveled and naked, looking like a beautiful blond goddess right out of a painting. She seemed surprised to see me, which was odd, as she'd known I was sharing a room with Jonah. So why question my arrival? Jonah had used me for companionship, only to dump me when a better model came along, playing upon my worst fears of being inadequate. Why? What had I done to deserve that?

I looked up at the moon and realized I was floating on my back. When had I stopped swimming? I should keep going.

I was getting cold.

Too cold to move.

I floated, drifting in the sea, wherever she decided to take me, staring up at the stars.

I was tired too.

Closing my eyes, I spread my arms, letting the waves lull me to sleep.

Twenty-Two

I awoke to the sensation of floating and an odd feeling in my ears and nose. *Water*, I realized, my eyes shooting open as I flailed helplessly, reaching for the surface. Salt burned my eyes as I scrambled. There was a weight in my legs that prevented movement. I held my breath as stars began dancing across my blurry vision.

"Whoa, whoa, Holly. Try to relax." I barely heard the words as I struggled. Hands wrapped around my arms trying to hold me still. "Holly, I need you to relax and breathe." With a whimper, I fought, clawing at the arms holding me. "It's different, breathing underwater," the voice continued calmly. "But you will get used to it, I promise. Breathe, Holly. It's okay. Just breathe."

When I could no longer hold my breath, I gulped, moaning as the salty water filled my lungs.

"Good. Again."

I did as I was told, but the pain was intense, little needles piercing my insides.

"Again."

When the arms loosened, I pushed them away, attempting to turn. My hands brushed against my shirt and hips, and I felt slick scales. One glance down and my breaths turned to screams. Just barely visible in the dim light was a long tail, complete with scales and fins on the end. It added several feet to my length and moved when I tried to move my feet.

"Holly! Holly! Please!"

I turned to find a man approaching again, a man who looked and sounded like Max. He reached for me, but I lashed out at him. "Don't touch me!" I screamed when he reached for me again. "Get away from me. No!"

"Holly, it's okay. You're okay. You're safe."

I could not understand why he was so calm. "I am not okay! I am a fish!" Frantically, I kicked my legs, trying to understand the mechanics of a tail.

"We know, sweetheart. We know—we brought you here."

"We? Who is 'we'?"

"Me, Jonah, a few others—"

"Jonah! Jonah? No!" I screamed again as he reached for me. My back collided painfully with a wall and I spun, feeling for a way out in the semi-darkness. Small shapes of light lined the bottom and I reached for one. Finding an edge and pulling myself down and under, I escaped beneath it as Max grabbed for me. His attempts were fruitless as I kicked toward the surface. Sunlight filtered through the waters in long lines that stretched down around me.

"Holly!" Max was still calling. I ignored him, reaching for the surface. "Holly, wait!"

A massive shadow passed above me, and I swam up toward it, slowing only when a second passed. It was not a boat or jet ski, as I originally thought, but something large with fins.

There was a directive shouted behind me, and I was suddenly hit hard from the side, arms wrapping around me, pulling me back down to the abyss.

"No!" I screamed.

"Holly, stop," Jonah's voice in my ear was harsher than I had ever heard him. I was whisked through the water down to a dark mass, which I realized was the hull of an old airplane. Fear gripped me again, and I struggled to free my arms. "No, Holly. Now is not the time. You must stay with Max. A fight with orcas is no place for a human."

Orcas. Humans. Things that didn't belong in the same sentences unless you were attending a *SeaWorld* show, which I most definitely was not. "What are you—"

"For the love of—keep her here, Max!"

"I'm trying!"

I was turned to face Jonah, his eyes as wild as his hair as it floated around his face. "You *will* stay with Max, Holly. That isn't a request—it's an order. Do you understand?"

"But—"

"Later." And with a flourish he was gone, out of the airplane and back out to open waters.

"Orcas? Max, what is he talking about?"

"Hunting pods passing through the area."

I held up my hands. "What are you talking about? W-what are you saying? Th-that this is normal, and you just fight orcas?"

"It's part of living in the ocean."

"What!" I wailed.

"Living in the ocean."

"You live here. Under the ocean. Like… mermaids."

Max grinned. "Yeah. I know it's a bit wild, but—"

"Wild? Wild. Max, this is *insane*. This-this… This is a dream. I—" Realization struck hard. "I'm dead. I'm—is this what happens when you die?"

"Holly, you aren't dead. You—"

I held up my hand, shaking my head. "I must be dead. I fell from a cruise ship, into the ocean. It was unbearably cold, and I couldn't swim anymore. I-I'm dead. Abby. Abby! No!"

"Holly." Max reached for me as sobs racked my body.

"No!" I wailed again. "Don't you dare touch me." I pulled myself to the back of the plane and curled into a tight ball. *Abby*, my heart cried. Abby would finish her life without me. I had secretly ensured that if anything were to happen to me that everything I owned would go to her, as well as making sure all my funeral arrangements were paid for. I had chosen to be cremated, not that my body would ever be found. She would always wonder what happened, and I would never get to tell her the truth. Death, it seemed, was not a paradise, but rather a very acute form of torture.

ooooo

"Holly, wake up."

I opened my eyes and quickly pinched them shut again.

"Come on, Holly."

"No. Leave me alone."

"Please. The danger has passed now. It is safe to venture out."

"No," I said, louder when he pulled on my arm. "Leave me alone. I don't want this. I don't want any of it."

"She thinks she's dead."

"Holly, you aren't dead," Jonah said gently. "You have been changed to an ocean dweller for your own safety. When the danger has passed, you will be able to change back. You'll be able to see Abby again, Kitten. I promise."

I glared at him. His brown hair was tied back again but his face was still blurry. Behind him his tail flashed, long and dark. "Don't *ever* call me that again."

His smile dimmed. "Holly, what—"

"And don't you *dare* ask me what's wrong."

I attempted to swim past him but he moved between me and the door. "Max, excuse us a moment, would you, please?" Jonah asked without turning. Max did as he was told, slipping out the door Jonah was guarding. "Holly, I don't know what is going on, but I'd sure like an explanation."

I wanted to punch him then, fury covering my pain. I wanted to ask why, but all that came out was a passive-aggressive, "You figure it out yourself." I tried to dodge him, and again he blocked my way, causing me to smack my head on an overhead compartment. "Ouch!" I shouted at him. "Let me out."

"No. You're going to tell me what this is about."

"I don't have to tell you anything. Oh, except that we are over. *So* very over. I should never have trusted you in the first place. I hate you, Jonah. Is that enough of an explanation?”

The man had the balls to look hurt. “Is this about changing you to a mermaid?”

“You’re responsible for this?” I scoffed. “Then, yep, that, too.”

“Holly! What is going on?” he cried. “I want to help you through all of this. But I can’t if—”

“I don’t want your help!” I shouted. The way my voice traveled through the water, slowing and stopping, was less than satisfying.

“Why not?”

“Because you slept with Layla, you awful, good-for-nothing, backstabbing asshole!” I turned and moved away, back to the hole I had found earlier, pulling myself beneath it, I emerged into open water.

“Holly!” I felt his hands on my fins before I slid away. Moments later, he was out the door and coming behind me. “Holly, what are you talking about? I never slept with Layla.”

“No?” I scoffed. “Huh, interesting. Because finding her in the bed we shared, naked, with a used condom on the floor—so gross, by the way—and you in the shower… looked pretty obvious to me.”

“I didn’t sleep with Layla.”

“Then, explain yourself, Jonah, because I’m apparently missing something.”

“I did *not* sleep with Layla,” he repeated. His voice had gone soft, all the fight leaving him. “I would never sleep with her. I promised—”

"You promised. Yeah. This is what I get for trusting someone I hardly know."

"Jonah," a voice called behind me. "Is this the girl you spoke of?"

I turned to see another fish-man approaching. His face was blurry too, but I could see that his hair was silvery gray and shimmered in the sunlight.

"This is Holly. Holly, this is my father, Master Jonah."

He put a fist over his heart. "Lovely to meet you. Jonah, you're needed in the cave."

"I should really stay—"

"Go. I'll bring Holly back when she's ready."

The healthy option would have been to stay and talk it out with Jonah, but I wasn't in a mood to do that. "Go. I'll be fine." My heart hurt, my head hurt, and my soul felt as though it had been pierced with a knife. Jonah had gone from friend to lover to enemy, and I needed him to step—swim—away until I could clear my head. I did not look back at him as his father put an arm around my waist and turned me away.

"Fish release a hormone when they are frightened," Old Jonah said quietly. "I can sense your panic, Holly. I'd like to help, if I can."

"I'm not a fish."

"You're as close to a fish as you'll ever be."

"Mermaids aren't real. They don't exist."

He spread his free arm wide. "I'd like to argue that point."

"No. This-this isn't real. I am either dreaming, or-or I am dead. And seeing as I fell off a cruise ship—"

"You aren't dead. You aren't dreaming, either. You are living in a reality unlike anything you can possibly comprehend."

"Mermaids aren't real."

"Because we have convinced you they aren't."

"What does that mean?"

He sighed, as though my question pained him. "It means we have convinced you humans that we aren't real to protect ourselves from you. Just like the gods and deities of old, we are thought to be only mythical creatures now. They've allowed that to transpire, simply so they can go on meddling without human knowledge."

"No."

"Yes. Masters at manipulation, the gods are. If they are caught, humans are left denying the experience, pretending it never happened. The higher beings delight in confusing and cajoling with thousands of years of practice. We have learned well from their practices."

"Why have scientists not discovered you all and where you live?"

"We choose remote places to live, and we have ways of camouflaging humans could not begin to fathom." His tone was becoming more and more condescending.

"Why am I here?"

"I'm told it was not a choice. If you had been left much longer, you would have died. Which leads me to my question. How did you come to be out in the middle of the ocean in the first place?"

"I was pushed into the water by a man named Creed."

"Why?"

"How should I know?" This man was as infuriating as his son. "If someone attacks you, do you ask why after they throw the first punch?"

"We don't punch down here."

"You know what I mean."

"Do I?"

I moved away from him. "Look, it was nice to meet you, but I just need a little time by myself. Please, excuse me."

"I'm afraid I can't do that." As I moved away, he grabbed my arm again. "You can't possibly think you know your way around after such a short time. And besides, there are rules."

"Rules?"

"I'll enlighten you, since it seems my son has not," he swam closer, but I moved away. "Stubborn girl. There are only a few rules we follow down here. You are to keep to your home during the evening and dawn hours, as that is when orcas and sharks are most prominent in this area. The midday Gatherings will be a great way to learn the ways of the sea, as well as learning what is expected of you. Your attendance is required."

"I don't plan on staying," I said, swimming past a massive boulder that appeared to be carved in the shape of an octopus. Many of the boulders had been carved into different animals. Over the years, coral had grown to cover them, bringing colorful fish with them. The result was stunning.

"You'll stay as long as we decide."

I stopped short. "Excuse me?"

"It is our duty to keep you safe. Beneath the water is safe. Until we can work out negotiations, you'll stay put."

"How long will that take?"

Jonah shrugged. "Time passes differently down here than it does up there. The ratios are different. One hour on land is about… two or three days down here. Theoretically, you could be down here for about three months and be back on land by the next day."

"Still, I'm not staying down here that long. I need to go back. Home."

"Aren't you in the middle of a trip to the small islands of the west?"

"No. I'm going home. To the mainland."

Jonah's father laughed cruelly. "You're proposing to just… Poof, show up at your home. No one will question how you got there or why?"

"I don't appreciate your sarcasm."

Old Jonah's brows raised. "Not sarcasm—it was a question. How will you explain yourself?"

"I'll figure something out. I don't want to go back on that ship."

"Why not?"

"Because not only did your son royally piss me off, but I also don't want to be pushed overboard by anyone again."

"You are staying here until you are allowed to leave. *If* you're allowed to leave."

"I have a sister at home who needs me."

"Humans are such selfish creatures."

"Excuse me?"

"Selfish," Old Jonah repeated slowly, as though I was stupid. "Selfish, in that they must always be loved and appreciated. They cannot simply exist and serve their purposes. Easily hurt, easily offended, easily influenced by others."

"I'm inclined to agree with you on certain points," I admitted, thinking of how trivial and snippy social media had made us. "But I disagree with the term selfish. Many of us simply pursue happiness. Being a servant, beneath one who doesn't care about feelings, doesn't sound happy to me. It isn't something I want for myself."

"Happiness isn't everything. And besides, what you want doesn't matter down here. We make the rules, not you."

Fury filled my breast as my hands turned to fists. "Who is your superior? I'd like to speak with him."

"Why do you think I am called Master Jonah?" He laughed at me again. "I believe there is a story familiar to you called Jonah and the Whale from your religious teachings. Since then, each first born son of the original Jonah bears his name."

"Your ancestor was swallowed by a whale," I asked skeptically.

"No, but again, that's what you humans were led to believe. The whale was the god of the waters. My ancestor, drowning in the water, bargained with him. Spare his life and he would worship him forever. The god not only agreed, but made him immortal beneath the waves, and gave him the ability to change humans into ocean dwellers, as we call ourselves."

I threw up my arms. "That's even less believable than being swallowed by a whale."

"Good. That means our efforts to distort history are working just fine."

"Why me? What do I have to do with all this?"

"Shouldn't you be grateful that you were saved from drowning?"

"What do I have to do with all this?" I repeated.

"You are part of a much larger game. Dispensable eventually, but necessary to achieve our goals for now."

"Yesterday I knew nothing about this world. Now I'm a pawn in the game? No. I'm not playing. I'm going home."

He moved quickly, preventing me from moving away from him. Gone was the mirth from his face, and his eyes glowed blue. "You will not speak to me so dismissively again. I am the master here."

"You are not my master."

He jabbed a finger in my neck. "So long as you have fins and gills, I am."

I shrank back slightly, for his eyes were terrifying. "You are not my master," I repeated, less firmly.

He grabbed my arms above the elbows, squeezing.

"Holly?" I turned to see Max swimming toward me.

Before I could respond, Old Jonah's lips were at my ear. "I will break you, human, and then I will own you."

Ripping my arms away, I swam toward Max.

Twenty-Three

"I've been looking all over for you," Max said gently. "Where were you?"

A glance over my shoulder told me Old Jonah was still watching. "I'm sorry I yelled at you before. Just get me out of here. Please, Max."

He wrapped an arm around my waist, tucking me into his side so that I could match him kick for kick. My abs began to throb, and I cursed myself for not working out on the cruise ship. The butterfly kick had never been my area of excellence, but swimming laps during the trip certainly would have helped.

"Jesus, Holly, I can feel your heart pounding. What happened?"

"I don't like him."

"Master Jonah? Well, he—"

"He is not my master."

Max sighed. "Things run a bit differently down here, Holly. He makes the rules."

"Then, get me out of here."

"I don't have that authority."

"Who does?"

"Jonah and Master Jonah. They make the rules around here."

Crap on a cracker. Of *course*, it would be those two. The one who disregarded all humans, and the one who betrayed me. "There has to be another way."

"I'm afraid not." Silence passed between us before Max spoke again. "You've gone from complete denial of your current situation to acceptance pretty quickly it would seem."

"Max, in a matter of days, I fell in love, was cheated on by my boyfriend, pushed off a cruise ship, almost died, and became a mermaid. There is no way I'm accepting any of this. What you see is survival mode."

"Right. Anything I can do to help?"

"Explain, Max. I need explanations."

"I-I'm not sure I have all the answers, but I'll do my best to help. Start with the easy questions, if you can."

"Why can't I see clearly?"

He stopped to look down at me. "You can't see?" When I shook my head, he replied, "I wasn't sure. You didn't say anything about it. I thought maybe—well, let's go take care of that. We will go to see Marida. She can help." We changed course, heading deeper into the waters, back toward the massive coral sculptures.

"Who carved those?" I asked.

"Our ancestors." Max chuckled. "Surely you have more in-depth questions than that."

"You said to start with the easy ones. Where are we going?"

"Marida is our local healer. She will probably have something for your eyes to help you see better while you are down here."

"You don't have any problems seeing?"

"I am from the water. My eyes were made to see down here. Adjusting eyes to air is much easier than adjusting to water."

I paused a moment to consider my next question. "So, this is your home. You are half-man, half-fish."

"I am."

"And you can change into a full human… whenever you want?"

"Yes."

"How?"

"It's like putting on or taking off a coat. I don't know how to explain it—when I want to change, I do."

"You're saying you could change to a human right now."

"Yes, I could."

"Do it."

Max laughed. "Do you have a death wish for me? We are in too deep waters for humans to survive, even for a few moments."

"Oh."

"Raincheck. If it will help you understand, I will do it when we are closer to the surface."

"Why am I here? Jonah's father said I was a pawn in a bigger game."

"I'm not privy to all their information, but aren't we all just pawns in a bigger game? The game of life?"

"I'm not ready to talk philosophy."

"Right, sorry."

"Why can't I go home?"

"You've been monitored for a long time, Holly. Something about your past ties you to us. I'm not sure what all the details are, since it was kept very quiet. But something happened that brought you to us."

"I was pushed in the water!"

"By who?"

"Creed. I don't remember his last name." His body stiffened. "You know him too, don't you?"

"I know *a* Creed. It could be a coincidence."

"Jonah knew him too. He avoided talking about it with me. Why?"

"You just aren't safe on land right now."

"Why not?"

"Holly," Max sighed. "I told you—I don't have all the information."

"Who does?"

"Master Jonah."

"Ha! I'm not asking him."

"Here," he said, pulling me down into a deep cave. "Marida, are you here? We need you."

A light filtered through the dark, growing brighter as a shadow enlarged. "What can I do for you, Max?"

"Not me. This is Holly, the human who just arrived with Jonah. She says she can't see."

"Ah yes, the weak human eyes." In the dim light, I could see a mass of dark curls. "You'll need a salve to help with that. I have some in my stores." She moved away and returned a few minutes later. "Come, you have no reason to be afraid."

I suppressed a scream as massive tentacles wrapped around my back, pulling me from Max's side. The light hovered closer, as though she was inspecting my face in the brightness. "Ah, pretty hazel. Hold still and keep your eyes open." I did as I was told, too scared to do anything else, and flinched as her fingers rubbed my pupils, like she was applying contacts. Almost immediately, the fuzzy, blurry vision cleared.

It was still dark, but her concoction made everything lighten somehow. Like I could see in the dark. The cave had light on either end, marking the two entrances, and water had long since carved out the space inside the rock. The floor was sand and pebbles, the walls lined with various items, crammed into niches and on naturally made shelves. The woman named Marida was impossibly long, with blue squid-like tentacles billowing out below and around her. Her hair was dark, more of a shiny navy blue with eyes to match, and her skin was a beautiful pearl color, with features so beautiful she would put any supermodel to shame.

"Welcome," she said with a kind smile, realizing I could finally see her. "Before you return to the human world, come see me. I will need to reverse the effects of the salve."

"Thanks."

"Come," Max said, putting an arm around me once more. "Let's get you back to the plane. Are you hungry?"

My stomach had begun growling earlier, but I needed more information. The ability to see had brought more than visual clarity. It had also brought a sort of calm, as though the sense of sight made me feel like myself again.

"Was Jonah's father telling the truth, that time passes slower here? Is this what Jonah was doing when he said he was working?"

"Yes, and often, yes."

"What about the catering business?"

"For the most part, it runs itself. With the time change, we can do so much more down here in a single land day. Like the day you got to California. He left around seven in the morning and returned, what, around… eight or nine maybe? Fourteen hours on land, give or take. On land. Down here, thirty-some days passed."

"So, you just… don't age?"

"It's complicated. The easiest explanation is that we age to our strongest selves and stay there much longer than humans do."

My head was beginning to ache with the amount of information I was being handed. "I don't understand."

Max patted my shoulder. "It's okay. Small steps, Holly, you'll get there. Open your mind and your heart. See the wonder and the magic here before you go home. You only live once, right?"

"This-this is a lot."

"I know. You're a smart girl, though. You'll get there."

We reached the edge of a sandy cliff, and my jaw dropped open in surprise. Amongst the massive coral reef were several large planes and shipwrecks. Man-made marvels amongst the beauty of nature. Animals of all shapes and sizes moved about like a colorful village. "How have humans not found this place? It looks like a vehicle graveyard," I breathed.

"We have our ways."

"How many, um, ocean dwellers are there?"

"A few thousand, scattered across the waters of the earth in small communities. This one is the largest with almost eight hundred."

A group of ocean dwellers passed as we watched. All men, and all with orca bottom halves. Like Max, I realized belatedly.

"Brother," one said. A few of the others echoed the greeting as they passed, barely glancing at me.

Max nodded back to them, putting a fist to his chest as they had.

"Who are they?" I asked. "Your family?"

"Not biologically, but we are close. This way," he said, crooking a thumb off to his right. I followed him to the edge of the clustered vehicles where a small plane lay on its side. The wings were long since rusted off, and coral grew heavy across where the windows might have been. We entered through the windshield of the cockpit, into the cabin. The seats were all gone, creating one big open space. Sand and patches of blue-green moss made up the floor. This was the place I had been in first.

"This is Jonah's and my place when we are here."

"You're roommates?"

"Yes. Master Jonah doesn't come here."

"Why not?" I asked, though it was not his presence I was concerned about.

Max shrugged. "He just doesn't."

"Where is Jonah—the younger one I mean."

"He said he'd come as soon as he could."

"Fantastic." I pulled myself along the ceiling of the cabin, grateful to give my bottom half a break. "Oh no! How old is this plane?" I asked, when I realized I had been sleeping in the small bathroom compartment earlier.

Max followed my train of thought and laughed. "Old enough. And any germs that were there are gone, thanks to the salty water. With the sand and the soft grass growing there, it works nicely as a bed."

"Does one of you sleep here?"

Max gestured to his massive bottom half, shaking his head. "We don't fit." He gestured to the space at the front of the cabin, with a bed of blue and green grass. "I sleep here. Jonah sleeps in the cockpit."

I looked down at my own body, running my hands over the scales. They began above my belly button, starting in skin tones and slowly darkening to the golden color. They shimmered with silver in the light drifting from the holes of sunlight filtering in from above.

"This wasn't supposed to happen quite like this," Max said quietly. "Jonah wanted to show you this place. With your photography background, he knew you would love this place for the beauty it holds. But… his hand was forced to bring you without giving you a head's up."

"Why did Creed push me?"

"I-I don't know. Creed is… one of us. Well, not really. I should say, he is an ocean dweller, but he does not belong to this village. His village is… at odds with ours."

"Why?"

"Many years ago, when Jonah and I were teens, their village was much larger than ours. They wanted our resources and, one night, they ransacked this place.

The whole coral reef was destroyed, homes destroyed, ocean dweller men murdered, women and children kidnapped. Most of the survivors had either been out hunting or on migration routes for trading supplies and came back to a reef with nothing of value left."

"Why?" I asked again.

Max shrugged. "I think maybe some of the elders know, but there are many secrets. Regardless, it started a war that has been carried on for many years now. As it happens, a plague struck their community hard and significantly diminished their numbers. They are hiding somewhere north and often send their people onto land to hide amongst the humans. Creed pushed you in because… well, he knows something about you that makes you an important piece of the puzzle. Maybe he thought you would drown, or maybe someone from his village was supposed to bring you to their village. Luckily, Jonah was able to get to you first."

At the mention of Jonah, my dark mood returned. "I'm surprised he bothered."

"What does that mean?"

I shrugged. "I'm surprised he didn't just let me drown. Had to continue the torture a while longer, apparently."

Max made the time out sign with his hands. "Back up. The last time I saw you two topside, you were too busy making goo-goo eyes at each other to even notice I left the room."

"Yeah, well, you won't see that anymore. Not from me, anyway." I gave him a summary of what had happened after the scavenger hunt.

"No. No, that's impossible," Max shook his head furiously. "There must be another explanation."

"Like what, Max? I'm all ears." I winced, closing my eyes at my harsh words. "I'm sorry Max. You've done nothing to deserve my anger."

"Holly, Jonah loves you. He told me months ago. And judging by the panic he felt when he got here with you in his arms, I know that hasn't changed."

"He told me he loved me too. Maybe he doesn't know how that whole process works."

"There must be some mistake."

"There isn't."

Max's brows furrowed, his shoulders drooping slightly as his hands clenched and unclenched. "I'm going to talk to him about this."

"Don't bother."

"Not for you, Holly. I want answers. The last few weeks, Jonah has been a different man—happier, more optimistic, stronger than I've ever seen him. On land, he is a colossus, answerable only to himself. Some might see that as awesome, but Jonah was also lonely as hell. Down here, he is subject to his father's wishes, and his actions are scrutinized as badly as any human government official. Unfortunately, his worst critic after himself is his father. He is Jonah, the next master of our community, and he has to act accordingly. The only time I saw Jonah happy, truly happy, was when he was talking about you, and Abby, and Cecille's café. There has to be another explanation for this, Holly. I'm sure of it." He sighed, dropping the conversation when he realized I wasn't going to budge. "Come on, I'll show you where the food is."

I followed him out of the plane and around to the side. Various species of seaweed were growing in large quantities with countless schools of fish flitting around it and us. I watched as Max gathered several items and rolled them up before handing them to me. Black on the outside, then green, then blue, then red, with something white and squishy in the center. I looked between him and the roll.

Max laughed. "It's like a… a deep-sea veggie wrap."

"What is that?" I asked, pointing to the white thing.

"Tuber." He reached down, pulled another out of the bed, and took a bite.

My stomach quailed at the word. "I'll admit I'm hungry, but I-I can't eat that."

"Aw, come on, Holly. It tastes like… like a… a water chestnut."

"It's still moving!"

He laughed, wiggling his at me before he took another bite. "And here I thought you would be grossed out by the seaweed first."

"Oh, I definitely wasn't done pointing out the things in your hand that I won't eat," I told him, putting my hands on my hips and glaring at the preposterous snack.

"Try it. I think you'll like it."

"No wonder Jonah went to culinary school," I grumbled, still not taking the wrap from his outstretched hand.

"Come on, Holly. It isn't bad, I promise. It's this or caviar," he said with a shrug.

Swallowing hard, I took the roll, carefully removing the squirming tuber and handing it to Max before rolling the weeds back up. "It's lettuce. Lettuce. Just a little lettuce," I muttered to myself, closing my eyes and taking a bite. The texture was more brittle than lettuce, and saltier, though the saltwater didn't seem to affect it. One of the layers had almost a soy sauce taste to it. If the tubers did taste like water chestnuts, it would be a sort of stir fry-like combination.

"Not so bad, huh?" Max said smugly, nudging my shoulder.

"I'm not giving you the satisfaction of answering that. I'm hungry."

"It's mind over matter, that's all. Note: we also eat raw fish, scales and all, like a granola bar. Just a head's up."

"Hard pass."

Max started laughing as a series of low water-thickened horn blasts sounded in the distance. "Come on. We are needed at the reef. It's a daily requirement that all dwellers are present and accounted for. A daily census, if you will, to ensure that everyone is safe. Only a few exceptions are made."

I followed him down into the reef, as animals of all kinds joined in the journey. Not animals—ocean dwellers. Half human, half sea creature. Small, large, thin, fat, young, old, and every color and pattern I could think of. I tried not to stare but failed epically. In the process, I lost Max in the crowd.

"Crap," I muttered, trying to see around fins and tails. I slowed, swimming further up for an aerial view. I saw no orca tails. No Max. No Jonah. The crowd was thinning, disappearing into a large cave, the entrance nearly hidden by overgrown coral. Only a few people would fit in the opening at one time, and the outward appearances suggested that many creatures could not possibly fit in the interior.

I could follow.

I probably should follow.

Or I could use the opportunity to explore on my own.

"You look lost."

Twenty-Four

I turned to find an older man approaching slowly. His face was impossibly wrinkled, his hair long and gray, and eyes the color of the water around him. Despite his age, his body was as strong and lithe as Jonah and Max. His bottom half spread out into a stingray, easily seven feet from one side to the other and a long flat tail complete with a spiny barb at the end.

"If I had to guess, I would say you were the new young woman from the world above."

A blush crept up my face. "Is it that obvious?"

"There are a few clues, yes. For one, you're wearing clothing that was not made down here. There are no fish quite the color you are, which means you are not from the reef. And also, no one down here can blush like that."

"Oh."

"What is your name?"

"Holly."

The man's smile was wide. "My name is Alfred. I am the reef's keeper."

"Keeper?"

"You'll notice, eventually, that the homes in the area have very little inside them. No personal items. I am the keeper of things. Anything to be kept safe, I'm the one for the job."

"Why don't people keep things in their homes?"

"Come. Let us swim and talk. I have a feeling our elders would not want you to be left on your own."

"It wasn't intentional. I lost Max on the way into the…" I tried to come up with the name before throwing my thumb over my shoulder to the cave. "Whatever they were doing."

"We call them Gatherings. Daily meetings to discuss issues, take attendance, and plan for the next day."

"Jonah, the older one, told me I should be attending them to learn more about your… culture. And rules."

"That would be a good place to start, yes, but I think you'll be excused. Only a few of us know about your arrival. Not everyone will take the news well."

"Why not?" I followed him back down to the reef, away from the Gathering point, into a separate valley, and under an overhang of red and pink curly coral. "Ouch!" I cried. Behind me, my fins had brushed against the edge of the coral. Chipping, it lodged in my back. The burning sensation was intense, as though I had rubbed my butt across a burning nettle.

"Ah, yes. Another defensive strategy." He reached past me and pulled the coral out, tossing it away. Blood drifted out, seeping upward before disappearing into the rock. "That will leave a mark, unfortunately. Sorry, I forgot to mention it."

Reaching back, I rubbed at the open wound before following him into the grotto, biting back an irritated response. Light filtered in, showing walls of various items and trinkets. Some were human, and some were pieces unlike anything I had ever seen before creating a huge, diverse collection. It was a scene straight out of *The Little Mermaid*, except it was a bit dimmer.

Alfred led me to the left side of the cave. "That… whatever it is you're wearing, is going to become a hindrance, if it hasn't already. Most of our women live without any covering, but I am told your kind lives more modestly."

I blushed again, remembering the number of boobs I had seen on the way to the Gathering. "Yeah, I'm not going to be going anywhere topless. I do not have a body to show off."

"Every woman has a body to be proud of. The female body creates life, whether it is eggs or live birth. Men cannot."

"Yeah, well, the women down here haven't met the wonders that are ice cream and Fruity Pebbles," I muttered.

"I'm not sure what that means."

"Never mind."

"Regardless," he said gently. "You *are* a beautiful woman and have nothing to be ashamed of when it comes to your body. But if you insist on covering yourself, let's see if we can find something more suitable for you to wear down here." He pulled down a large turtle shell full of seashells that varied in size.

"Oh no," I replied laughing, when he held it out for my inspection. "There is no way I'm wearing any of those."

"Why not?"

I lifted a white oval shell out of the group. "How would I even keep these in place?"

"We have many different kinds of seaweeds down here. Some we eat, others we use. There is a clear thin weed we use for tying things. With a hole in the sides, it is very simple really."

I shook my head. "I could not wear this. Not in a million years."

"You can't continue to wear that either," he said, nodding to my dress. "If you need to move quickly, this large bundle will hinder your movements."

"I'll figure it out."

Alfred considered the knot at my thigh for a moment before holding up a finger. "Might I offer another suggestion?" At my nod, he retrieved a knife-shaped coral and untied the knot.

"What are you doing?"

"Cutting this. There is a lot of material here. If you cut it, say, here, you would have enough to cover your upper half, plus you would have enough for another covering or to make a pouch."

"What about when I return home? I would be naked from the waist down."

"When you don't even know when you'll be returning? What are your priorities? Survival should be at the top of that list." When I didn't respond, he slashed at the skirt, easily removing it from the bodice.

He held it while I gathered and tied what remained near my hip, so that the fabric would not float upward. "Thanks," I said, taking it from him.

"You'll need a few other items to get by down here." He moved about the cave easily, bringing me a small piece of the same coral he had used for cutting and a large over-the-shoulder pouch made of soft moss.

"Thank you." I added the skirt fabric and donned the bag, thinking about Max's history lesson. "Do you keep things—I mean, is it because of what the other tribe did when they attacked?"

Alfred's eyes lit with anger, and his tone was harsh. "Those villainous cowardly scum. They ransacked the place, taking countless items, priceless pieces that we held dear. That was a dark day for us. Very dark. Everything was gone." To my surprise, he sniffed, covering his face with his hand. "What you need to know down here, Holly, is that the wound they dealt us is still deep. It festers amongst those of us who saw it happen. We live with the guilt of not being here when our families needed us most. I lost my entire family that day—my wife and my daughter. The men had gone for a routine hunt and returned to devastation and death."

The pain in his voice was unbearable. "I'm so sorry, Alfred," I said softly. "I understand the loss of family. I also bear those scars."

"Mine is not the only story of loss. We mate for life down here, Holly. I'm told your kind are more… flexible."

"Some are, not all. A lot of us mate—or plan to— for life as well."

His eyes were ice. "We are not flexible. We mate for life. When our mate dies, we feel death too. And yet, we have to wait for death to find us, so that we might be reunited in the afterlife."

I thought of Jonah and wondered if maybe he was mistaken. If he was a creature of the water, maybe he already had a mate. Or maybe he was taking advantage of the relaxed human rules of monogamy. When that thought came, I dismissed it. Surely, he wasn't *that* awful. And yet, I could not get the sight of that used condom out of my head.

"Why have they brought you here, Holly?" Alfred asked after regaining his composure.

"I don't know. No one will tell me. They only say that I have something to do with this quarrel between your community and the other."

"What can Jonah possibly be thinking? If they found you on land, it could mean that you are one of them. If you are, that will not bode well for anyone," Alfred seemed to be talking more to himself than to me, but I listened in, hoping for any theories. "If you are one of them, hidden amongst the human population for self-preservation, can the elders hold you ransom?"

"I'm not. I would know, wouldn't I? If I was a mermaid—I mean, ocean dweller?"

Alfred shrugged. "Maybe, maybe not. It depends on how they approached it. It could be that your mother or father was an ocean dweller."

"Max said the attack happened during his lifetime, that he was a teenager. We are similar in age, and by that time, my family was all dead except a sister."

"Time passes differently here. How old are you, Holly?"

"Twenty-six."

He considered this a moment. "Down here, you would be considered much, much older."

"I don't understand."

"I don't expect you to, but know that this feud began in your lifetime."

"I am not an ocean dweller."

Alfred shrugged. "Jonah and Master Jonah had a reason for bringing you here. What was it?"

"I don't know. I was hoping someone could answer that question and a few others."

"I hope you find out soon."

"If I do, I'll do what I can to find out what happened to your family."

Alfred shook his head sadly. "I've accepted their fate."

My heart ached for his loss. In the silence that followed, he began moving about the cavern, straightening and organizing shelves. I floated past him, feeling as though I was inside a vault, admiring shells of all shapes and sizes, knowing they held these people's treasures. I wanted to peek inside a few, just to better understand the people here but I resisted the urge, knowing how much I appreciated my own privacy.

There was a small opening, nearly concealed with black coral, where the sand met the rock. A flash of light that caught my eye. I swam down to look. Light streamed in from the other side of the rock. I reached out to touch the coral, quickly. When nothing happened, I touched it again, a bit longer.

"I would advise you not to go in there," Alfred said, as he passed. "That is where we keep prisoners. It is empty currently, but it is not a part of our life I would recommend seeing on the first day."

My brows rose. "You guard people's things this close to your prison?"

"I am the keeper. I keep the good and the bad."

"If anyone escaped, wouldn't they be able to grab a few things on their way out?"

"If they got past the barriers on the inside, which is unlikely. Follow me, I have a few things I think you'd enjoy." We moved to the back of the cave, through a second and then third rock arch. "Over the years, dwellers have been bringing me things from above. We do not have many humans passing through here, so I don't know what they all are. Jonah and Max are among the few who go between land and sea, but they are often too busy to explain. Our paths rarely cross. I'd love to use your knowledge, if you're willing."

"Sure."

In the blink of an eye, the old man became an excited child. "Excellent. Maybe you can help me find a use for some of these things."

My stomach churned uncomfortably when I saw the stash of items he had in the next space. I knew humans had been awful to Earth's oceans, but seeing the stacks of items in the cave just solidified it. Some of the things were grouped together—plastic bottles, glass, piles of fishing lines. There were piles of other things too, odds and ends like sunglasses, phones, shoes, and jewelry.

"Like this. What is this?"

I burst out laughing. Of all things… "That's a toothbrush, Alfred. We use them to keep our teeth clean. Oh, no! Don't!" I cried, grabbing his arm as he lifted it to his face. "You don't know where that has been. Don't put it in your mouth."

He studied it a moment before setting it aside. "These have been particularly useful to me, to remove scales from fish. Especially when they have the little pick on the end."

"You don't have that here? Something to clean your teeth I mean?"

He shook his head. "Saltwater keeps them healthy." He dug another item out of the pile. "And this. Tell me, how do you use this?"

I took the browning volleyball from him. It was filled with water so had kept its shape throughout its underwater adventure. "See if I can do this," I muttered. It wasn't easy, but I managed to serve the ball, sending it across the open space. Despite its weight, it moved fairly quickly, hitting the wall with a thump. "It's a volleyball. A game we play on land."

"For children?"

"For anyone who wants a little exercise."

Alfred stared at me, confused. "I understand the word but not the meaning of your phrase. Why?"

I rummaged through the items, finding a soccer ball. Pushing it back and forth from one hand to the other, I tried to explain. "Walking on land requires much less energy than swimming. Over the years, our food has also taken a negative turn as well. Food people create, rather than hunting and gathering. As a result, many people have gained weight. We need to exercise more to combat that. Sports, swimming, yoga, Pilates… anything to get us up and moving around. Each of these round objects—that white one, this one, that orange one over there... Oh, and that brown, odd-shaped one. Those are the balls we use for the sports we play. Each one has its own set of rules."

"No," Alfred breathed excitedly.

"Yes!" I giggled. "Like this one, for example. Soccer. The ball stays on the ground and is kicked. You are not allowed to use your hands." I dropped it near my tail to kick it away from him, squealing when I realized someone was in the entryway, exactly where I had kicked the ball. Hands came up, catching the ball before it could cause any damage. "I'm so sorry!" I cried, starting to swim for the entrance.

Jonah glided into the light, tossing the ball back to me with a grin. "Nice shot," he said.

Holy crap. A whale shark, I realized. When I could not see, I thought his tail was dark gray. It was actually midnight blue, almost black, and covered in white spots. Paired with his dark tattoos, the white of the spots became almost iridescent. He breezed through the water like he was made for it. *He was made for it*, I reminded myself.

"Ah, Jonah. Welcome. I was just asking Holly about some of the items from the land folk."

"I'm afraid your questions will have to wait."

"Of course," he said, excusing himself with a nod and a friendly smile.

"Holly, we have some things to discuss."

Crossing my arms, I lifted my eyebrows, shaking my head. "No…" I said thoughtfully. "Nope, I think we are done talking."

"Maybe you were, but I'm not."

I turned away from him, rummaging through the piles of items, looking for something, anything to put between myself and Jonah.

"Holly."

"Leave me alone, Jonah. I'll stay here. Just come back when you can bring me back to land."

"Holly."

I continued as though he had not spoken. "I'll just help Alfred clean up this stuff, sort through the useful and non-useful things."

"Holly!" His voice echoed off the walls around us. It was odd, hearing an echo underwater. It traveled slower. Not only that but I didn't think I had ever heard him yell before. "Will you please listen to me?"

"There isn't anything you can say to me that I don't already know!" I shouted back.

"Besides the fact that I didn't sleep with Layla? Because I didn't."

I wanted to believe him. I wanted to believe him so badly. "Prove it, then."

Jonah faltered. "What?"

"Prove it. Prove to me you didn't sleep with Layla."

"How?"

I threw my arms up in frustration. "I don't know, Jonah! All I know is that one minute you're telling me you love me and the next moment there's a naked woman in your bed!"

"I was in the shower. I didn't even know she was in there."

"How did she get there, then?"

"I don't *know*, Holly! One of the scavenger hunt items was to find something barbecued. I let Isaac into the kitchen where we made dinner and for the photo, since it was our last one, he dumped a bottle of barbeque sauce on my head because Isaac wanted me to pose so we could call it 'hot sauce,'" he grinned, but it faded when he saw my scowl. "I showered while I was waiting for you. When I came out, Layla was just getting her shoes on and said you had come and gone. She said she didn't know how she had gotten in our room. As soon as I was dressed, I went after you. I went to your booked room, and every bar and club in the place. When the sun started to come up, I went back to Layla. She was not feeling well. She thought someone might have drugged her and she started to worry that you had jumped to conclusions. On my way back to the room, I overheard a security guard talking with Creed. Asking whether he had seen anyone jump over the side the night before. He declined to comment until... Well, until I intervened. When he told me it was you, I jumped ship and came for you as quickly as I could." He moved toward me, stopping when I moved back. "I almost didn't make it in time."

"How did Layla get into our room?"

"I don't know. Someone must have had the key. All clues point to Creed, but I don't have proof. Yet. But I will find out the truth. I promise."

"Your promises mean little," I said in a small voice. I saw the pain my words caused, but I steeled my heart. "You promised you wouldn't hurt me. You promised you trusted me. You promised to tell me the truth."

"I have."

"Why not tell me about all this? About your home?" I asked, spreading my arms out. "I told you I could cope with changes if I had a head's up."

Jonah's anger seeped through the calm exterior. "Would you have believed me? 'Hey Holly, I'm a merman, just so you know. Oh, and Max and Isaac are too.'"

"No," I admitted. "I wouldn't have believed you. But at least, floating out in the ocean, all alone and freezing, I would have at least had some hope to hold onto. Do you know what that's like—facing death with no hope of salvation?" A sob escaped as I covered my face with my hands.

"Holly, please let me help."

I shook my head vigorously. When I felt his hand on my shoulder, I shrank from it.

"Holly, I love you," he said softly. "I love you like I have never loved another being. When ocean dwellers find their mate, it hits them, w-with a wave. It isn't just physical, it's emotional. A wave of love, to pride, to protectiveness, to elation. When I met you, I couldn't stop thinking about you. My life revolves around making you happy. Your smile kept my heart beating, your laugh kept my soul alive. It-it's something so foreign to me, to be entirely dependent upon someone else for my own well-being. Finding a mate has become the stuff of fairytales and legends amongst humans, but it's not fiction here. When we find a mate, it is like… like a lightning storm inside our bodies, and it's for keeps. It is my job—my life's work—to keep you. To keep you happy, safe, and loved. You want me to go away, but I-I can't. I can't leave you like this. I need to make it better. Tell me how I can make it better."

I made myself very small when he tried to touch me again, his words only serving as salt on my wounds. I wanted to yell and scream at him, to tell him how much pain I was feeling. I wanted to tell him that he would never understand and that he should go screw himself. After years of fights with Abby, however, I had learned that some things were just better left unsaid when one was furious or hurting. A raging fire needed no kindling.

"Holly, please talk to me. Tell me what you need."

I could hear the pain in his voice, and I grudgingly gave him credit for staying and not giving up. Not many guys would have done that. "I need time. I want you to leave me alone so that I can try to understand this—all of this."

"Ask me. I will answer any questions you have," he urged.

"No. I don't want you. I don't want you to be here. I don't want you to talk to me. I don't want you to touch me."

"Holly, please."

"No. You claim to know me so well, then you know I need time."

"Jonah?" there was a voice behind Jonah. I didn't look up.

"Leave us," Jonah snapped.

"Forgive me. Master Jonah requests your presence."

"Leave us!" Jonah shouted.

"Just go," I hiccupped. "I need to be alone."

"Holly, look at me." When I didn't move, Jonah pulled my hands from my face, lifting my chin. His eyes were vividly green, brows furrowed, jaw clenched. "I need you to hear me. I am sorry. More sorry than you'll ever understand. This whole situation… this wasn't supposed to happen. I wanted to tell you about this life on my own terms. I wanted it to be fun, easy, a-and this isn't. This is going to be messy and dramatic, even without whatever you think happened with Layla. There isn't much I can do anymore except to make sure life is as easy as possible for you while you are here. If you want to be mad, I-I've more than earned that, keeping this secret from you, but I'm worried about what the next few days will bring. We need to be a team to get through this. Knowing you're down here, and that I can't keep watch over you all the time, keep you safe…" he groaned, putting his forehead to mine while he gathered his thoughts. "This is going to test me in ways beyond your comprehension. Please, if you must be mad, promise me one thing. I'm in no position to ask for anything, but I must. Please, stay safe. Alfred and Max are safe. Isaac is safe. If they ask you to do something, please do it. If you won't do it for me, do it for Abby. Promise me you'll be careful, for Abby's sake."

I removed his hands. "Sure, bring Abby into it," I snapped. "You know my weakness and use it against me."

"Not against you, for you. Promise me, Holly."

"I owe you no promises."

His shoulders sagged. "No. No, you don't."

"Go, Jonah."

He left reluctantly, glancing back at me once more before he disappeared. When he was gone, I hugged myself, letting out the shudder I had been holding back. I wanted to believe him, truly. I wanted to believe Layla had not betrayed me either—that someone had set Jonah up. I wanted to believe everything. And yet, his actions held the destruction of everything I had allowed myself to believe.

I was not whole after all.

I would not be whole again.

Not for a *very* long time.

Twenty-Five

"Holly?"

I looked up to find Alfred hovering anxiously in the entrance to the cave.

"I-I couldn't help overhear your conversation with Jonah. I won't pry beyond saying I have never seen Jonah so upset, and I have known him his whole life. I wanted to give you your space, but it is getting late. Are you hungry? Can I get you anything? Oh, what are you doing here?"

I looked down at my work. I had been organizing the piles of garbage into things Alfred could use and things that were trash. It served a dual purpose—to take my mind off of my pain, as well as feed the monster inside me that was my creativity. Not only that, but it soothed my guilt as a human who never thought about where garbage went when it left my house in the garbage truck. Having made the decision not to return to Jonah and Max's home, I hoped Alfred would let me stay with him. "I hope you don't mind. I kept myself busy."

"I see that," he chuckled. "And no, I don't mind at all."

"Jonah said you were a person to be trusted. While I am in severe disagreements with Jonah right now, I will trust his judgement on this because I have no other choice." Taking a deep breath, fighting to keep the tears at bay, I continued. "I was wondering if I could stay here for a while."

Alfred considered my request before shrugging. "I don't see any harm in it. I stay here alone, and unless there are prisoners, there is no danger here for you. If we do take prisoners, though, we will have to reconvene."

Bubbles rushed from my lips as I sighed. "That's more than fair. Thank you, Alfred."

"Our lives, I'm told, are much simpler than yours. Our needs are few—food, shelter, community. Perhaps you could learn a few things from us, just as we could learn from you." He sighed, giving me a sad smile. "I need to find some food, and I need to visit Marida if you'd like to come with me."

I wanted to say no, but my stomach was growling. At my nod, I followed him out of the cave. My body ached and made me clumsy as again, I brushed against the pink coral. Swallowing my angry words, I brushed the coral away quickly before hurrying after Alfred. I envied his gracefulness. He glided with the ease of a stingray, barely needing his arms to maneuver. Behind him, I was huffing and puffing along, breathless by the time we got to the edge of the reef.

The sun had set while I worked in the cave. I had severely underestimated the number of bioluminescent creatures in the reef. It was like a firefly gathering on steroids, almost easy to forget the time of day. My mind raced with photography ideas, devastated that I did not have an underwater camera to capture the magnificence.

Marida lived, I remembered, off the reef near the large octopus sculpture. I would need to memorize the statues to figure out where everything was, as there were no other distinguishable markers. Alfred lived near the shark sculpture, and Jonah and Max's plane hull was near the sculpture of a family of turtles.

"Marida?" Alfred called, gliding smoothly through the opening in the rocks.

"What can I do for you, Alfred?" Marida asked. I stared in surprise. In the daytime, she was beautiful. In the dark, her hair and tentacles glowed with thousands of tiny, twinkly blue lights. She was gorgeous.

Alfred listed off his needs, and Marida gathered everything. It sounded as though they were speaking in a different language. Different types of coral, weeds, and a few bones were all I caught. It was hard to look away from the beautiful woman, as she lit the space like neon under a dark light.

"Thank you," Alfred said when she gave him everything.

Marida turned her eyes to me. They glowed blue—not scary like Old Jonah's, but a calm, soft glow, like the rest of her body. A tentacle lifted my chin, so she could study my face. "You are in pain."

I blushed fiercely, shrugging. "I'm okay."

Her head tilted, studying more. "Your… side? Stomach?"

"I'm good."

"We would rather have you all well rather than limping along. Down here, that does not help your survival. What hurts?"

"I'm okay. I just—my stomach muscles hurt a bit. I swim regularly, but not all day long. I'm sore, that's all."

"You're also hungry."

I barked a laugh. "Deep sea cuisine is taking a bit of getting used to."

"Here," she said, breezing away and returning to put a small jar in my hand. "These will help with the muscle pain. Consume one each morning when you rise. And you must eat."

"I'll do what I can."

"Perhaps tomorrow you can get some of the sweet coral we grow not far from the reef."

Max had mentioned something like that. "Anything is better than caviar or tubers," I replied, shuddering.

Marida was not done assessing me. "There is more pain. In your heart," she said softly. "Unfortunately, I cannot help it—that's for you to fix."

Was she talking about Jonah? "Yeah, well," I sighed. "That ship has sailed."

"Your heart suggests it hasn't."

I shrugged. "Thank you," I said, holding up the jar. "I appreciate it. If there's anything I can do to return the favor, I'm happy to help." Quietly, I followed Alfred back out into the night. There were a few other ocean dwellers passing through, nodding or putting a fist to their chest as Alfred passed. Alfred returned their greetings. They then turned to me, with mostly curiosity. Some raised a fist to their chest, but most others looked away quickly.

"Why do you do that?" I asked Alfred quietly when he thumped his hand to his chest again. "What does it mean?"

"There is an old saying. Not many use it anymore. United by our hearts, we are one school. It means that very few of us here can survive without the help of others. Together, we are stronger than any power the ocean yields. It is a message as much of love as solidarity, unification, and strength."

We made our way back across the reef as the world glowed around us. A squeal of delight floated across the reef, and we both turned to find two ocean dwellers swirling together, shooting toward the surface. There were whoops and cheers from the reef where a small group had gathered. The two spun and danced through the water with such grace. It was like watching a dance in slow motion, slowly moving faster and faster until—

I gasped as they breached the surface, disappearing before reentering the water in a burst of bubbles. Twice more they did it before returning to the crowd. The joy surrounding them filled my heart.

"What was that?" I asked.

"The mating ritual," Alfred said, his face mirroring the happiness I was feeling. "Looks like Tamar and Alana finally worked up the courage. It's been a long time coming."

My face heated. "So, they just… mate… in front of everyone?"

Alfred's laugh was hearty. "No. That is to be done privately. The ritual is an announcement to the rest of us, telling everyone they are no longer single units. Tamar and Alana are mated now, for life."

"It was like a marriage ceremony."

"I don't know what that is."

"Sorry," I said quickly, looking back at the group. "I think we have something like that on land, if I understood you correctly. That was beautiful."

"It is. So short, but those moments stay with you for the rest of your life."

Black with white dots drew my attention. Jonah was there with his father, not far from the group. Neither father nor son was looking at the happy couple, though. Both were staring at me. I looked at Jonah, wondering. Did he plan to do that with his mate? Had he already? Would he have wanted to do that ceremony with me, if we had stayed together for the long haul?

I broke the connection first, turning away. It was going to be incredibly difficult to get over someone who didn't want to end things. And someone I was, for the time being, completely dependent upon for survival.

Twenty-Six

The next morning, I awoke with a start, holding my breath and swimming toward the ceiling of the cave. It was disorienting and took a long time to calm my breathing. I was also very sore. Digging through my bag, I found the little jar Marida had given me the night before and took out one of the tiny pink jelly-like lozenges.

"Please don't be a jellyfish, please don't be a jellyfish," I muttered, as I brought it to my lips. With a deep breath, I popped it in, chewing and swallowing quickly. Not a fishy taste, I realized thankfully, but extremely sour. I sat for a moment, braiding my wild hair and tying it with a hair tie I had found the day before in the pile of human leftovers. Curls were already escaping by the time I finished, but I hoped it would at least keep most of my hair out of the way. Pushing off of the floor, I was surprised that most of the aches dissolved. Hunger, however, was a major issue.

Alfred was not in the next chamber or the next, so I ventured to the cave opening, considering my choices. Old Jonah had said certain times of the day were not safe to be out. However, with Alfred gone, I reasoned if he could leave, it was probably okay for me to do so as well. I stuck my head out of the hole, careful to keep the rest of my body pinned to the ground to avoid the pink coral. Resting my chin on my arms, I watched in wonder.

The morning was beautifully bright. Animals meandered past, alone or in small groups. I watched as the little Nemos and Dorys passed by, searching for their families, and an army of starfish vacuumed the sea floor like little scullery maids. Small sharks passed by leisurely. Nurse sharks and reef sharks, Alfred had told me the night before. Harmless to ocean dwellers and humans. It was still surreal and intimidating to be so close to them, having heard so many horror stories about the massive creatures. Light shimmered from the sky above, making fins and scales sparkle, and creating more glitz and glamour than a 'Miss America' contest. A group of sea turtles drew my attention, floating lazily above me, and I grinned, thinking of the laid-back, hippie personalities humans had given them in the entertainment business. It was easy to see how they had come to that conclusion.

"Holly?" I jumped with a squeal and then yelped in pain as the pink coral lodged in my back. A hand pulled me from the entrance of the cave, quickly brushing off the coral. "Sorry," Jonah said softly. "I didn't mean to startle you."

I removed myself from his grasp, reaching back to rub the sore spot, unable to meet his gaze.

"What were you doing down there?"

"Just watching. I-I didn't know if it was safe to come out. Your dad said no morning or evening, but I have no idea what that means when I can't tell time down here."

He hesitated before holding out his hand. "Can I show you? I can teach you."

I hated needing to rely on this man, still so angry and hurt about Layla and all the secrets he hadn't told me. And yet despite everything, I still loved him. This fact was only amplified by the sizzles that shot through my body when I put my hand in his and watched as his fingers gently turned it over.

With his free hand, he pulled two small rocks from the pouch at his waist. They looked like tiny marbles, with beautiful intricate blue and green designs inside the translucent outer shell. "These are called Time Stones," he said, putting one in the center of my palm. "You need to hold one up so it can catch the sunlight first." I gawked as he did what he said. After a moment, the stone lit, as though it had sucked the sunlight into itself, glowing bright green. "Keep your hand stretched out, make it as large as you can," he said. "You have to drop it so that it hits the other one."

"Will it hurt?"

"No," he chuckled. "When you drop it from… about chin height, it will bounce off and tell you the hour, similar to a sundial." He did as he said, and the rock bounced to lay near my thumb. "Your middle finger is twelve o'clock. Your wrist is six. We stay out of the open reef between six and eight, morning and night. As you can see, it is around eleven."

"That's… amazing." Jonah released my hands so I could examine the little stones. They were so smooth, and the one still glowing was slightly warmer than the other.

"Keep them," he said when I began to hand them back.

"Thank you."

An awkward silence passed between us. I looked up at him, watching him struggle for something to say. It was excruciating. "You should probably go. I wouldn't want you to keep your dad waiting."

His eyes darkened. "Holly, I need you to know... my father and I, we don't see eye to eye on everything that happens down here. We have agreed on less and less over the last few years. I need you to know that."

"Does that include me too? One of you wants me down here, and one of you doesn't?"

He flinched. "There was... always a plan that you would come here, eventually, but neither of us were prepared for it to happen so soon."

"Why? Why me? What do I have to do with all this?"

"I-I can't tell you that."

"Why not?"

"I can't tell you that, either."

That anger returned, rolling into my chest with the current around me. "What *can* you tell me?"

"To be careful. Please, be careful, Holly."

"Be careful of what?"

He reached out to run a hand up my arm, dropping it when I brushed it off. "Everything," he said with a sigh. "Be careful of everything and everyone. Isaac, Max, and Alfred. They are the only ones you can trust."

"What about Marida?"

He shook his head. "Marida is a loose cannon. She does what she wants, when she wants, and helps others when it benefits her."

"So, I… shouldn't take the medicine she gave me? Because it helped."

Jonah's brows furrowed. "Why did you need medicine? What's wrong?"

"Nothing—I am just sore."

"From what?"

"Swimming."

"What did she give you?"

"Jonah!" Max called behind us, floating in with Isaac and a group of other orca-backed men. "Hey, Holly! Jonah, your father requests a private meeting with you before the Gathering. I thought maybe Holly would want to join us on patrol to see the reef."

"That isn't a good idea."

"Aw, come on, Jonah," Isaac said, winking at me. "There aren't any predators out today, and Holly should learn from the best how to defend herself out here."

The idea of having to defend myself was terrifying. On the flip side, it meant I would not need to depend so heavily on others to survive. "What do I need to bring?" I asked before Jonah could argue.

"Just your pretty little self," Max crowed.

"Holly, please be careful," Jonah said quietly.

"You told me to trust them," I said with a shrug. When Jonah failed to respond, I swam away from him out to the group of men. We swam in school fashion, myself in the middle and the others around me. The current their powerful bodies created drew me along with them, so that I hardly needed to propel myself. I felt protected and quite safe, and the grin that spread across my face was impossible to withhold.

"What's so funny?" Max asked, catching my glee.

"This is the closest thing I've experienced to swimming with dolphins."

Several of the ocean dwellers around me roared. "Whoa!"

"Hey!"

"Dolphins, seriously?"

Max hushed the group. "Humans don't swim with orcas," he told the guys around him. "She meant no disrespect."

My face blazed. "Oh, no! I didn't mean it like that. I always wanted to swim with dolphins. Never had the opportunity. I only meant—"

"Dolphins are pests!" said the guy above me.

"What he means is, dolphins are like… new puppies. Always up in your face, needing to know what's going on, pestering incessantly."

"I'm sorry," I said again. "I didn't mean anything—"

Isaac was still laughing. "We got you, Holly. You're good."

Between orcas and dolphins, humans had been taught to believe that dolphins were the friendlier species. And yet, the orca men around me had forgotten my transgressions by the time we were out of the reef, laughing and teasing each other like a band of brothers. Soon, all that stretched out in front of me was sand, as far as I could see, with random spikes of sticks and rock protruding from the ground.

It wasn't California, I realized. It was the ocean that knew how to grow her men. All built like gods, with long hair and chiseled features. To be a woman down here was to enjoy never-ending eye candy. Trying to imagine what Cecille would say to this crowd kept a smile on my face.

"Alright, Holly. Since we don't know how long you'll be down here, we want to make sure you can protect yourself, whether it is from another ocean dweller, or a predator, or whatever," Max spoke while the others began pulling out coral spikes out of the sand. "First things first, you know that the water is not like the air. You can't just throw a punch—it won't be effective. We have found that swinging your weapon is most effective. If you don't have a weapon, use your resources."

"For example, your lower half is a stonefish. Heard of them?" Max asked. When I shook my head, he grinned. "Your kind are poisonous."

"They are—I am?" I said, trying to look at my back.

"Yes," he said, gesturing to the pointy spikes along the fin that ran down my back to where my knees had been. "This is where the poison comes out. Before you ask, I have no idea how to do it—I wasn't blessed with the gift. All I know is that when you are angry or scared or injured, we all need to get out of your way."

"Well, that's cool, but how—I mean… Why are they on my back?"

"To protect your organs. If you are swimming and presenting your front to an opponent, they could easily attack your core. And you really wouldn't be able to protect yourself."

"What do you suggest?"

We spent the remainder of our time debating, before deciding that somersaults were the best option. Not unlike flip-turns in competitive swimming, I learned to execute them quickly, while still protecting myself. As the horns for the Gathering sounded, we traveled back to the reef, setting up a practice schedule to span the next few days. Upon returning to the reef, some of the emotional weight of the last few days lifted, and I basked in the new confidence in my own body. Being unique amongst the ocean dwellers had its perks, and being proud of my body felt empowering.

The orca dweller named Bo had given me a seafood sushi roll, similar to Max. They had all laughed as I handed the tuber back to him before eating the rest.

"You'll need a little more protein in your diet, if you want to build up your muscle, Holly," Max told me.

I made a face. "You're telling me I need to eat these raw, slimy, gross, *still alive* things, just to beef up?"

"What is 'beef up'?" Bo asked. All morning he had been very interested in my mannerisms. Isaac flexed and pointed to his bulging bicep. "Ah, yes," Bo nodded, "you need to eat those. Packed with nutrients."

"Hard pass."

"What is 'hard pass'?" Bo asked again.

"Means a resounding no," I responded before turning to Max. "Side note, how do they all speak English? Have they all been on land at one point in time to learn?"

Max shook his head. "We are not speaking the same language as you. The water translates. You hear what we say in English, we hear what you say in the language of our people."

"Which is…?"

The sound he made was a series of screeches and clicks. "The name for it basically translates to 'sea words.'"

Before I could ask more questions, two sharp horn blasts sounded in the distance. Gone was the lighthearted air. Dwellers on their way to The Gathering scattered as fish do when startled, leaving the reef bare in minutes.

"What—" I began.

"Two quick blasts mean predators," Max said, putting an arm around my waist and pulling me with him to fly across the reef to Alfred's cave. "Stay here until you hear two long blasts."

"But—"

"Not negotiable, Holly, sorry. I must go help my brothers. Stay here." He left me at the entrance, turning to race after the others. Unfortunately, the fight was coming to him, and quickly. I froze, unable to look away.

A large group of enormous great white sharks were whizzing through the water, the longest being the length of a bus. The ocean dwellers were shouting to each other, each holding weapons to use in defense. With the fight came a cloud of blood, moving slowly into the reef. I saw Jonah and his father amongst the men, and my heart plummeted. He was not close enough to see clearly, but he did appear to be moving without injury. In his hand was a large length of coral that he wielded like a bat, whacking any shark that approached him, moving out of the way with lightning speed. Yet another type of dance, this one dark and deadly.

There was a flash from the corner of my eye, and I turned in time to see one of the bigger sharks heading toward me. Startled from my frozen state, I made a dash for the opening between the corals. I screamed as the pink coral pierced my skin, arms, back, and fins. The shark collided with the coral at the same time as I entered, smashing coral and rock down into the entrance. Like that, I was blocked in the cave. There was another loud rumble and I scrambled in further to avoid more falling rock. The shells were falling from their ledges, and items scattered across the sandy floor. My heart was hammering, and my breathing was coming in short bursts, too quick to get adequate oxygen to my brain. When a third earth-splitting rumble sounded outside, I scrambled for the back of the cave, trying to slow my racing heart. Alfred was nowhere to be found.

I swam up to the openings in the rock. There were many to allow ample light into the space, but most were no wider than the length of my arm. None of them had a good view of the fight. I could hear shouting, but I couldn't see anything.

Until blood began drifting into the holes.

I retreated back down into the belly of the cave, trying to ignore my rolling stomach. The blood continued to seep in, drifting down through the water like eerie smoke tendrils. I swam around nervously, back and forth, trying to think of something to distract myself. Making bargains wasn't my thing, but I tried anyway. "They spoke of the god of the waters. Poseidon? Is that your name? Please, let this be over soon. Please. I have nothing to give, nothing to barter, only my gratitude. Please keep them safe—Jonah, Max, Isaac, Bo, everyone. The sharks may be your creatures too, but please, let them find food elsewhere."

I repeated the mantra as blood continued to waft in. Needing to block it, I found several flat pieces of colored plastics. Light green plastic plates, clear plastic totes, red transparent lunch trays, blue five-gallon bottles that had been once used for drinking water. One by one, I filled each of the holes. I sang to drown out the noise outside and tried not to think about what was happening. Only when I was finished filling each hole did I take in my surroundings. With the sun streaming in above, I had created a kaleidoscope of lights. Each ray sent a color down to the cave floor in a different direction, creating a rainbow across the sand and art out of trash.

I needed to keep myself busy and distracted. With no more blood coming in, it was easier to relax, but only slightly. I then began sifting through the piles of items Alfred had gathered, debating which could serve as weapons, in the event I needed them. Old table and chair legs, discarded steak knives, even a baseball bat. It made me fully understand the extent to which humans had gone to destroy the environment. Mentally, I made a list of all the things I would do when I got home to combat the garbage in the ocean—not using plastic cutlery or plates, skipping straws and coffee lids when I could, and repurposing furniture instead of donating it or throwing it away. The creatures of the deep did not need or deserve this.

A rumble of rocks and debris sounded from the mouth of the cave. I grabbed the metal bat I had located, hurrying to put my back against the wall next to the opening.

"Holly? Holly, where are you?"

My breath came out in a whoosh as I lowered my weapon. "Jonah?"

He was there before I could move, hugging me to his chest as he swore under his breath. "Thank goodness," he whispered.

Carefully, I removed myself from his grasp, putting distance between us despite my soul's desire to stay. "Is everyone okay?" I asked, as Max, Isaac and then Alfred appeared as well.

"A few bumps and bruises, but we'll be fine," Max replied.

"I like what you've done with the place," Isaac said with a grin.

I swallowed hard. "There was—there was blood coming in. I hope you don't mind," I said to Alfred.

"Mind? No-no, I don't mind at all," Alfred mumbled, staring up at the lights in amazement. "I wonder why I didn't think of that sooner."

"How did you guys get in?" I asked.

"We had to dig the entrance out," Max replied. "Took a bit—the shark really did some damage."

"Why were you out of the cave?" Jonah cried. He was only barely concealing his rage. "I told you to stay safe, and you deliberately—"

"I didn't *deliberately* do anything!" I shouted back.

"She froze up, Jonah," Isaac said quietly. "I saw it happen. She wasn't able to get into the cave before the fight reached the reef. She just froze until one of the sharks came at her." He turned to me with a grin. "Fast moves, Holly. That was a very close call. Well done."

"Not an experience I'd care to repeat again," I admitted.

"You will not repeat it again," Jonah snapped. "From now on, you'll be staying with Max and I—"

"No."

"No?" Jonah repeated in surprise.

I folded my arms over my chest. "That's right, no. I won't. I'm staying here. This cave is much safer than a decaying airplane."

"Dammit, Holly!"

"Jonah," Max said quietly, putting a hand on his arm. "Holly is right. This place is safer than ours. We are too far off the reef, and there is no way the plane would have held up against a shark that large. Here, she's in the center of the reef, protected by rock, and surrounded by others who can help her."

Jonah glared at me for only a moment before brushing off Max's hand and exiting the cave with a snarl.

When he was gone, I dropped my arms, letting out the breath I was holding.

Isaac chuckled. "Max told me he was riled up. I didn't realize how bad it was."

I went to Alfred, who was still gazing up at the lights with a soft smile on his face. "I'm sorry your home was damaged."

He surprised me by pulling me into a hug. "Reefs heal and regrow. I'm glad you're alright."

"Where were you?"

"I was on my way back from seeing Marida. When I heard the horns, I was closer to her than here, so I returned to her shelter."

The entrance to the cave was significantly larger than before, I discovered when the two men left. No more pink coral to bite on the way in or out. "I'm really sorry," I said again.

"Holly, your back needs tending. Let me help."

I did as I was told, turning so Alfred could apply a salve to my scratches, and tie the loose ends of my top so they would continue to stay in place.

"You remind me of my daughter," Alfred said softly. "She was older than you are now when she was taken from me. But you have her tenacity, her energy. She was creative like you too. I'd like to think you two would have been good friends in another lifetime."

I smiled over my shoulder at him. "I hope it is okay, me staying here with you."

"You make me feel almost whole again. I'd like you to stay as long as you'd like."

"Thank you, Alfred," I said quietly, feeling a tightness in my throat as I thought the same about him.

Twenty-Seven

Days turned to a week and then two. I wanted to get back to the surface and home to Abby, but as the shock of the new environment and truths wore off, I began to enjoy my time, even going so far as to create a routine of sorts. Each morning, I found a milk jug lid from the pile and added a lid to a small jar, to keep track of the days I had been beneath the surface. I spent the morning creating something useful from the garbage. It had taken me nearly the entire two weeks to create a neat little bed. I dug holes in the sand for four tires, burying them halfway in so they wouldn't move. I then twisted and tied plastic bags together, making a sort of hammock. It turned out very well and was quite comfortable. When I showed Alfred, he tried it out and immediately asked that I make him one as well. I happily agreed.

When the predator quarantine was over each morning, I emerged to find some breakfast. Alfred had taken me to the different parts of the reef, teaching me which corals, algae, and weeds were edible. I continued to refuse anything that moved on its own accord. Then, if they were available, Max, Isaac, and their pod showed up and took me out to practice my self-defense skills. With the ultra-clean diet, swimming constantly, and the added exercise they put me through, I had to tie and retie my shirt to fit, even going so far as to remove my bra, because it was too loose.

After the shark incident, it became apparent that I was being kept away from the Gatherings. Each day, something came up that excused me from attending. Self-defense classes running late, Alfred needing me for one thing or another, even Marida summoning me to her cave. I approached Alfred, asking him why, but his answers were vague before he quickly changed the subject. The men in the orca pod—Bo, Peleg, Zale, and Leven—did the same.

The other ocean dwellers all avoided me, which I tried not to notice. When they saw me approaching, they dispersed before I reached them. I asked about that too and received equally pathetic answers. Eventually, however, some of the orca pod's families began traveling out with us. All but Zale, Max, and Isaac were mated, and Bo and Peleg had small adorable ocean dweller toddlers, who were delighted when I decided to bring some of the balls along one day, teaching them how to throw and kick them. This brought smiles and laughter from the mates, though they still avoided talking to me directly.

In the evening, I would continue crafting before heading out with Alfred to find dinner or visit Marida. Occasionally, we would see the mating dance being performed, and I'd watch with a little pang of jealousy. Almost every time, Jonah and his father would be there, watching me, and I would hurry away, blushing fiercely. Neither father nor son had sought me out after the shark accident. Avoiding one man left me relieved. Avoiding the other tore my heart apart.

ooooo

Sometime during week three, I began to sense a mood change in the orca pod. Where they were usually happy and carefree, laughs came less often. The children and the mates stopped coming, and occasionally one of the males would be missing as well. Even Isaac and Max showed signs of distraction and darkness.

"What is going on?" I demanded one day when I was able to wallop Max two rounds in a row. Occasionally, he let me win, but he had hardly been defending himself at all.

"What do you mean?" he asked, rubbing the spot where my fin had collided with his chest.

"I'm not an idiot, Max. I know something is up. What is going on?"

"We aren't supposed to tell," Isaac said, a warning to Max in his tone.

"She's going to find out eventually," Max argued.

"Find out what?"

"Things are… a little tense," Max said quickly before Isaac could argue. "Between our reef and the one to the north."

"The one that attacked here before? The one that Creed is a member of?"

"Yeah. We have been trying to negotiate a deal, as we have things—necessities—that they could use."

"If you're going to tell her, tell her what they want," Isaac growled, a sound that was very unusual, coming from one so happy as him.

"They want you, Holly," Max said quietly, unable to meet my gaze.

"Me?"

"Remember that first night on the ship, when Creed sat with us and was trying to flirt with you?" Isaac asked. "That's how they wanted to get you. They wanted Creed, who holds some sort of leader position within their ranks, to seduce you, make you his mate. It is an unspoken rule amongst the ocean dwellers, not to take another's mate. Not that Creed would follow that."

"But-but they didn't follow that rule. Alfred said his mate and daughter was taken from him by their village."

"Yes," Max replied. "And it began a very long feud we wish to end."

"Giving me to them would end it?"

"Some think so, which is why you haven't been brought to the Gatherings as of late. It has been for your safety."

"She can't go!" Max exploded, throwing up his fists. "She is Jonah's mate!"

"I know that," Isaac snapped. "Those of us closest to Jonah know that you are his mate, Holly, but since the mating ritual has not been performed down here, it isn't official."

"I am not Jonah's mate!" I cried, blushing furiously. "We *were* a couple until he lied to me."

Max shook his head. "You still have feelings for him. And he never stopped loving you. What's more, he has worried himself sick over all of this. He will no longer see us, his friends. He stays shut up in meetings with his father, day in and day out. I don't understand it.

Why not fight for you? Why not stand up to his father? The mating ritual would declare you his before all ocean dwellers. If you guys did that now, you could work out your differences later, but you'd both be much safer."

The idea of having an undersea wedding when the bride and groom weren't even speaking to each other was laughable. "Why won't he talk to you?" I asked.

"I don't know," Isaac said, pinching the bridge of his nose as he sighed. "The older generation—Master Jonah, the elders—they want revenge for what was done to them and their families. They are asking the younger generation to fight a war they began. Many of us are tired of fighting. We just want peace, to live our lives as we wish, not being constantly trained for a war that might never come."

"Master Jonah is a decent leader, but he has always tried to manipulate his son. He wants Jonah to be harder, a warrior, a leader trained to fight, mentally and physically aggressive. You've met Master Jonah," Max said, "and you told me you didn't like him."

I shuddered. "He told me he wanted to break me."

"He wants Jonah to be like him."

"That isn't what you need in a leader," I said, glancing back at the reef.

"Or want," Max agreed.

"What will you do?"

Isaac spread his arms. "Why do you think we have been training you? It was much our idea as Jonah's— young Jonah, that is. If Master Jonah knew about this, he would be furious." I hadn't realized what I was doing was meant to be a secret, and Isaac read my face accurately. "Don't worry. We have been covering for you. Master Jonah has been so busy anyway that he has hardly noticed. Messengers from the north have been coming and going, but the elders and the Jonahs are the only ones who are privy to their information. Gatherings have been question-filled, but no answers have been given."

"I still don't understand. Why me? What do I have to do with all of this?"

"There are many theories," Max replied with a shrug. "All of them have significant holes."

"Many dwellers here believe you were once one of the northerners," Isaac added.

My jaw dropped. "I'm not. Three weeks ago, I didn't even know these places existed."

"We know that, but they don't," Max replied. "They are scared, thinking you'll spy on us or somehow bring another raid. Those of us who know you have tried to defend you, but we are whispers in an enormous cavern. Our words mean little."

"Wait a minute. Hold on," I said, holding up my hands. "Why were you on land, then? If it has been so tense down here, why bother coming up?"

"I was sent to be Jonah's backup," Max said, suddenly unable to meet my eyes. "We were sent to find some of those the northerners hid among the people. We did find a few, but most of them had been brainwashed, and we realized that our efforts to return them to the water would be fruitless if they didn't believe we even existed."

"I don't understand," I said in a small voice, dreading where this conversation was going.

Max sighed. "Cecille… is one of us. She had long since chosen to live on land but agreed to be a contact person, if we ever needed one. Jonah happened to be visiting her for some other business when you came in looking for a job. They are related, but maybe not as closely as you were led to believe. It was simply a way for Jonah to get nearer to you without drawing suspicion because Jonah's bond with you was instant. He waited for you to warm up to him, taking things slowly. He didn't want to scare you with the intensity of what we feel when we make a bond. You know how the rest played out."

"He didn't know until later," Isaac said, taking up the story, "that you were the one that both villages were looking for. When he found out, he reached out to Max and me for help. Max helped from afar, and I helped when you got on the cruise ship."

"When did he learn about this?" I whispered, the familiar lump rising in my throat.

"Holly—" Max began.

"When did he find out? How long has he known?" Both men fidgeted, exchanging worried glances. "*When did he find out?*" I shouted.

"A couple weeks before you left on the cruise, our time," Isaac said gently.

"The day before you got to California, your time," Max added.

I felt the breath leave my lungs in a rush as things clicked into place with a chilling revelation. That night in his apartment, talking about board members and inherited companies. Jonah had been talking about me. I was the little company. I had heard the passion and the urgency in his voice. How he had struggled with the weight of the job to protect and the need to help the inheritance—me. Absorbing the company into his own was to bring me beneath the waves permanently, without Abby. He knew I would not go willingly, and he had fought against needing to do that. Shock turned to fear.

"Holly?"

My breathing was increasingly shallow, causing my lungs to burn. "He's going to keep me here. I'm not going to be able to leave," I gasped. "He's going to—"

"No, Holly," Max said quickly, reaching for my arms. "He isn't. He would never agree to something you didn't want."

"He-he told me. I can't breathe. I-I need to—" I clutched at Max's arms, fighting the weight on my lungs.

"Breathe. Breathe, Holly."

"I-I can't—"

Max took my face in his hands and put his head to mine. "You can do this. You are stronger than your anxiety, stronger than your fear. Your mind is a powerful thing. For any negative effect it can cause, it can create one just as powerfully positive. Think of Abby. Think of your photography. My favorite was the one in the woods, sometime in fall, when the light was shining through the trees like little fingers of light, reaching toward you. Take yourself there, Holly. Imagine walking through the woods, nothing but you and your camera and your imagination. Are there—oh, yep, there are a few squirrels in the tree…"

He continued on a little trek through the woods, pointing out details I had no choice but to view in my mind. When he felt my breathing slow, his details became sillier, ending with a blue rabbit with eight lucky feet. "Good girl," he said when a small giggle escaped me.

I removed myself from his grasp, taking several deep breaths. Exhaustion was setting in, as was hunger. "Thank you," I told him quietly. "I-I would like to go back to the reef."

We went slowly, Max and Isaac making small talk about hunting or the currents or a passing creature. I only half-listened, replaying my conversation with Jonah in my head. A little company—that had to be me. The board members—the village elders, perhaps? And how had I been involved, exactly? And how had I gone through life without knowing? Did this have something to do with my dad?

What if my dad was one of the elders? That theory made the most sense. I had not met any of the elders. Would I know him if I saw him? My mom and Gram had flat out refused to tell me about my dad, or Abby's. It resulted in a fight time after time that Abby and I both stopped asking. When they were gone, Abby had attempted to do a little genealogy. All searches had come up empty.

One thing was for sure, I needed to get into the next Gathering, incognito. And I hoped Marida would be able to help me.

"You want something to change you to a different animal?" she asked, her tone equal parts wonder and confusion. "I don't understand."

"Marida, I am worried about my place here," I said quietly. "I do not know what the future holds for me, but-but I need to get into the Gathering. I need to hear what the plan is, because no one will tell me."

She studied me a moment before shaking her head. "You have no concern for your own well-being. You worry about others." When I blushed in response, she added, "While that is a noble trait, it can also be very dangerous."

"I need to be at the Gathering. I have questions that need answers, and no one will give them to me."

"Why not ask, then, for a simple truth serum?"

"You make that?" I breathed, but then shook my head. Giving Jonah a truth serum, while intriguing, was asking for more information than I could handle. "I just want to go into the Gathering unnoticed, hear what information is being given, and leave."

"And what makes you think I can do that?"

Her tone made me feel sheepish. "I-I don't know."

"If I did, who could I make you look like? The creatures around here know each other. Strangers stand out."

My shoulders slumped. "If you can't, or won't, I guess I can understand. I've been told you don't pick sides, and that's more than fair."

She cocked her head as she studied me. "What information do you seek?"

I considered for a moment how much to tell her. "I want to find out if my father is one of the elders."

"That was not your main reason for attending the Gathering."

"No, but there are many reasons. Everyone has secrets."

"True enough." She gave me a small smile, her teeth white and even. "You still do not trust me, do you?"

I threw my arms up. "After today, I don't know who to trust anymore."

"Let me tell you one of my secrets. There was once a young ocean dweller who dabbled in the ocean's mysteries with her mother, a vain creature whose need for beauty and acceptance knew no bounds. She had learned from her mother and her from her mother's mother, how to use the ocean's resources in different, more mystical ways. But attaining beauty was an impossible task, eluding her at every turn. Squid are not like other creatures. They stay hidden with the other ugly creatures of the deep. They live alone and die alone, ocean pariahs. My mother wanted to change that. She began traveling closer to the surface, interacting with the other ocean dwellers, trying to make friends. All was well until my mother began killing them, one by one. She raised me to believe that I was superior to them, poisoning me. First my brain, with her lies and manipulations, and then with foods tainted with her magic. I would wake up now and then with different features than before. My body, once a red-pink color, slowly changed to blue. My hair was white like the moon, my skin pale and spotted with pink. You see, I was beautiful then. I am beautiful now, too. The point is, I was never given a choice."

"What happened to your mother?"

"She was sentenced to death by the elders for tampering with their politics. I was allowed to live because I was so young and naive, but they made me swear never to follow in my mother's trek."

"Weren't you angry?"

She shrugged. "I could be angry and slowly kill the elders off, one by one. Or I could be gracious that they saw the good in me that my mother never could. I chose the latter."

I digested the information she gave me before sighing. "You told me that story to explain why you can't help me."

"Or because it is a story that is a well-kept secret among the elders. This is the first time I have spoken of it since it happened."

"I won't tell anyone."

"I know. I can see that you are a trustworthy person, capable of compassion and forgiveness when it is warranted. So, I cannot help you change your appearances, for the promises I made to myself and to the elders."

Back to the drawing board, then. "Okay. Thank you, Marida."

"I can tell you, though," she said, as I began to turn away. "Your father is not among the elders."

"He isn't?"

She shook her head. "None of the elders have children. If an elder chooses the family lifestyle, he relinquishes his position. It allows the elders to focus on the good of the reef, without having biases or distractions. The leader is the only exception to the rule, as he must bear the next Jonah."

Frustration bubbled out of me. "How do I fit into this mess, then?" I cried.

"After what happened with my mother, they rarely give me information. I dwell quietly in my cave, trying to avoid any negative attention. They ask for my resources, and I give freely. Then, they go on their way."

"Thank you, Marida."

She inclined her head with a gentle smile. "I will always be here, if you need me."

Twenty-Eight

By week four, all self-defense classes had stopped completely. I noticed more ocean dwellers circling the reef like patrols, in groups of two or three, and all armed with weapons. Alfred invited me to venture out less and less often, bringing me food rather than allowing me to go get it myself. I adapted my schedule accordingly, using various trash items to wield rather than the stakes from the sand bar. I finished Alfred's bed, for which he was most grateful, and moved on to sorting out small storage containers. Between Alfred and Marida, they were almost always in need. The remaining trash pile had decreased in size with my efforts, though I wondered if it would ever disappear completely.

Using an old garbage bin and a few bricks to hold it down, I began adding things that could serve as weapons. A few knives had been discovered amongst the items, as well as the bats and chair legs I used to practice. I had decided after my talk with Max and Isaac that it was better to be prepared, just in case.

By week five, I was unable to leave the cave at all.

"I'm sorry, Holly," Alfred said when he brought the news. "There is a fight larger than any of us going on, both in the reef and beyond. The reef residents fear what is to become of them and where the future will take us. It is safer for you to stay here, out of sight, until this has passed."

"Alfred, I just want to go home. With me out of the way, won't that solve everything?"

Alfred shook his head. "No, unfortunately. You hold something of value to the northerners, and they will hunt you, on land or sea, to get it back, whatever it is."

"I'm a prisoner of war, then."

He embraced me in a tight hug. "You will see your sister again. I promise. We just have to wait this out together. You have many allies here who know your story."

I listened to him on the first day, busying myself with various tasks.

I listened to him on the second day, organizing the piles of trash and belting out any song that came to mind from Cecille's jukebox.

I listened to him on the third day, reorganizing the piles and volleying balls against the walls of the cavern.

I even managed to listen to him on the fourth day, though I spent much of the day pacing and cursing Jonah for bringing me to the reef.

By day five, I could not take any more. I needed to get out. When Alfred left for the Gathering, I ventured out. I wasn't planning on going far, just out to the seaweed beds to get my own food. The warmth of the sun shining down into the reef was lost in the cool waters, but it still felt good to be out in the direct light. There were no ocean dwellers roaming about, but the reef was a never-ending rollercoaster of movement, schools of fish flocking together.

With the basket I brought, I gathered enough seaweed to last the day. Maybe Alfred would let me go out with him after dark, when I would draw less attention. Even if he didn't, I wanted to enjoy the little bit of time out and about. I returned to the cave, munching on a roll of seaweed. With one last look around, I sighed and went back inside. No one had seen me, and no one would know. I had been quick and efficient and had not strayed from my mission.

As I was putting my things away, I heard a loud thump sound, followed by another. The Gathering lasted much longer than ten minutes, I knew. And when the sound registered as the shells holding personal items hitting the rock wall, I grabbed the nearest weapon—a baseball bat, and held a knife behind my back. Carefully, I kicked through the water. When people came to gather belongings, they never came in. They called for Alfred from the entrance of the cave and waited while he gathered their items.

With the element of surprise on my side, I hugged the shadows to examine the situation. There were two male ocean dwellers, examining each shell before tossing the contents behind them and moving to the next one.

"Hurry up," the first man told the other. "We need that jar."

My heart hammered. I recognized that voice—it was Creed. His body was a brilliant silver that shimmered even in the low light. Both men were built slightly smaller than the men of the reef, but not by much. I had worked with Isaac and Max, discussing tactics for two opponents instead of one, but we had never practiced them. Unarm and fight, those were my two goals. A moment of fear sizzled through me before anger took over. This was the man who had tossed me out of a ship and left me for dead. He was the reason I was stuck beneath the waves, instead of going home to Abby.

I swam at the pair when they were close enough, swinging my bat at Creed while presenting my backside to the other man. Both cried out in surprise, the second man screaming in pain, holding his chest, where blood was oozing from a large wound. I made to strike Creed again, but he caught the bat and kicked his fins hard against my belly. The breath was knocked from my lungs.

"You!" he shouted. "What the—"

I rolled but he darted out of the way to avoid the poison. The second man fled with a moan.

"You were supposed to be brought to our village! My men said they would be following the ship!" Creed shouted. "I was so careful. You were supposed to be *my* mate, to unite the two greatest clans in the ocean. Too bad I have a field of degenerates to work with on my side."

"I would never mate with you," I said breathlessly, keeping space between us as he tried to circle me.

Creed laughed cruelly. "Down here, you don't have a choice."

"That's a lie."

"So was Jonah sleeping with that whore Layla, but you believed that, didn't you?"

In my moment of surprise, he darted forward, catching me around the waist to pin me against the wall. My head hit the rock hard enough that stars danced across the cave. Over and over, he jabbed an elbow into my side before crushing my neck with his forearm. "Females believe anything we tell them, Doll," he said into my ear. "Funny how easy it was to convince you Jonah betrayed you. Separate the weakest fish from the school and go in for the kill. You, Doll, are the weakest fish."

My hands grasped the walls, searching for a weapon. Landing on a piece of hard coral, I broke it off and swung hard, catching him in the ribs. With a grunt, he doubled over, and I was able to move out of his grasp.

Creed shouted as blood seeped from the wound. He darted to the floor, where I had dropped the knife earlier. Coming up with it, he grinned maniacally. "If I kill you, they can't have you either. I'll never let them win. Never!"

He charged at me, but a flash of gray flew between us, a large tale swinging wildly out toward Creed. The younger man screamed, and I saw a large white barb lodged near his collarbone. Alfred crashed into the rock and was still. I turned to go to him, screaming when a white-hot pain seared through me. Creed was retreating quickly, his blood adding to Alfred's inside the cave.

I reached back, trying to find the source of the pain. Creed had managed to stab me in my distraction, the knife lodged in my lower back, ripping open the skin and scales. When I tried to remove it, I nearly blacked out from the pain. It would have to stay in until someone could help me.

"Alfred," I moaned. It hurt to move, but I forced myself down to where he lay, face up in the sand. A large gash across his chest stretched from his left shoulder to his right hip. His eyes were closed, but I could feel a light pulse at the base of his neck. "Alfred, please."

"Marida…" I heard him moan.

Marida would help. "Yes," I whimpered, pulling his arms around my shoulders so that I could pull him up. If we could get out of the cave, someone would see us. "I will get you to Marida, I promise."

As a human, I imagined Alfred would not have been much taller than me. However, with a body of muscle, and several extra feet of stingray behind him, it took everything I had to struggle out of the cave. It would have been easier to carry him on my back, but I remembered what Max and Isaac had taught me, that my poison would be more prevalent if I was angered, scared, or injured. And I was all of those things. I resorted to pulling him along in a hug and drag system. Adrenaline coursed through me, giving me more strength than I could have ever imagined. We reached the mouth of the cave, only to find that no ocean dwellers were available. I shouted for help, but no one came. Even the fish were scared off, likely from the scent of blood. I was going to have to take him to Marida myself.

Stifling a sob, I pulled him along, trying not to think about what his body was being scratched on beneath us. I considered leaving Alfred, bringing Marida to him, but if an ocean dweller found Alfred before I returned, assumptions would be made, alerts raised. I would look like the culprit, knife in my back or not.

Marida's cave was less than a half mile away, a swim completed in ten minutes on a good day. But this was not a good day. I used coral landmarks to keep myself on track.

First, the pink coral on the little hill up there.

Good. Now, the gray star-shaped one there.

Closer. Now, the little green coral that waved like hair in the water.

Some of the swim was lost. I would look around, wondering how I had gotten there. But I focused on my goal. When I saw the edge of the reef, I began to sob and call for Marida at the same time, my voice coming out as a breathy squeak.

There was a whoosh above me, then another. I looked up, and my heart dropped. Sharks, big ones. Most likely drawn by the smell of blood. Vaguely, I registered the sharp blasts of a horn, impossibly far away. No help would come before we became shark lunch, and I would not have enough time to reach Marida's safely. Yet the thought of leaving Abby kept me going. I would not leave her to live alone. Not today.

Not today.

"Not today!" I screamed when a shark plowed into me, separating me from Alfred. I rolled clumsily, my poison catching the shark in the face. It darted away, and I turned to see the sharks nosing Alfred, attempting to find an appendage to chew on. "No!" I shouted. I swam back as quickly as I could, covering Alfred's body with my own, tucking his arms under me so that the sharks could not reach them. Twice they pulled at his large fins, but I kicked out with my tail, trying desperately to protect him. Closing my eyes, I buried my face in the nape of his neck, praying.

Not today.

Not today.

Twenty-Nine

"Holly? Holly, wake up."

I opened my eyes slowly.

"There you are," Marida said kindly. "You gave us quite the scare."

Why was I in Marida's cave? I wondered groggily. Creed. Alfred. Sharks.

I bolted upright and let out a scream of pain.

"Well, I guess those stitches will have to be re-tied," she noted calmly. "You're safe, Holly. All is well."

"Where-what-I—" I sputtered.

"Your fear will make this job a bit more dangerous. The first time, you were unconscious, so I was able to work around your poison."

"Where is Alfred?"

"Recovering in his cave."

"He's okay?" I breathed.

"Yes, thanks to you, it would seem."

"How?"

She felt my body relax and guided me back down to the bed of soft algae I had been lying on, turning me so that she could examine the source of the blood seeping up around us. "I'm going to apply a salve that numbs first, and then I will need to sew your wound shut again. I need you to hold very still."

I did as I was told, whimpering as her hands neared the wound site. "How did we escape the sharks?" I asked quietly.

"The charge of the orca brigade," Marida replied. "Followed by Master and Younger Jonah."

My breath came out in a whoosh. "I remember hearing the horns, but I didn't think they'd make it in time."

"Your decision to lay on top of Alfred bought them enough time. The sharks wanted the soft flesh Alfred had to offer—his upper body, and the underside of his fins. They could not get to it with you lying atop of him. Your spikes reach up your back far enough that they could not get to your soft flesh without injury either. Sorry," she said gently when I flinched. "You only ripped a few stitches. I'm nearly finished."

"Creed. Did they find Creed?"

"Who?"

"Creed. He's one of the northern village's leaders. He and someone else came into Alfred's cave looking for something. I did my best to defend the belongings, but—"

"I must warn you, that is not the conclusion the elders came to. They believe you are a spy for the village to the north. There are two dweller warriors outside my cave now, waiting to take you to see Master Jonah when you are well enough."

"What! I'm not a spy!" I cried.

"I do believe you, but you'll need to convince them. You said they were looking for something. What was it?"

I tried to remember the conversation. "They only said a jar. Whatever it was, they were not successful because one ran away when I attacked, and Creed left empty-handed after he took a barb from Alfred. They could ask Alfred—he would be able to support my story."

"It sounds as though Alfred may be only able to support half your story. He was not in there when the men were searching. He cannot speak for your involvement."

Panic seized, and my breathing increased. "I didn't do anything," I whispered. "I was only trying to help."

Two tentacles caressed my face, and I felt the weight lift from my lungs with an odd tingling sensation. "You must remain calm, Holly. I can buy you some time. The warriors are on strict orders to bring you to see the elders when you are well. You are not well yet, and I do not need to tell them the minute you can swim again. Rest is warranted, as is food, to regain your strength. Eat, sleep, and come up with a plan when you are well."

I nodded. With her tentacles slowly drawing down, hairline to chin, she was able to dispel the worry enough for me to eat a small meal before exhaustion overtook me.

ooooo

A beautiful tune woke me later. It was dark, and Marida was floating around the cave, humming softly. She sensed my movement and smiled over her shoulder. "Hello. Welcome back."

"What was that you were singing?" I asked.

"Ah, an ancient lullaby of sorts. Have you not heard of the sirens of the deep?"

"You're a siren? Well, I suppose. You fit the bill."

She laughed. "Saltwater gives us healthy voices. Healthy voices sing prettily. Don't be surprised if you have a better singing voice when you get home."

"If I ever get home." I pulled my hands down my face with a groan. Pain, exhaustion, hunger, frustration assaulted me with a pounding headache.

"Eat this for the pain."

"Thanks." I chewed quickly and made a face. "Oh, that's terrible."

"Of course, it is. It's feces."

I choked. "What?"

"Feces<" Marida replied, matter of fact. "It is from a fish I haven't named. The poop is easy enough to find, but the fish who leaves it is one of the most elusive. I've only seen one in my lifetime."

"You asked me to trust you. And you feed me poop?"

"It has healing properties that extend to injuries beyond the usual aches and pains. Horrible taste, but effective."

As she spoke, I felt the effects almost instantly. Warmth crept through my body, reaching to every niche with a gentle caress, taming the streak of fire down my back and the intense ache in my side. Even my head stopped pulsing with pain. "Wow…" I breathed. "I want to hate you, but I can't."

Marida laughed again. "You're welcome." She then passed me a jar of seaweed. "Eat. Your body needs to rebuild its strength. It's been almost three days since the attack, and you haven't eaten much." She contented herself to talk while I ate, carrying the conversation one-sided. "The warriors outside my cave will not allow any visitors, but several have come and gone. Many of the orca pod and Alfred tried to come, but only Jonah and Master Jonah were allowed to enter. They came early this morning, together. They weren't here long—just asked after your health and a general timeline for your recovery. I didn't promise anything, which infuriated the elder."

I remembered Creed's cruel trick, feeling myself blush crimson. "I owe Jonah an apology."

"I doubt it. He is no longer angry with you."

"Can you… can you read minds, then?"

"No. I don't know what you're thinking right now. I can, however, feel your emotions. Anger, pain, desperation. I make assumptions, based on what I feel."

"That seems… burdensome."

She shrugged. "More often than not, it's helpful. Alfred could not come in to see you, but I went to the entrance of the cave when I felt his anger approaching. I tried to reason with the warriors to let him enter but they refused. 'Tell Holly,' he said."

"Tell me what?" I asked when she appeared to be done talking.

"That he came. That he tried to see you but was refused entrance. He, too, knows of my abilities. He knew that I would be able to convey his nonverbal message to you. He is grateful to you and angry at the turn of events that have come since. He, too, loves you unconditionally."

The lump in my throat grew. "Thank you," I said quietly.

She shrugged. "No need to thank me."

When I was finished eating, I got up and moved around the cavern, gritting my teeth at the pain. Her magic poo pills were doing their part, but I was still incredibly sore. Marida kindly declined my offer to help her, leaving me to my own devices and advising me to stay well inside the cave to avoid being seen by the guards. I needed a plan, but I had no idea what to expect when I left the cave.

All I knew was that the time had come to leave the reef. I needed to get back to the human world, as soon as possible.

ooooo

It came to pass that Marida could no longer hide my physical improvements. With her unusual senses, she was able to tell me when to return to my algae bed, to lie quietly and still as though I was sleeping. Elders or Master Jonah came to inquire and left angry that I had not come to yet. Marida was a master of deception, telling one believable lie or another to keep them at bay.

By the eighth day, the guards came for me while she was applying the salve. They had overheard Marida telling me that it was passably healed.

"Time to go," the first said, reaching for me.

Marida's tentacle snapped, and he snatched his hand away. "She can swim on her own. No need to drag her like a prisoner."

The man rubbed at his wrist with venom in his eyes. "Fine," he said through gritted teeth, "though that's the last time I take orders from deep sea scum."

I gave Marida a quick hug, whispering my thanks.

"The time to escape is not now," she whispered back, tucking a jar of the magic poo into my small bag. "Go see the elders. Argue your case. Someone will listen."

I nodded. Not escaping would hopefully buy trust I could use later. If I couldn't convince the elders that I was a neutral party first.

My body was still aching, the wounds aggravated and screaming for attention by the time we reached the Gathering cave. Unlike Alfred's compartmentalized cavern or Marida's dark space, it was one great area, similar to a sporting arena. All sides and floor were rock, and near the top, long wispy underwater trees branched out, reaching through a large hole in the top. It was the perfect cover—allowing light in without drawing attention to the space hidden beneath. Holes the size of doorways lined one wall, but we were too far for me to see inside them.

"This way," the warrior to my left growled, pushing me ahead, where an adjacent cave was waiting, a guard on either side of the entrance. This one was brighter and held nearly twenty men with the tails of a variety of sea creatures—octopus, stingray, whale, and shark. All large predators, I noted.

"Holly, welcome. We have been waiting most anxiously for your arrival." Old Jonah came forward with an icy smile. "How are you feeling?"

"I've been better," I muttered, scanning the crowd. The younger Jonah was in the back of the group, staring at me with an eerily blank look, as though he didn't recognize me.

"Has Marida not taken care of you?"

"She did just fine. I was forced to leave before I could heal completely."

"I see. What were your injuries?"

I gritted my teeth, reminding myself this was the time to appear calm. "Head, ribs, and back."

He turned to the group behind him. "This is Holly, the one we have been searching for," he announced. "Unfortunately, her behavior suggests she has not been as loyal to our reef as we had hoped. But, let it not be said that I was not fair," he said, turning back to me. "I would very much like to hear your side of the story of the events that happened in Alfred's cave."

With a pit in my stomach, I retold the story. I included the fact that I had left the cave without asking Alfred, hoping it would count toward my honesty. I omitted what Creed had told me about Layla, saving that for when I could talk to Jonah privately. I told them they had been searching for a jar and had not found it, how Alfred had saved my life, and how I had done my part to save him. When I was finished, there was a murmur of voices, each leader speaking with his neighbor.

"Alfred was able to verify that he saved your life and that he had a vague memory of you pulling him out of the cave," one of them said.

"I was trying to get him to Marida's. No one was in the reef, and I did not want to leave him alone."

"So, you pulled him along, causing more injury."

"I didn't mean to hurt him. I was trying to help!" I cried, willing him to understand.

"By bringing him to the deep-sea creature?" the man said with a sneer.

"By bringing him to someone he trusted."

Old Jonah guffawed. "The squid siren is not to be trusted. She and her kind forfeited that right long ago."

"With all due respect, I said someone *he* trusted, not someone *you* trusted."

"Are you suggesting your dear friend Alfred would rather side with Marida over his own leaders?"

"No! Stop twisting my words!" I shouted, my temper rising. Old Jonah's eyes flashed with satisfaction. That was what he was trying to do, I realized. He was trying to get a rise out of me, to show the elders my ugly side. What I didn't understand was why? Calming myself, I tried again. "When I was trying to help, he said Marida's name. Being that I had never met any of you previous to this, I heeded his word because I knew she could help us."

"Alfred's wife and daughter were good friends with Marida, before they were taken," another man from the group said softly. "Her story is plausible." A few of the others nodded. Younger Jonah continued to stare blankly.

"Nevertheless, how do we ensure she is on our side?" Old Jonah asked.

"I don't want to be on any side—I just want to go home."

"I'm afraid that is impossible. Things have reached a precipice, and we need your loyalty, your fealty, and your submission," he replied.

I remembered his words. *I will break you.* "I just want to go home."

"This is your home now."

"No, it isn't. My home is on land."

"Perhaps you ought to tell her the story," another man said. "It's clear she doesn't know it."

"What story?" I asked, looking at the shark man who spoke when Old Jonah did not answer. "What story?"

"Your family's story," he said.

"I only have a sister. My mom died when I was twelve, my grandmother when I was eighteen."

"That is what you were led to believe," the shark man said.

"I beg your pardon?" I said incredulously. "You mean—"

"Who is the leader here?" Old Jonah shouted. The men all darted backward a foot, like a school of fish when a pebble is dropped into the water nearby. "She will not be able to comprehend the tale, and so we will not share it. The issue here is that Holly must prove herself not a spy."

"I'm not a spy!"

Old Jonah twisted to me, his eyes glowing blue again. "And how do we know that? You say you were defending the keeper's cave. How do we know you did not lead those men right to the cave? How do we know you weren't helping him look and had a deal to injure the keeper if he caught you?"

"Because I didn't do that!"

"Jonah tells me you were acquainted with the one called Creed. Was he one of the men who searched the caves?"

"Yes, he was. I didn't know the other man."

"She admits she knew her alleged attacker," the elder Jonah cried victoriously.

"Yes," I said quietly, speaking to the others when I realized Old Jonah would not listen to me. "I knew Creed. I met him on the cruise. He attempted to get… close to me, but I did not allow that to happen. I refused his attempts at friendship and avoided him when I could. Jonah could vouch for that."

A few of the leaders looked to the younger Jonah, but he continued to watch wordlessly before exchanging worried glances with each other. Something was wrong with the younger Jonah, and they knew it too.

Old Jonah approached, and it took everything not to flinch away from him. "Jonah will not speak for you. He knows where his true loyalties lie," he said softly.

"What have you done to him?"

"I've improved him. He was too soft."

I looked over his shoulder at Jonah, my heart filling with dread. What had he done? Drugs? Poison?

"Ah, I can see I've scared you. He won't remember you, just as your mother and grandmother didn't remember."

"What—"

"We must remedy this situation," Old Jonah said before I could ask, turning back to the others in the room. "We must calm the reef dwellers. We must convince them there is nothing to fear with this human. We must make her an official reef dweller, once and for all."

"What do you propose?" One of the men asked.

"A mating."

Murmurs circled again. "With who?"

"Me," Old Jonah replied.

"No!" I screamed.

The older Jonah spun to me. "You dare defy me? It is as much for your protection as anything else. You ought to be thanking me."

Panic and desperation were making my chest hurt. "No! I will mate, if that is what I must do, but not you. Younger Jonah. Please."

Old Jonah threw his head back and laughed. "As I said before, he does not remember you. Go ahead, examine him yourself. Human life was making him weak, soft. So, we erased his memory of that life. You're in that life, and so you no longer exist."

I didn't hesitate when he gestured for me to go to him. With a lump in my throat, I approached cautiously. "Jonah?" I whispered.

He didn't move or even look at me. Upon closer inspection, there were light bruises on his chest and face that I had not seen before. His body was rigid, his hands bunched in fists, and it looked as though he had lost some weight.

"Jonah," I said again, taking his hand, moving so that I was in his line of sight. "Jonah, talk to me, please."

"He doesn't say much these days," one of the elders muttered quickly, quiet enough that Old Jonah could not hear.

I kept my eyes on Jonah's face, running my hands up his arms, willing him to show any sign of life. "Jonah, I'm so sorry about what happened with Layla. I-I didn't believe you, but I do now. Please, talk to me."

"That's enough," Old Jonah was saying. "Take her to the holding cave."

I felt them approaching and knew my time was running out. In a last-ditch effort, I wrapped my arms around him and kissed him, full on the lips, in front of everyone. The guards wrenched me away from him, causing pain to shoot up and down my side, but it was nothing compared to the pain of Jonah's blank look. His eyes moved, watching me be dragged away, but beyond that, there was no change.

Old Jonah was grinning triumphantly. "The next Gathering will be reserved for the announcement of our ritual, which will take place at dusk tomorrow. I very much look forward to it."

I let them pull me away, offering no more than dead weight, and kept my eyes on Jonah for as long as I could see him. We left the cavern and went to Alfred's cave. Many of the ocean dwellers stopped to watch our procession, shaking their heads with disgust before carrying on their activities.

"Holly!" When the guards shoved me into the cavern, Alfred was there, wrapping me in a hug.

I had spent much of my time with Marida, thinking about what I would say to the man who had saved my life. How I would hug him and tell him I loved him. In the moment, however, all I could manage was a whispered, "Save Jonah," before I was pulled away from him, and forced into the small hole in the wall reserved for prisoners. I had no choice but to follow the dark, narrow tunnel toward the light.

Pain registered as I reached for the opening, and I screamed in agony. I had passed through a shrink-wrap-type of coral, like the clear plastic on a tissue box. It wrapped around my body as I swam through, covering my skin with a burning, awful film. I clawed at my arms and chest, willing the pain to go away. Almost immediately, angry red bumps flared over my skin. I wailed again, trying to wipe off the pus that covered me. Vaguely, I remembered Alfred warning me of the prison's barriers, keeping them from the keeper's side of the cave where Alfred resided.

I wanted to escape. I wanted to process what had happened in the cave. But all I could do was curl up and sob, willing the pain to go away.

Thirty

Sometime in the early morning hours, when the pain was finally manageable and the cave was brighter, I was able to look around. The view that met me was dismal indeed. Coral and seaweed stretched up the walls, and all of it was bad news. Thanks to Alfred's careful teaching, I recognized the pink corals that burned, poisonous seaweed, and the clear demon algae growing across any hand-sized holes. Since the guards removed my bag before shoving me into the cave, I was facing an impossible task with no tools or allies to help me.

Abby, as always, was my beacon of light. And yet, with each passing minute, I lost a little more hope. If Old Jonah mated with me, there was no chance I would ever be able to go home. And if I could not go home, that meant I would live out the rest of my days seeing my stepson, wishing things had been different. The younger Jonah's blank looks haunted me. Part of me wanted to rage. He promised he would protect me and love me through it all. That shell of a man in the cave was not Jonah, and it was clear he had been broken in a way I could not understand. All I could do was hope that someday he would return to his senses. If he did, I prayed he would not be like his father. And yet, if I was mated to Old Jonah, part of me wished the younger's mind never returned.

If only I had stopped and listened to Jonah on the cruise. Then, we could have worked out what had happened. If only I had taken Max and Isaac's suggestion, to mate with Jonah for safety, and to work out our differences later. I could have stayed with him and Max in their airplane. No Creed, no injuries, no sharks. If only I had just listened to stay out of the mess.

ooooo

The sun was still bright when there came a great crash from above. Rock and debris rained down into the cavern, and I did my best to avoid it.

"Holly, come quickly," Marida hissed, her face appearing in the new hole.

I hurried up and out. Her tentacles surrounded me, covering me almost completely as we flew through the water like a speedboat. I gripped her tentacles, but it was unnecessary. Marida was in complete control.

As light became dark, I was released from my bondage to get my bearings. "Marida, what—" I froze, coming face to face with three of the village elders.

"You're safe here, but not for long," the first man said. "We must speak with you, quickly, before we send you on your way. We are expected for the sunset mating ritual."

"The one I am supposed to be a part of?" I asked.

"Yes. You won't be there, though," the shark man replied.

"I-I don't understand."

"We don't have much time," the one nearest the cave entrance snapped. "Tell her, and let us be gone."

"We are releasing you from this place, Holly. Many of the elders believe your story, that you were unaware of the issues happening within our reef. We believe Master Jonah has gone too far, and we want peace restored. That should always have been the goal, but things have gotten clouded with lies. Our Master is not himself, driven by this need of revenge for what was done to us so long ago—too long ago. We cannot do anything but hope, until his death, that things stay civil enough. Then, the younger Jonah can take over, and we will be able to mold him into the master this reef needs."

"What happened to him?"

"Master Jonah has been poisoning him since his return, slowly increasing the dosages, to create a man with no feelings, no original thoughts, and no memory."

"Why?"

"He knows his age is a factor and wants to ensure the next Jonah continues to rule with ruthlessness and strength. Beyond that, I believe his pride was seriously injured, as ruler during such an attack as the northerners brought."

"But why? Why risk bringing me out here? He could have you—"

"Poisoned? Killed? Fed to the sharks?" the man said with a small smile. "All yes, but we seek the greater good."

"Hurry," the watcher called again.

"We will cover you and create a believable story. We will protect all involved, as well as the younger Jonah. You have no need to worry."

"What will you do?"

"It's best if you know nothing of our plan." He produced two small items from the pack over his shoulder. "You must promise to do your part. The green tuber will make you feel very sleepy. You will fall into a deep sleep here and wake up on the cruise ship. The red tuber is if you would like to forget your time down here. We have only two rules we implore you to follow. You must tell no one—*no one*—of your time down here. And you must never try to return to the ocean. If you do, we will not be able to protect you from the consequences."

I took them, feeling breathless. "I get to go back?"

"You must go back. And now, before anyone finds us."

"Marida?" I asked, looking around.

"Eat the tubers," the elder said. "You will have about two minutes before the potion takes hold."

I removed the tuber, took a deep breath, and quickly chewed and swallowed the awful substance. "I want to say goodbye to Marida."

"I'm here, Holly."

When she emerged from the shadows, my jaw dropped in awe. Behind the surprise, my heart plummeted, as I realized what was about to happen. "N-no. No, Marida, don't do this. No!"

Marida looked at me with my own eyes, a soft, sad smile on a face that was mine. "It is what needs to be done. I will be you for this night, and tomorrow, Master Jonah will learn that he has mated with the wrong—"

"No! No, you said you couldn't-wouldn't change. Y-you told me it was forbidden. Your mother—"

"My mother died in vain. By changing my appearances, just this once, I will not. By taking your form, I protect many people."

"No," I sobbed, wrapping her in a hug. "No, please don't do this for me. Please."

"When these men came to me for help, I volunteered. To be seen as a martyr for peace, I would happily take that over 'deep sea monster.' I will do this, for you, and for Young Jonah, and for the good of the reef."

"I won't let you," I wailed.

"I'm afraid you have no choice. You will be beginning to feel very tired. Here, lie here. You will wake up in your suite. No one will miss Jonah. His belongings will be gone, and it will be like he was never there. Creed was also erased from history. When you return to your home, you will find that Cecille has employed a different cook. She will remember, though, but I would advise you to forget Jonah. Make up a story to tell your sister, and move on with your life."

"Marida—" I said, fighting the exhaustion.

"Goodbye, Holly. Be strong." She removed my hands from her arms and turned to the elders, who each took an arm like she was their prisoner.

"No! No, no, no, n—" Too tired. Too…

Thirty-One

I awoke in the tiny cabin that had been assigned to me for the contest. Even in my groggy state, I remembered immediately. I was lying atop the blankets, naked from the waist down, with a vial in my hand that contained the end of my pain. Tears rolled down my cheeks, saltier than any ocean, from a sorrow deeper than any natural chasm. I knew that it was done. No matter how long I had been sleeping, Marida would already be mated with Old Jonah. He might even know that she was not me. Would he have her killed, just as her mother had been? Was she already dead? And what of Alfred, Max, Isaac, or Jonah, or the elders who had helped me? What happened to them?

"Jonah," I whispered, rolling to my side to hug my knees.

My phone buzzed, somewhere nearby, but I ignored it. I knew it would be Abby, but I did not want to talk to her. Abby would demand to know why I was crying, and she would never believe me. The elders made me promise not to tell anyone, and I knew I couldn't without sounding like a mental patient.

The voice of relief, knowing that I could return to Abby, was strong, but my heartache was louder. I had sacrificed the love of my mate for the love of my sister.

"Why? Why me?" I sobbed. Hadn't I lost enough already? How many more people would I need to grieve for before the higher beings decided I was finished?

ooooo

I laid in the bed until I could no longer hold my bladder. Maybe a day had passed, maybe not. I didn't care. When I passed the mirror, I stopped to stare. My reflection bore a face void of color except around my puffy eyes. My cheeks had sunken in slightly, and my hair was wild. I stripped off the remains of my dress to find a chiseled body, and a turn told me that I would always bear the markings from the coral and from Creed's knife. Emotions washed over me, disbelief, agony, and then a raging fury at the turns my life had taken.

Pulling on the nearest clothing, I ran from the room, down the hall. I took the stairs two at a time, brushing past a young couple. They grumbled their irritation, but I hurried down to the deck. The ocean breeze was cool, and paired with the hefty breeze, my skin broke out in goosebumps. I ran to the back of the ship where Creed had thrown me overboard.

For a moment, the urge to jump threatened to overwhelm me. To return and save Jonah, to bring him home with me. To care for him and nurse him back to health. But the elders had warned me that they could not protect me if I returned. If I jumped, I would not become an ocean dweller—I would be a victim to the aquatic elements.

Taking a shuddering breath, I hurled the glass vial over the railing, and watched as it hit the water far below with only the tiniest of splashes. I did not expect to see any fins or human bodies surface with its entrance, but I watched anyway, staring at the place it had entered the water until my tears blurred it.

On a deep, deep level, I finally understood Alfred's words. Losing one's mate was a torture worse than death.

And yet, no matter the pain, I never wanted to forget.

Abby

One

"What the hell?"

My voice echoed in our empty apartment as I scrolled through the folder marked 'cruise' on Holly's computer. At first glance, the thumbnails displayed a series of photos taken by someone who excelled in macro and light photography. Admirable, to be sure, but photos of condensation slipping down a glass of champagne did not create any red flags. There was one of Holly, a rare selfie in a beautiful bathroom. I did pause then, absorbing the joy in her face that I hadn't seen since she returned home from her cruise. She looked genuinely happy, and I knew this moment was important to her because she rarely took selfies, and never took them in a bathroom, no matter how beautiful it was.

No, it was the photos later, hidden between photos of a beautiful woman lounging on a beach chair and a wild storm, that drew my attention. "What the hell?" I cried again, flipping between several shots of Holly dancing with and kissing a man, their silhouettes outlined by a massive storm behind them. I zoomed in, to study the man holding my sister. "That's Jonah!" I screeched. Jonah had been our coworker, and the two had gone on their first date a few days before Holly left. "Jonah was on the cruise?" Both of them were gazing at each other like nothing else existed, and the kiss… *wow*.

Honestly, I had not meant to pry. I loved my sister, and we had respected each other's privacy, usually only reserved for gift-giving, or other fun surprises. This was different. This was a mission of investigation to figure out how to best help Holly.

Something had broken my sister on that trip, and I was livid over it.

I had my suspicions that something was up before she got home from the cruise. She would not video chat with me and avoided talking to me on the phone. Her texts were vague, and she used more emojis than she ever had before. Upon her return, her hug at the airport was painfully tight, as though it had been years since I'd seen her last, rather than just two weeks. On top of that, I marveled at and worried over her new, thinner frame. She said it was due to eating healthy and working out, but I wasn't sure. She had always been pretty active and didn't overeat, but it was virtually impossible for anyone to lose that much weight in just two weeks.

The thing that scared me most of all was how quiet Holly was. After years of slowly removing them, the walls around her heart were back up, and impenetrable. She refused to discuss the details of her trip, only that she had not won the hundred thousand dollars from the photography contest. No cruise stories, no tales from Hawaii, nothing. Something had happened that hurt her deeply.

I gave Holly the idea of space, while still keeping an eye on her. She needed reminders to eat, but would pick at her food—sticking with fruits and vegetables only, leaving me to eat our cherished Fruity Pebbles or ice cream alone. When we were at work, she moved slowly, often pausing to stare out the window blankly. The only time she moved quickly was grabbing dishes from Kevin, the cook, and distributing them to their tables. Cecille, our boss at the cafe, watched her like a hawk, worrying over her as I did. Her efforts to seek out the problem were equally unproductive.

Most nights, when she got home from work, she would skip our evening swim and go to her room. More than once, I watched her take the nighttime ibuprofen, and when I listened at the door, I could hear her crying softly. Nightmares plagued her too, screaming incoherently and thrashing like a fish out of water. When I roused her, she would tearfully thank me and send me back to bed, insisting she was fine. I was quite sure, on those nights, that she stayed awake until morning, judging by the dark circles under her eyes.

It had taken years—*years*—for her to get over the pain and trauma of our childhood. She had seen our mom die in a car accident. In high school, she was drugged and raped by boys she thought were friends, found out she was pregnant, and attempted to commit suicide. I had prevented that last part and helped her through the doctor's appointments that ended the pregnancy. Not even a year after that, she found Gran dead on the bathroom floor. At only eighteen, she became my legal guardian. We had grown up, moved on, and moved away from the horrible town to Hartford, Wisconsin. Holly had even found a great guy—Jonah, Cecille's nephew and former cook—who she was falling for hard. As a finalist in a photography contest, she won a free cruise, and had made a few new friends along the way. Things had been going so well.

And now, nothing.

I had theories of course, and most of them revolved around Jonah Seeley. He had resigned his position at Cecille's shortly after Holly left for Hawaii. That left Cecille short-handed and me furious. How could he take my sister out, treat her like a queen, and then just disappear? He was something of a celebrity in California, the state's most eligible bachelor. Seeley Catering in California, my internet searches revealed, had also recently changed hands. Jonah had stepped down, and a man named Max Something-or-other had taken over. No one knew where Jonah was. As July became August, gossip columns suggested rehab, but Cecille assured me that was not the case.

And then, to find him in these pictures, placing him on the cruise with Holly, and not coming home with her… "Dammit, Jonah, what did you do?" I scrolled through the rest of the pictures, surprised that there were very few after that. The time stamps said they were captured less than halfway through the trip. *Had something happened that night, then?* There were a whopping thirty photos after the silhouettes, and none of them were up to Holly's normal quality.

I replaced her computer and camera, stewing on the new information while I waited for her to get home from the bank. *Why hadn't she told me that Jonah was on the cruise? Had they fought, prompting him to leave Cecille's as well?*

I had, of course, asked Cecille why Jonah had left, when she announced his resignation.

"He had some family matters to attend to," she said sadly. "He asked me to keep things private."

"Did he tell Holly?"

She shrugged.

I took matters into my own hands that evening, coercing Holly to at least go for a walk around the neighborhood with me. "Did Jonah talk to you before he left?" I asked. "Cecille said he had some family things."

She was quiet for a long time. Crickets had begun singing beneath the warm evening sun. The light breeze kept the humidity bearable. "Yeah," she said, her voice soft and shaky. "He told me."

"Have you talked to him since he left?"

Holly shook her head. "He asked me not to."

I had to take several deep breaths to prevent my anger from seeping out. "That sounds… difficult."

A glimmer of her old self shone through. "You're doing well to suppress your feelings," she replied knowingly.

"I'm trying."

Holly reached for my hand and gave it a squeeze. "You've been doing a good job. I don't say it enough, but I appreciate everything you've done for me the last few weeks."

I squeezed back. "I just wish you'd talk to me."

She didn't respond, but I wasn't discouraged. As always, acknowledgement of what I was seeing was always her first step toward improvement. From experience, I knew these things took time.

ooooo

In the weeks that followed, I applied to colleges. I was already leaning toward a two-year school to complete some of my undergrad credits closer to home before pursuing a bachelor's degree, and Holly's emotional upheaval when she returned from the trip only solidified my decision. It would allow me to stay at home with her and continue working part-time for Cecille. I was confident my grades were good enough to be accepted, with advanced math and English courses on my plate for senior year. We gathered all the necessary school supplies and started meal prepping—making and freezing extra casseroles, stir fries, and crockpot meals in the days leading up to school. It had been our little tradition since I started high school so that we could work together on the busy nights to do what needed to be done without worrying about long nights of cooking.

Mid-August, swim practice began too, eating up my early mornings. Holly rose with me, having taken up running since her trip. She rarely swam anymore, but would still come to the pool when I practiced. Sometimes I would catch her staring into the water as though she could see something there, often with tears she would quickly dash when I asked.

The weekend before school started, she took my senior photos at the local park. I knew it was one of Holly's favorite places for photography, as it had a little of all the elements—a small pond with a bridge, a few rock formations, tall grass and wildflowers, and paths into a small, wooded area. We brought a few different tops along, and I wore a light tank top underneath to change easily between takes. I applied light makeup and left my hair down, waving in the gentle breeze. Holly's hair was wildly curly, the color between caramel and chocolate. Mine was black coffee and much thicker, so that it only curled below my chin to where it ended at my elbows. My eyes were darker too, matching my hair color. Holly's were a pretty hazel.

"Your skin and the red of that shirt will make your hair and eyes stand out," Holly said with an affectionate smile. She always seemed to sense when I was being hard on myself.

"It's your photography skills that make the magic," I replied. She snapped a few more pictures, asking me to move every few shots. "What about that couple who wanted to hire you for their engagement photos?" I asked. "The couple from the cruise?"

She stared at me in surprise. "You remember that?"

My laugh was a loud guffaw. "Of course, I remember it. You were super excited about it. I remember things you tell me, sometimes."

She ignored my joke and recovered only slightly. "I thought… never mind." I watched as her face suddenly closed and her jaw tightened. "I don't know if I'm going to do that."

"What? Why not?"

"I-I'm not sure they still want me to do them."

Patience, I reminded myself. "Why not?" I asked again.

"Well, for beginners, they know I didn't win the contest. Another photographer did, though."

"So? They met you. They formed a relationship with you. Didn't you say they wanted your work with light photography? Why not reach out to them?"

She shrugged. "It doesn't feel right."

"But you are so good at what you do, Holly," I cried. "Please! If you want me to go with you, for moral support, I will. I think this will be really good for you."

"We'll see," she said. "Now, I need you to lean back a little bit more, and smile."

ooooo

Of course, I was worried about Holly and her emotional welfare, but I was going to wait until she decided to share what was going on to act. Beyond checking social media every so often for updates on Jonah's whereabouts, I did not intrude. I only helped where I could in Holly's and my daily lives.

The night before school started, I returned to the apartment after a swim to find Holly curled up on the couch, fast asleep. She had a little more color in her cheeks and had been running regularly, taking better care of her body. Still eating small amounts, but I counted each victory.

I reached over to wake her just as her phone's screen lit up. Two consecutive messages came through, both from the same number.

Hey, Holly, it's Isaac. We would really like to talk to you about engagement photos. Give me a call. Please.

Amanda has convinced herself that it is you or no one. I know that everything that happened was difficult, but we need you. I need you.

My hand paused. Two options: wake Holly and gauge her reactions, or open her phone. It shouldn't have been a dilemma, but I needed my sister back. If he knew what happened on the cruise, maybe he could help me. I didn't open her phone, but I took mine out and punched in Isaac's number to save. Then, I gently woke Holly. "Hey," I said softly. She opened her eyes with a mumble. "You should go to bed, so you aren't sore. Your phone just lit up."

She sat up slowly, stretching before reaching for her phone. I watched carefully as she read the messages and then set it back down on the coffee table, screen side down. No reaction except leaving her phone behind as she headed to the bathroom. "What do you want for breakfast tomorrow morning?" she asked.

I followed her, disappointment filling my heart. "Cereal is fine."

"Are you sure? What about coffee?"

"I'll get everything ready before I go to bed."

"Senior year," she said with a sigh, as she looked at me. "Last first day before college."

"That sounds negative," I decided, making a face. "I'd like to think of it as the first of the last stretch before I become an adult."

She smiled. "I can't wait to see where life takes you."

"Us—where life takes us. Even when I'm in college, we are still in this together. Deal?" I asked confidently when I saw her smile waver.

"Of course."

Pulling an old trick out of my hat, I started humming the song "Lean on Me." It was a song that had always made her smile when I sang it. "Come on," I coaxed between the lyrics. "I know you know the words."

"Abby," she sighed.

When I only sang louder, taking her hands to dance around the tiny bathroom with me, a giggle escaped her. "Come on, you can do it!"

She grinned helplessly, and joined in for the next verse and I froze to stare at my sister. Holly had always been a good singer, easily matching her pitch to mine. This time, however, the sounds coming out of her were beautiful, flawless notes, infinitely better than she had ever been before. "Whoa, Holly! What—how did you do that?" I screeched.

She blushed crimson at my amazement. "In Hawaii, they said being exposed to salt water and salty air would improve singing abilities. I guess they were right."

"If you sound like that, I'm going to need a flight out there, stat." I reached for my phone, pulling up a karaoke version of "Amazing Grace." "Try this one."

"Abby…"

"Humor me. Please, Holly."

She rolled her eyes and began singing. Three songs later, all sung in nearly perfect pitch, I had to scrape my jaw off the floor. "That is *crazy*, Holly. Seriously. What am I even doing going to college? We should go on the road, performing in bars and coffee shops until someone hears us and wants to make an album."

"You aren't skipping college."

I scoffed, putting my hands on my hips. "Well, I'll hurry my ass up and graduate early."

She shook her head with a chuckle. "I don't know if it's a permanent change."

"Who cares—it is amazing!"

She brushed her teeth while I showered, singing throughout. Holly didn't join in again, and slipped out before I was finished. I found her curled up in her bed under the blankets, sleeping. She left her phone on the coffee table, so I plugged it in for her before heading to my bedroom. Isaac's messages were still on the lock screen, unopened.

"Dammit Holly, what is going on?" I hissed under my breath.